His Sweet
Obsession

by

Twilla Kay Lamm

The Wild Rose Press, Inc.
PO Box 708
Adams Basin, NY 14410-0708
Visit us at www.thewildrosepress.com

Publishing History
First Edition, 2025
Trade Paperback ISBN 978-1-5092-6110-9
Digital ISBN 978-1-5092-6111-6

Published in the United States of America

Dedication

For Gary

Chapter 1

Washington City, 1866

"Morning, Doctor Clay." The whiskery old man grasped the horse's bridle and flashed a near-toothless smile.

"Good morning, Sam." Sabrina dismounted, and the saddle shifted left with her weight. She dropped her right foot onto the soft dirt of the paddock. "Missy needs a good rub and an extra bucket of grain." She stroked the mare's silky brown side.

"Yes, um."

She stepped from the barn and tugged the wide brim of her brown hat down and shaded her eyes against the sleepy-eyed sun bursting above the pink horizon. The heels of her boots slid against the rocks on the ground. Over her left shoulder, she heard a rooster crow while the spring breeze lifted the edge of her tan riding skirt. The gust carried the faint scent of cloves from the yellow forsythia bush at the edge of the yard.

She wiped her boots at the door and entered the plant-filled foyer of her family's three-story home. Antique furnishings from her Virginia home physically connected her to her ancestors who arrived from England in the seventeen hundreds.

A maid, wearing a black dress and white apron, entered the foyer. "Glad you're home, Miz Sabrina."

Using a dust cloth, she skimmed the glass front of the family's grandfather clock.

The brass pendulum swung *tick-tock-tick-tock,* and the notes carried softly through the corridors.

Releasing a deep sigh, Sabrina set her medical bag on the round, marbled-topped table at the bottom of the staircase. "Good to be home, Jasmine." She rotated her shoulders and worked her hands from her riding gloves, then tossed them on the table. "I need food baskets sent to the orphanage and tell cook to add some fruit pies."

"Miz Sabrina, you look plumb worn out."

"Long night. All I want is breakfast and a bath." She flopped her hat over her gloves, and her stomach rumbled. "I'll be in the library." From the corner of her eye, she glimpsed her younger brother on the staircase, two steps from the bottom. "Bobby? Why aren't you at the bank?"

"Because Mother had one of her spells last night." He descended to the bottom of the stairs, a slight frown marked his forehead, and he stuffed his hands into his trouser pockets.

She pressed her lips together, smoothed curly strands of hair from her forehead, and tucked them in the chignon low on the back of her neck. "Imagine that." She strode toward the library, snapping her boot heels against the wooden floor. The sound ricocheted from the high corners.

Bobby trailed. "Carolina is with Mother. She says Mother hasn't eaten since sometime yesterday."

"My night was a long one." Sabrina slumped into a wing chair near the cold fireplace. "Brother..." She propped her feet on a nearby footstool and toed off her right boot. "When Mother gets hungry, she will eat."

She dropped the left boot onto the floor and stretched and massaged her arch.

"How can you be sure?" He eased into a chair.

"She always conveniently has one of her weak spells when she doesn't get what she wants." Sabrina scrunched her toes.

"Mother doesn't want you going to Fort Greer." Bobby traced his chin with his right thumb.

"No, she doesn't. But, right or wrong, I am going." She kneaded her calf muscles.

"You sense some sort of a military cover-up?" He rested his right ankle on his left knee.

"Possibly, but whatever the truth…" She raised her shoulders. "I must know." A little voice inside her head taunted an old proverb, *let sleeping dogs lie.*

"I know you loved William." Bobby toyed with the cuff of his trousers. "But…maybe something happened out there. Something we don't know about."

"William was a physician dedicated to healing. He would never have taken his own life." Their last conversation replayed in her head. "William asked me to go with him, and I said no. Maybe if I had gone…" She sighed, brushing her fingertips across her mouth.

"Some things we control, and some things we do not." He dropped his foot and leaned forward, resting his arms on his knees. "You shouldn't blame yourself for what happened."

Jasmine entered with a breakfast tray, transporting the delicious aromas of coffee and fresh baked biscuits into the room. The maid set the tray on a low table, then streamed coffee into blue-rimmed china cups.

"What about the hospital?" Bobby added sugar to his coffee.

"Doctor Anderson will take over." She flashed her thoughts to the hospital their grandfather designed and built. "Drew is an excellent physician." She removed a china plate from the stack, scraping the bottom against the next one. "The only thing I know for certain, Little Brother, is…I'm hungry." She dropped a fluffy golden biscuit into the center. "And tired." From a pint-sized pitcher, she poured a dollop of honey. "Right now, I'd give anything for a good night's sleep."

"Amen"—he massaged his left shoulder through his white shirt—"to that."

"Is your arm hurting?" She recalled how handsome he appeared in his Union uniform and how scared she was when they received the message; *your brother has been wounded.*

"Grandfather called it phantom pain." He rotated his shoulder while reaching for a biscuit.

"I suppose we all carry ghosts from the war." She dipped the edge of her biscuit into the golden syrup and allowed the excess to dribble back onto the blue-banded plate, then took her first bite. The rich honey coated her tongue, releasing sweet girlhood memories of helping Grandfather tend his beehives.

"Do you have any idea how long you'll be gone?" Bobby placed a biscuit onto his plate.

"No." She licked her right index finger before wiping it on the thick blue napkin. "I can't believe he is no longer with us." She focused on the painting of the silver-haired gentleman mounted above the fireplace. "I don't know what would have happened if he and Grandmother hadn't given me a home."

"Mother thought she was doing what was best." He poked his right thumb into the side of the biscuit and split it in half.

"Of course she did."

"Homer said you had an emergency at the orphanage." He smeared butter on his biscuit and added a teaspoon of blackberry preserves.

"Appendectomy." She placed her lips on the edge of her cup and sipped. The hot liquid simmered over her tongue, heating a path down the back of her throat. "Every time I believed I had her fever under control, it would spike again. But…barring any complications, I expect little Dorie will recover."

"You are a good doctor, Sabrina. Grandfather would be proud." He bit into his biscuit and washed the bite down with a mouthful of coffee.

"I owe him everything." She sopped the last half of her biscuit in the honey. "Being a woman, the medical colleges refused to admit me. Grandfather hired tutors and trained me himself and then petitioned for me to be allowed to sit for the medical exams. I passed every test they presented. I showed them being a woman does not make me inferior." Sabrina cradled her cup with both hands, allowing the warmth to seep into her chilled fingers. "Then, the old tyrants refused to grant me a certificate."

Around a bite, Bobby shook his head. "I had no idea. We were at Fort Union, and Grandfather's letters did not mention any of this." He lifted his eyebrows. "But you did get one?"

"I did. Grandfather called in every favor he was owed and demanded I be recognized as a physician." She felt her eyes burn with unshed tears. "I miss him terribly." She downed the last drop in her cup.

"We all do."

She inhaled deeply, then exhaled. "William and I were planning to be married, and I have a certain obligation." The bottom of her cup *clinked* against the saucer. "If you'll excuse me, I hear my bath calling."

"Please, Bree." Bobby stood and laid his napkin on the table. "Carolina has been by Mother's side most of the night."

"Very well." The last thing she needed was another quarrel with Mother but... She dropped her napkin onto the tray. "You run along to the bank." She looped her arm in his. "I'll see about your wife and our mother."

"Thanks, Sis." He kissed her cheek.

Minutes later, on stockinged feet, she entered the darkened bedroom and smelled an oily kerosene scent. Her pregnant sister-in-law sat in a high-back chair near the only lamp burning.

Carolina rapidly shifted her hands, looping and pulling yarn over the wooden knitting needles, creating a blanket.

"You should be resting." Sabrina leaned over and pecked her sister-in-law's cheek.

The petite blonde-haired Carolina smiled, stroking her belly. "Rest? Not when he's flipping and flopping like a fish out of water."

Sabrina lifted her brows. "What if he is a she?"

"In that case...I hope she'll be just like her Auntie Bree." Carolina rested her hands in her lap.

Sabrina lovingly squeezed her sister-in-law's hand. "Hardheaded and stubborn?"

"Smart and strong."

"Perhaps now"—Mother's scratchy voice grated from the canopied bed—"if the two of you are finished, I can get the medical attention I require."

Sabrina drifted closer to the high shadowy bed and identified the pungent odor of camphor...her mother's cure-all. Mother's wrinkled face, outlined by brown-gray unkempt hair, almost disappeared into the white bedsheets. When had she grown so old?

Carolina heaved her body upward. "Shall I fetch you a cup of tea, Mother Clay?"

"Bobby is worried about you." Sabrina made eye contact with her sister-in-law. "Please go and rest."

"At times, I swear my sweet husband is the one having this baby." She shoved her knitting into an oversized bag and walked to the door, exiting the chamber with a final *click* of the knob.

Sabrina folded her arms across her chest.

The windup clock on the bedside table *ticked* away the seconds.

"I'm glad you finally decided to come home and take care of me." Mother laced her fingers on top of the sheet.

"My services were required at the orphanage. I told you." She rubbed her forehead and sighed.

"After you left, I had one of my dizzy spells." Mother lifted her chin. "And...you weren't here."

"You need to eat." Crossing the chamber, Sabrina inhaled deeply. She clutched the bell cord dangling in the corner. "We both know when you don't eat, you get lightheaded. When your body talks, which is what it is doing, you need to listen." She jerked the call rope, feeling the rough texture rub the palm of her hand.

"I'm not hungry." Mother flattened her lips into a thin, hard line.

Sabrina returned to her mother's bedside. "Soon, little feet will be running along these old halls." She smoothed the multicolored counterpane edged with white eyelet lace. "And there will be grubby, pint-sized handprints on everything. Aren't you excited to see your first grandchild?"

"Of course, I'm excited, but I'm worried sick about you." Mother grabbed Sabrina's left hand. "You have no idea the dangers you will face."

She drew her hand away. "My mind is made."

"Could you fluff my pillow?" Mother wrinkled her chin and leaned forward. "I do believe the feathers have turned to stones."

Sabrina removed the top pillow from the stack and gave it a firm shake, then a punch.

Mother blew her breath out. "I've lost everyone—dear Mama and Papa, Warren, and now...you."

"The problem with your assessment is..." Sabrina shoved the support behind her mother's back. "I'm not dead."

"No." Mother pursed her lips. "But you're leaving me, and you won't be here when I need you."

You weren't with me when I needed you.

A maid arrived.

Sabrina ordered tea and toast and then crossed to the window and jerked the velvet panels apart.

High above, brass curtain rings screeched along the metal rod and like cream pouring from a pitcher, golden light flowed through the pane.

She opened the window and held her face in the warmth. Carriages rattled along Pennsylvania Avenue, harnesses *jangled*, and drivers shouted and whistled, coaxing their teams into a faster gait. She soaked in the outside.

From the garden below, a perfumed cloud of floral

scents drifted in a light breeze.

A hummingbird hovered, drinking from an orange trumpet flower and flashing his ruby-red throat while songbirds chittered from the tree branches.

People strolled by and conversations and laughter floated from the walkway.

Sabrina heard the distant *bam-bam-bam* of a hammer, reminding her of the beating of a human heart.

The war was over, and after a year, life was returning to the nation's capital.

Down the street, she could see the roof of the White House, and she propelled her mind back to April 14, 1865. She tapped her thumbnail on the front of her bottom teeth, feeling her throat thicken.

She and Grandfather had sat in the audience at Ford's Theater. During the final scene, the audience's laughter filled the hall, and then a pop, like the air from a paper bag being squashed, came from somewhere. A man jumped from the president's box, caught his foot on the draped flag mounted on the front, and dangled for a moment. Then he dropped to the stage floor. *"Sic Semper Tyrannis!"*

The South is avenged.

"The president has been shot," were words shouted from the balcony. "We need a surgeon."

The crowd surged to its feet, and frightened people shoved and stampeded their way out of the theater.

She and Grandfather followed the men transporting the president across the street to Mr. Peterson's house. Everything humanly and medically possible was done, but the following morning, Mr. Lincoln died. He, too, gave his life to the war. Then a couple of weeks later, Grandfather passed. "Why don't you enjoy your tea and toast outside on the porch, Mother?" Sabrina rubbed her shoulder.

"Daughter, you must listen."

"Not now, Mother. I'm tired." Sabrina stalked from the window. "We can talk later, but I won't change my mind." She passed the foot of the bed. "Uncle Nathan is coming for supper."

Mother flipped upright. "During my first five years of marriage, we lived at four different posts. You have no idea what can happen on the frontier."

"I wasn't with you, because you left me behind." She felt knots form in her stomach, fighting the familiar pain of having been abandoned and unloved by her mother.

"I swear, even to this day"—Mother gripped the edge of the bedsheet—"you refuse to understand."

"I understand just fine." Sabrina jerked open the door. "I was crippled, and you did not want me." She closed the door, and feeling old pain, she wilted against the barrier. Hot tears sluiced. She wrinkled her chin and yanked a handkerchief from her white shirt sleeve. If only she could wipe away the ache embedded in her soul. *I will never forgive you, Mother.*

She had been born with her right leg inches shorter than her left, and when she was only a few weeks old, Mother had placed her in the care of her grandparents. Grandfather created special splints, and as she grew, he used longer boards, pulling her leg in the process. But with the braces, walking and running were impossible, and dancing only a dream. She lifted the hem of her tan riding skirt and wiggled her toes, then pirouetted down the hallway, humming an Irish jig, and spun into her room, gasping for breath. "I'm not crippled anymore,

Mother."

She removed the metal hairpins from her chignon and dropped them into a porcelain cup on her toilette table. When her hair hung free, she leaned forward and brushed from her nape to the ends. Next, she undressed, leaving her clothing piled on the floor, then stepped into the water-filled copper tub. Gliding down into the warm, lilac-scented oasis, she sighed. She used a hand-sized sponge and dribbled water over her shoulders and felt her muscles relax.

When Grandmother died, Grandfather sank into a deep depression and wanted to give up medicine. Not long after, talk of war spread through Virginia. He felt his duty was to come to Washington City and build a hospital.

She scrunched deeper into the water and dipped her head backwards. After the strands were soaked, she scrubbed her head with the bar of lilac-scented soap, releasing the heavy scent of summer.

In the beginning, people were suspicious of the two Southern doctors, one of whom was female, and their plans to provide medical treatment to anyone who needed help. But when the war became a reality, no one paid much attention to who they were or where they came from—only grateful for the care provided.

Miss Dix supplied nurses to the hospital. The nursing supervisor did not believe pretty women would make good nurses, and a woman doctor was not acceptable...plain or pretty.

One day, a soldier, suffering from battle fatigue hallucinations, pointed a gun, thinking she was his enemy. Miss Dix was the only available nurse, and together they calmed the patient and administered a sedative. After the incident, Miss Dix accepted her and became a strong hospital supporter and ally.

She poured clean water from a pitcher and rinsed the suds from her hair while last night's conversation with her friend, Martha, replayed.

"Your granddaddy and I grew up together, more years ago than this old woman cares to remember. One day, Charley come to our house long about suppertime. Mama asked him to eat with us, and afterwards, we sat in the creaky porch swing, and old Charley finally spit out what was eating on him. He and his daddy had a big spat over him going to medical school. Your great-granddaddy had different ideas for his only son. Wanted him to be a farmer and raise tobackee. That day, ole Charley was feeling lower than a snake's belly, wondering if he was doing the right thing. Kind of like you are about going out there to that fort. Sometimes, there ain't no way to tell if something's wrong until you've already done it."

"I'm afraid William committed suicide because he didn't want to marry me."

"Now that's just plain nonsense. I've known a few men to run off, but lordy, I ain't never known one of them to up and kill himself over getting married."

"I'm never going to love anyone the way I loved Mathew."

"I know seeing Mathew marry your baby sister weren't easy. But he's dead now."

"So he is." Sabrina stepped from the tub, gathered her towel, and crossed the room, drying as she walked. After dressing in her favorite floral-cotton gown, she opened the drawer on the bedside table and removed a piece of pecan praline from a lidded bowl. She popped the morsel into her mouth and padded to her Queen Anne desk in the corner. The buttery caramel coated her tongue, and the fight with Mother faded. She retrieved William's letters and arranged the correspondence in sequence.

Dear Sabrina,

I take pen in hand to write a few words. Most of the fort's buildings are made with bricks of red clay. The scarcity of trees, reminds me of the ocean, but without water. A south wind blows constantly, waving through the high buffalo grasses. I dream often of Nelson Springs and the way the fields grew before the war. Must close for now and post this letter.

Your devoted, William

She scanned the second letter.

It has been a most horrid day. The drinking water is contaminated, and the men have come down with dysentery. I fear an outbreak of cholera. I have finally convinced the commanding officer to dig a new well away from the privies.

Nothing out of the ordinary appeared in William's first two letters. But something had happened, he was dead.

Chapter 2

That evening, wearing a black dress gathered at the waist, Sabrina proceeded into the dining room with her family.

A large painting of the family's Virginia home hung on the wall above a mahogany sideboard, and the glow of slim candles, burning in silver candleholders, painted the room in muted halos of light. A centerpiece of freshly cut flowers, arranged in a pink vase, emitted soft floral scents of early summer.

Uncle Nathan, dressed in his navy-blue military uniform with ropes of gold braid, sauntered to the head of the table. His salt-and-pepper hair, combed straight back, gleamed in the candlelight.

Sabrina and her sister, Vivian, sat to his right.

Bobby and Carolina took the chairs on his left.

Staffordshire pink china made each place setting a miniature work of art while delicious aromas steamed from several food dishes sitting on the white tablecloth.

Uncle Nathan anchored the roast to the platter with a long-handled fork and sliced the meat with a large-bladed knife. He maneuvered a serving of beef onto a plate, then passed it right. "I'm sorry Polly wasn't able to join us."

"Mother doesn't want me to go to Fort Greer." Sabrina handed the plate to her sister.

"No one wants to see you put yourself in danger."

He continued slicing and serving.

"Why is it dangerous?" Carolina sipped water from a crystal glass.

"Fort Greer is in Indian Territory. And, at best, the situation with the Indians is uncertain. I fear in another year or two, we are headed for an Indian War." Uncle Nathan passed a plate to his left.

"Maybe you need to reconsider, Bree." Bobby set the plate in front of his wife.

"I would like William's grave properly marked." Sabrina sipped her water.

"When a loved one dies on a battlefield"—Uncle Nathan handed Bobby a plate—"families often place markers in private cemeteries as a sign of respect." He slid into his chair and reached for the crystal bowl of boiled potatoes. He dipped a helping, then handed the bowl to Sabrina.

"I feel I have a duty." She scooped the small, red-jacketed potatoes from the dish and rolled them onto her plate, then gave the dish to Vivian.

Uncle Nathan dug a spoon into the salad bowl. "Your mother knows what duty is. She followed my brother from post to post. Wouldn't let him go alone. Very dedicated woman."

"What I don't understand is"—Vivian passed the potato bowl across the table to Carolina—"if William was looking forward to getting married, why did he go and kill himself?" She twitched the muscles at the edge of her mouth and dipped her head.

"Perhaps." Mother's gravelly voice charged from the doorway. "Sabrina must go to Fort Greer because of guilt." As she trod closer to the foot of the table, her stiff black bombazine gown rustled with every step.

15

Sabrina bit the inside of her lip. She did feel guilty about not loving William, but was it wrong to want a family and children? She flicked her gaze across the table. Had her brother said something to Mother?

Bobby slowly shook his head, holding eye contact for a moment before rising and going to aid the family matriarch into her chair.

"I have done nothing to feel guilty about, Mother." Sabrina sipped her water and beneath the table, she crossed her ankles.

Uncle Nathan rose and sliced another serving of beef. "I'm glad you're feeling well enough to join us, Polly." He handed the plate to Sabrina.

"Nate, talk some sense into your niece." Accepting the plate, Mother set the dish a little too hard on the table, creating a *clunk* against the wooden surface.

"Polly, Sabrina is a smart woman and knows her mind." He eased back into his chair and lifted his goblet of wine. "Very much like someone else I know."

"Thank you, Uncle." Sabrina lifted the corners of her mouth, feeling some of the tension in her shoulders evaporate.

"All I'm saying is"—Mother snapped her napkin before placing it across her lap—"if you loved the man, you would have gone with him." She scooped a serving of carrots and peas onto her plate. "The problem I had with Doctor Nelson…was…he refused to look people in the eye."

The dish *thumped* against the table.

"Can't trust a man who won't look you in the eye, Daughter."

Sabrina clenched her ankles. "William was a good doctor, Mother." Using her napkin, she dabbed the cold sweat beading along her upper lip.

"What did you know about him?" Mother glared at her eldest child.

"Everything I needed to know." Sabrina forced air through the knotted muscles in her chest.

"In the two years you worked with the man..." Mother placed her elbows on the edge of the table and narrowed her gaze. "He never came to supper, never took you anywhere, and then all of a sudden, he up and wants to marry you." She tilted forward.

Bobby blotted his mouth. "Mother, they worked together every day, and just because he didn't socialize doesn't mean he wasn't a good man."

"Robert, the man was hiding something." Mother sipped her wine.

"I apologize to everyone." Sabrina laid her silver fork beside her plate and then rose. "William loved me, Mother." She set her napkin on the table. "Is that so hard for you to believe?" She marched toward the door.

"You were wrong once before, Big Sister."

Hearing Vivian's voice, Sabrina paused in mid-step, rotated, and flattened her lips. "And you know all about that, don't you?" She bit the inside of her mouth, feeling a sharp stab between her shoulder blades. She mashed her lips together and flipped her back, then strode from the room.

****

In the library, Sabrina paced, jamming the heels of her shoes into the carpet and creating muffled *thumps* while the hem of her black gown whirled around her ankles. With each step, she discovered new words describing her sister—selfish, malicious, vindictive, hurtful, and plain nasty.

Sweet Mathew. His green eyes had reminded her of spring grass and his boyish smile melted her heart. She eased the corners of her lips up. And his curly blond hair looked like little springs all over his head. She lifted the crystal paperweight from the marble-topped table and glided her hand over the smooth bent surface, feeling the coolness against her palm.

One summer night, when the hot temperatures had become unbearable, she and a group of nurses visited a local shop and bought lemon ices. They strolled to a nearby park and people-watched, and then some musicians began playing. The toe-tapping fiddle music encouraged an impromptu dance.

Cadet Mathew Stark and some of his buddies from West Point were in the city on leave, and they were seeking female companionship. Mathew asked her to dance. From the moment she had stepped into his arms, the night turned magical. Later, as the dawn highlighted the eastern sky, they said their good-byes, and he promised to write. Over the summer, his letters arrived, and when he came to Washington, they often attended one of Mrs. Greenhow's teas or soirées. By Christmas, she was in love.

She shifted the crystal weight from her right hand to her left and floated her fingers over the glass surface.

Memories of the most perfect, unforgettable night shimmered, Christmas at West Point. She had worn a full-skirted, black velvet gown with a rhinestone-studded bodice, and Mathew had worn his uniform with three vertical rows of shiny buttons down his chest.

Dancing in his arms, she floated in a cloud of happiness around the ballroom floor. When the clock *bonged* midnight, he stopped beneath the sprig of mistletoe and kissed her. At that moment, she fell deeply in love, forever. He proposed, and she said yes.

A spring wedding was planned, but in January, she received distressing news. A cannon Father was loading misfired and exploded, and he was killed. Since she had never lived with her family, she had not known her father well, but she loved him and due to her family's mourning, the wedding was postponed.

Mother and Vivian moved into Carter Hall, and when Vivian became pregnant and married Mathew, her lovely dream of becoming Mathew's wife faded like summer disappearing into fall. A few months later, Vivian miscarried, and the following month, Mathew fell down the stairs and broke his neck. And to this day, she suspected her sister might have shoved him.

She elevated the paperweight toward the burning double-globed oil lamp. The flickering light spotlighted tiny bubbles trapped inside. Like the bubbles she was trapped, and until she knew the truth about William's death, she could not go forward.

The aroma of Grandfather's pipe tobacco lingered like a patina coating the room. *I need you, Grandfather, your wise words, and your gentle counsel.* She set the paperweight on the edge of the fireplace mantle, then crossed the room to the chess board which reflected their last game, still in progress, and frozen in time. She lifted the white knight and held the chess piece close to her face.

Grandfather had complained of heartburn and said he needed to lie down.

After giving him a dose of bicarbonate, she kissed him good-night. The next morning, he was gone.

As a young girl playing chess, she discovered

patience, and as a woman, she learned the importance of studying a situation before she acted. With each choice comes a consequence—sometimes good, sometimes bad.

The day William proposed, they were picnicking at Wild Flower Meadows. After eating, they strolled along the banks of the river, holding hands. He told her he was leaving Washington and didn't know when, or if he would be back. He picked a single yellow jonquil, and as he handed her the ruffled flower, he proposed.

Later, when she told Grandfather, she had expected his blessing. But instead, she received a warning about considering the matter carefully.

"Marriage to the right person can be a challenge, but marriage to the wrong person will be a disaster."

A few short days later, Grandfather passed away, and William left Washington City.

"*Harrumph*, may I come in?" Uncle Nathan drifted deeper into the room.

"Certainly." She traced the grooves along the ivory horse's mane with the tip of her right index finger.

Uncle Nathan swooshed into a well-worn leather chair and removed a silver cigar case from his trouser pocket. "Mind if I smoke?"

She shook her head and cradled the chess piece in her hand. "I always thought of Grandfather as a knight, gallant, and noble." She slipped into the opposite chair.

"He was a fine man." Uncle Nathan clipped off the cigar tip and laid it in a dish on the low table in front of him, then struck a match and lit his cigar. "Back in Virginia, our families were neighbors, and Warren and I would often see your mother at parties." He puffed, releasing the strong odor of his cigar. "The first time I laid eyes on your mother, Warren and I were attending a ball at the Elgin plantation. We were all kids back then. We thought we knew everything and didn't know anything." He held his cigar between his fingers. "Polly wore a yellow dress with all kinds of sparkling little do-dads." He flicked his ashes into the ceramic dish. "I had a soft spot for your mother, and I admit I was a little jealous when my brother and she married. As you know, your father and I were only half-brothers, but I loved Warren and wished him and Polly nothing but the best."

"I'm surprised you never married, Uncle." She rotated the chess piece in her hand feeling the coolness against her palm.

"Takes a special woman to marry an army man."

Rising, she set the chess piece on the table. "A glass of wine, Uncle?"

He nodded. "I know you think you owe William something, but you don't." He rotated his cigar to the other side of his mouth.

Sabrina crossed to the round table holding an array of liquor decanters. "He has no family, his parents died when he was young, and he was raised by his aunt, who is deceased, as well." She lifted the crystal decanter, feeling the sharp indentions press into her palm similar to the uncertainty pressing into her mind. The burgundy liquid splashed into the bottom of a *V*-shaped glass.

"Let's suppose for a moment, Nelson did commit suicide." Nathan laid his cigar in the dish and accepted the short-stemmed glass. "You are putting yourself in danger to find information you already have."

"I can't believe he killed himself. But if he did…I must know why." She resumed her seat and feelings of responsibility swooped.

Swirling the burgundy liquid, Nathan watched the churning for a moment. "Secretary Stanton feels he owes you a debt. Otherwise, he would not agree to this."

The fruity aftertaste registered on her tongue. "A debt?" She wrinkled her brow. "I don't understand."

"The secretary's cousin speaks highly of a woman doctor who saved his life…and his leg." He removed a folded letter from his pocket. "Stanton has granted you permission to be the post surgeon at Fort Greer. Here is your contract and a copy for you. Your signature and the date are required on both."

The forms rustled in her hand, accentuating the uneasiness circling in her brain. "Thank you, Uncle."

"Don't thank me yet." Nathan massaged the bridge of his nose. "Before you sign…I have something to tell you—and you need to listen."

Gripping her wine glass, Sabrina opened her mouth to facilitate her breathing, focusing on each of her uncle's words.

"I love you with all my heart. You are more like a daughter than a niece"—he inhaled deeply—"and now I am breaking my oath to the United States government."

"Uncle Nathan?" She flattened her free hand over her racing heart.

He slanted closer. "I must have your promise this will go no further."

"You have my word." She set her glass on the table beside the chess piece. "I shall tell no one."

"We believe…during the war, Nelson was passing information to the Confederates. On several occasions, he was seen meeting with Doctor Samuel Mudd."

"They were doctors"—she furrowed her brows—"Maybe…"

"Sabrina, Doctor Mudd was found guilty of being involved in the Lincoln Conspiracy."

She tightened her gaze. "Please tell me you are not suggesting William was involved in the assassination." She licked her lips and swallowed the knot in her throat.

"As much as I wish I could…I cannot. At this time, we have too many unanswered questions." He sipped his wine. "If he was involved—that could be the reason he is dead. When you go out there snooping around, this could put you in danger, too."

"Mother was right." She felt icy tension slink into her stomach. "William was deceitful."

"It would appear so." Nathan tapped cigar ashes into the dish.

She scraped her bottom teeth along her upper lip. Was William involved with Doctor Mudd? Did William spy for the Confederacy? *If these things are true, I must know.*

With the contracts in her hand, she marched across the room to the opened slant-fronted desk. She located the ink well, removed the stopper, and slipped a nib on the end of the pen. She dipped the pen into the ink. *Is this a mistake?* In bold slanted letters, she scrolled her name across the bottom of the contracts. Blowing and fanning the sheets in the air, she returned one copy to her uncle and folded the other one.

"Very well." He pursed his lips. "You have made your decision." He released a deep sigh. "I shall request the secretary write a letter of introduction."

Outside the doorway, footsteps approached.

Mother strode into the room. "I have found a solution."

Sabrina raised her eyebrows. "You are locking me in my room until I see reason."

"Don't be ridiculous. If you won't change your mind, I shall go with you." Mother claimed a spot on the floral sofa and smiled, folding her hands in her lap. "I've already instructed Homer to retrieve our trunks from the attic."

Sabrina sipped her wine. "I will be serving as post surgeon at Fort Greer for an indeterminate time."

Mother widened her eyes, raised her brows, and pursed her lips. "Women do not serve in the military." She faced her brother-in-law. "Nate, what is going on here?"

"Polly." He held his hands up, palms side out. "Your daughter has received special permission from the Secretary of War. Stanton is granting her request."

"This cannot be happening." Mother tapped her forehead with the palm of her right hand.

"It is." Sabrina floated her fingers over her mouth. "Do you wish to reconsider?"

Mother crossed both arms over her chest. "No. I don't believe I do."

Vivian bounced into the room, and her pink full-skirted dress swung with every step. "Guess what? I'm going with you."

Heaven help me. Sabrina emptied her glass in one big gulp.

Chapter 3

Three weeks later, the stagecoach clunked into another Kansas pothole. Sabrina clutched the leather strap near the top of the coach door. Her teeth rattled, and her body bounced on the hard seat. The edge of her corset bit into the left side of her ribcage. Out the window, the vast open country wove in and out of view. In his letters, William described the scarcity of trees.

In Franklin County, Virginia, her family's home nestled near the foot of the Blue Ridge Mountains. On stormy days, clouds blocked the mountains, but on sunny days, the uneven ridges along the top appeared like broken blue glass against a lighter shade of sky, and trees blanketed the slopes.

The stage jolted over another bone-jarring rut.

In Washington City, they had boarded a train, but a week later, the party switched to coach travel. The explanation being the tracks destroyed during the war had not been repaired. The frustrations of dealing with finding transportation and accommodations for the night, in addition to the unappetizing food, had more than once made her want to give up and return home.

Mother kept the conversation lively, telling stories about traveling by wagon train to Fort Union in New Mexico.

In all honesty, she was glad Mother was with her—Vivian, not so much. Jittery sensations nipped, planting doubts about her decision and with each passing mile, she felt the chance to change her mind slip like water through her fingers, and she recalled what Martha had said, *There ain't no way to tell if something's wrong until you've already done it.*

"I'm glad that grimy old peddler decided to ride on top." Vivian lifted the speckled netting covering her face. "His breath smelled so bad, I believe something crawled in there and died."

"Fort Hex," was shouted from the driver's box.

"At last." Mother dusted the dirt from the lap of her black traveling suit. "I believe I'd give my eyeteeth for a cup of tea." She repositioned her elaborately feathered hat.

"A bath is what I long for." Vivian fanned her face with a gloved hand. "I'm as wilted as a rose in August."

The *rumbling* coach wheels ground to a stop.

"Hurry up, gents," the driver called to the soldiers. "Got passengers. Three ladies from back East. Help 'em out."

The coach door *squeaked* open.

A ginger-haired soldier, in a blue uniform, stood gawking at Vivian, his eyes wide and his mouth open.

"You are most kind, sir." Vivian flashed a smile and fluffed the white-blonde curls hugging the side of her face.

"Young man." Mother waved a hand in front of the soldier's face. "I am waiting."

"Sorry, ma'am." The freckle-faced soldier snapped to attention and aided them to the wooden sidewalk.

Sabrina watched the skilled military group working together.

Three privates expertly removed the team of six

mules from their harnesses and collars, then guided fresh animals into proper pulling positions.

A frisky pair tossed their heads and *hee-hawed*, jerking against their reins.

A tall, bull-sized soldier whistled sharply through his front teeth and bottom lip. "Whoa. Hold up there." He fought for control. "You fleabags ain't going nowhere 'till I say so."

As the stagecoach driver grabbed the mailbag from beneath the seat, the coach wobbled and *squeaked*. "Don't forget the boot, gentlemen." He dismounted and exchanged bags with a tall corporal.

Sabrina followed her mother and sister across an alleyway to the front of a general store. Wooden barrels contained an assortment of hoes, shovels, and pitchforks fanning into the air like a farmer's bouquet while the earthy scents of freshly dug potatoes and onions perfumed the air.

Customers gawked, sidling in and out of the store.

A wisp of a woman, wearing a straw hat with white ribbons dangling, stopped. "Polly Clay? I do not believe my eyes. I never expected to see you here."

"Bless my soul, Millie Hunter." Mother embraced the woman. "My goodness, it's good to see you again, dear. Are you living here?"

"No, we're at Fort Greer. James is the commander there." Mrs. Hunter slapped at a buzzing fly near her face. "I came here with some of the soldiers to visit with my cousin. You remember Coretta, don't you, Polly?"

"Of course. Millie, you are not going to believe this, but we are on our way to Fort Greer. Sabrina is under contract to be the post surgeon there."

Mrs. Hunter smiled. "I can't believe we are going to be together again. It will be just like old times." She shifted the cloth sack, she was holding. "I come over to the store for some sugar, and I'll be returning with a surprise. Polly, I want to hear about everything."

Sabrina glanced around at the row of crudely constructed buildings. "Mrs. Hunter, I need to check with the commanding officer, Colonel Young."

"That'd be Henry, Coretta's husband." Mrs. Hunter pointed to a small structure across the parade ground. "His office is right over yonder, dear."

As her mother and sister headed one way with Mrs. Hunter, Sabrina headed in the opposite direction. She crossed the dirt roadway and pebbles and dirt clots shifted and crunched beneath her half-boots. Arriving at the commander's door, she brushed the dirt from her navy-blue dress, adjusted her matching bonnet, squared her shoulders, then knocked.

"Enter," a deep baritone voice called.

She opened the door and faced a distinguished man seated behind a wide desk, wearing the military patches of a colonel.

The middle-aged man, with sparse gray hair, stood. "Good afternoon, ma'am. I'm Colonel Young. How can I help you?" The thickset colonel motioned her to a chair in front of his desk.

The unpadded seat mashed her sore backside, and she squirmed. "My name is Doctor Sabrina Clay." She fished the secretary's letter from her handbag. "I've been assigned the position of post surgeon at Fort Greer." She handed him the letter.

As the ruddy-faced colonel read the note, his frown lines deepened and his face darkened. "This is highly irregular, ma'am. I have never heard of a woman being a doctor." He raised his bushy eyebrows and squinted. "And then to be assigned military duty?" He shook his head. "Something's not right."

"I assure you, my papers are in order." She shifted her body and crossed her ankles.

"I don't mean any disrespect, ma'am." He handed the letter back. "Papers can be forged."

Sabrina felt dots of heat prickle into her chest, then spike upward. "I did not forge this letter." She returned the document to her crocheted bag and drew the strings tight. "Your orders, Colonel Young, are to provide me with a military escort."

"So…they are." The colonel's face spurted bright-red, and he shot to his feet. He flattened his lips into a straight line. "I shall send a letter immediately to the War Department and verify your story."

"Please do." She mashed her lips and wrinkled her chin while blood pulsed in her ears.

"In the meantime, we have a detail from Fort Greer picking up supplies." He skirted the corner of his desk. "My wife and I would be…honored…to have you as a guest in our home."

"My mother and sister are traveling with me, sir." Sabrina breathed through her mouth. "My mother and Mrs. Hunter are old acquaintances."

"In that case…" With more force than necessary, the colonel claimed his hat from the coat tree. "If you will excuse me, I shall see to your trunks."

The office door slammed.

She closed her eyes, inhaled deeply, and then let the air float out. *Is this a mistake?*

A wooden cabinet occupied the corner behind the

colonel's desk, and on the wall, hung a multicolored map showing Kansas, Indian Territory, and Texas.

She sauntered closer and straightened the wooden frame.

Dark lines marked state and territorial boundaries.

She positioned her right index finger on Fort Hex and skimmed downward, locating Fort Greer farther into the southwest and almost into Texas. She slid her finger to the eastern section of Indian Territory and read the labels, *Cherokee, Creek,* and *Choctaw Nations,* and in the middle, *Seminole* and *Chickasaw Nations.* In her history lessons, she had learned about the controversy surrounding President Andrew Jackson's decision to move the Indians west. She traced the north fork of the Red River. "*Cheyenne, Kiowa, Comanche.*"

Behind her, the door opened, then closed.

Firm footsteps thumped.

Sabrina turned, expecting Colonel Young.

"Let me guess. You're Doctor Clay." A tall soldier wearing well-worn, knee-high boots and a dirt-crusted cavalry uniform, batted his black hat against his thigh, flicking dust particles into the air. He tossed his hat on the desk.

She identified the bars on his blouse. "Captain."

"Ethan Reed—from Fort Greer."

Extending her right gloved hand, she passed the desk. "Nice to meet…" He had the most amazing blue eyes which were shifting from light to dark, reminding her of summer storm clouds.

The broad-shouldered man scowled, bringing his thick eyebrows together. Instead of offering his hand, he crossed his arms over his chest and perched on the corner of the desk. "So, you're a doctor. I bet you aren't married, are you?" He twitched his lips into a smirk.

A gradual burn started at the top of her head and boiled down to her shoulders. "Whether I am married or not is none of your business and has nothing to do with anything." She pressed her lips together and narrowed her gaze.

"Single women aren't allowed at military forts. Except..." He raised his eyebrows and pursed his lips. "In the capacity of...how can I say this for your delicate ears?" He idly played with a pencil. "Soiled doves."

Her heart pounded. "My ears are not as delicate as you believe, Captain Reed." The heat waved into to her stomach. She squeezed the muscles around her eyes.

"Good." He stood. "I'm sure we can get you return passage on the next coach heading east."

"Now—how can I put this for your delicate ears?" She clenched both her fists and glued her arms to her sides. "I am a doctor. I have a contract with the United States government. I will go to Fort Greer...with my mother and my sister...who are unmarried, as well." She breathed in short gasps and clamped her gaze on his chilly blue eyes. "You—cannot—tell me what I can or cannot do, sir. My contract...and your orders...are signed by Secretary Stanton."

Knock-knock rapped against the door.

"Enter." Captain Ethan Reed hardened the muscles in his face and secured his gaze on her.

She stuck out her chin and locked her arms across her chest.

"Begging your pardon, Cap'n." The private held his salute. "The colonel said we were to help this here lady, sir."

Ethan transferred his gaze to the private, then

stood. "This…is no lady." He saluted, and then returned his gaze to her. "She is a doctor. Understood, soldier?"

"Y-yes, sir."

Sabrina swallowed the knot pounding in her throat and lifted her chin, then swept toward the door. "Good day, sir."

Behind her, the sharp snap of a pencil vibrated.

"Of all the nerve." She tromped down the wooden steps.

"Ma'am, are you all right?" The freckled-faced private offered his hand.

"I didn't quite expect that kind of reception." She placed her hand in the soldier's gloved one. "My name is Doctor Clay, and you are?"

"Private Todd, ma'am." He gave her a half-grin, revealing a gap between his two front teeth. "Cap'n Reed's a good man."

"He's rude, arrogant, and bullheaded." She took a deep breath around the excited beating of her heart.

Private Todd escorted her toward the general store. "Yes, ma'am. But I'd give my right arm to be under his command. I've put in for a transfer to Fort Greer, and I hope I get my papers before the cap'n leaves."

"Why in God's name would you want to be under the command of a lunatic?" Not slowing her stride, she blotted the moisture from her upper lip with her gloved hand.

"Cap'n Reed's a war hero, ma'am. Risked his life to save some hoopty-do general."

"So, he's brave. A lot of men are." Beneath her left foot, she felt the gravel shift.

"Yes, ma'am, and he's a fine officer. Won't ask his men to do nothing he won't do hisself."

At the pile of baggage, four soldiers loaded trunks, several hat boxes, and various other items her sister had deemed necessary, onto handcarts.

Sabrina yanked her medical bag from the stack and then trooped behind the soldiers.

Did you expect this to be easy? The squeaking cart wheels taunted.

Private Todd knocked on the front door of a white, two-story frame house.

A woman with silver-gray hair and a friendly face appeared. "You must be Polly's other daughter, the doctor. I'm Coretta Young. Please do come in, dear."

Sabrina crossed the threshold. "I hope we're not intruding." She removed her gloves and glanced around the well-furnished parlor, feeling the stiffness in her body release.

"Of, course not." Mrs. Young wiped her hands on the yellow apron she wore over her blue floral dress. "We're having our July social celebration tonight." She addressed the soldiers. "You boys, take those things around to the back. Wind Flower will show you where to put them."

Mrs. Young took Sabrina's things and laid them on a nearby table.

How can that colonel have such a nice wife?

In a stuffy, cramped kitchen, aromas steamed and bubbled from pots on a cast-iron stove.

Around the room several women worked on food preparations, and introductions were made.

Mrs. Hunter chopped carrots. "I was so shocked to hear about that awful assassination." She added the slices to a blue bowl. "Polly, have you heard anything about poor Mrs. Lincoln?"

"Last I heard…she's living in Chicago with her sons." Mother peeled the skin from a cucumber. "Losing one's husband is never easy."

A young girl, who had been introduced as Annie, stared at Vivian. "How excitin' to be an actress. I would love to be on stage and wear beautiful clothes."

"In the theater"—Vivian elevated her nose and flipped her gaze—"we refer to them as costumes."

"I want to be an actress." Annie brushed the end of her auburn braid over her mouth.

"Some people are born to be on the stage"—Vivian fluffed the gathered skirt of her blue-and-gray-plaid gown—"and some people aren't."

"What plays have you been in?" Annie's freckled face glowed.

Vivian cocked her head. "I've starred in several Shakespearean productions."

"Starred?" Annie widened her blue eyes. "Golly."

"As a matter of fact…" Vivian scooted a tall stool to the center of the room and perched. "I was playing in *Our American Cousin* at Ford's Theater the night President Lincoln was killed."

A hush enveloped the room.

"Did you see the president git shot?" Annie held her braid.

"The only people who witnessed the shooting were in his box." Vivian curved her lips into a half-smile. "As I recall"—she glanced around at her audience, raised her right arm, and pointed with her hand to the side of the kitchen—"I was standing in the wings, then bam—and Johnny dropped from the president's box."

"Johnny?"

"John Wilkes Booth." Vivian lifted her lips in a

faint smile. "He caught his foot in the regimental flag which was hanging there, and when it ripped, he fell."

"They say he broke his leg." Annie tossed her braid over her shoulder.

"He stumbled across the stage and ran by me." Vivian described the scene with hand gestures, and her voice grew animated. "I tried to ask him what was going on, but he just kept running. And then...Mrs. Lincoln screamed, and somebody shouted the president had been shot." Vivian buried her face in her hands and sobbed. "It was awful, just awful."

Sabrina found a red-checked apron on a peg behind the door. *What a performance.* She tied the neckties and pulled the apron flat over her navy-blue dress, then tied the apron strings behind her back. *Does being a good liar make you a good actress?*

Vivian slipped from her perch. "Mrs. Young, could I please lie down?" She wiped her tears from her face on a kitchen towel. "I seem to be getting a headache."

"I'll show you to your room, dear."

Vivian sighed. "Would it be possible to have some bathwater?"

Unbelievable. Sabrina elevated the corners of her mouth.

"Millie." Mother stirred the simmering contents of a pot on the stove. "Do you ever hear from Geraldine Riddle?"

Mrs. Hunter added more carrots to the bowl. "I got a letter...I believe...about six months ago. She and her husband are still at Fort Union."

"Mrs. Hunter, what do I do with these potatoes?" Sabrina pointed to a large pot of steaming on the table.

"Mash them. We'll use them for a potato salad."

The ladies chatted.

Sabrina found a water glass and then conversed with Mrs. Young's daughter, Frannie. "When is your baby due?" She used the butt end of the glass and mashed the potato chunks.

"Doc Morgan says any day now." Frannie lovingly stroked her stomach. "I was sure sick at first, but then got better." She frowned. "But these last few days, the baby's been kinda still. Mama says I'm not to worry. Everything's normal."

Sabrina stirred the potatoes into a fluffy cloud. "Do you have a name?" She added a dollop of butter from a crock bowl sitting on the table.

"If we have a girl, Cora after Mama and if we have a boy, George Henry. George is my husband's name and Henry for Daddy."

Breezing back into the room, Mrs. Young hugged Frannie and kissed her cheek. "Please don't overdue, darling." She uncovered a rising lump of bread dough and punched the rounded top down. "Millie and I were recalling just this morning how our families used to get together for weeks on end. Our homes were always full, and at nighttime, we children would sleep on pallets scattered all over the floors."

"Those times all died with the war." Mrs. Hunter packed smaller food items into a clean metal dishpan. "Sabrina, I forgot to tell you, Graham is here. I know he will be thrilled to see you."

Sabrina watched the glob of butter melt into the potatoes. *Does he know about William and me?*

Chapter 4

Entering the mess hall, Sabrina ambled around the rectangular room admiring the decorations.

Festive ribbons of red, white, and blue cascaded over the walls while kerosene lamps, lanterns, and fat candles created circles of light. Long tables lined the south wall, and bright yellow sunflowers stood in glass jars for centerpieces.

Behind a blue-fabric-draped table, Mother smiled and laughed with the other women as she emptied a food basket.

Sabrina skirted the edge of the dessert table and noticed an oblong platter of pecan pralines. She tugged the corners of her mouth up and slipped a morsel inside, enjoying the smooth buttery sensation melting over her tongue. She sauntered between the groups, introducing herself while chatting and making small talk, then crossed the room and joined her sister, who was sitting near the door. "How is your headache?" She slid into the chair.

"My what?" Vivian frowned.

"You left the kitchen earlier because you claimed you had a headache." She scooted her medical bag beneath her chair.

"Oh, yes, my headache." Vivian continued to scan the crowd. "Completely gone."

Sabrina focused on Vivian's gown. "Couldn't you

have found something more suitable to wear? After all, this isn't some big stage production."

"What's wrong with the way I'm dressed?" Vivian brushed the lap of her red satin gown.

"Don't you think…the color is a little…?" Sabrina raised her brows.

"Vibrant?" Vivian smiled and tilted her head to one side. "Exciting?"

"I was going to say shameful." Sabrina shifted her position in the seat of the straight-back chair.

"I like being pretty and wearing bright colors. Just because you don't"—Vivian wrinkled her nose—"is no reason for you to be so mean." Vivian batted her green eyes at a group of soldiers standing near the regimental band. "You could fix yourself up a little." She twirled one blonde curl with her index finger. "Maybe find another man."

"I don't need a man in my life." Sabrina stiffened her spine. "I have my career."

Colonel Young stepped to the makeshift podium.

The crowd clapped.

Sabrina squinted at the man and pursed her lips. *He practically called me a liar.*

As the opening dance, the colonel announced "The Officer's March." He and Mrs. Young led the parade.

Captain Reed and Mrs. Hunter marched behind.

The captain wore regimental-blue, with a double row of shiny brass buttons, and held his partner's hand in his white-gloved one.

Mrs. Hunter quickstepped in a wide-skirted gown of calico with varying shades of green.

Graham Hunter held Mother's hand high, as he guided her around the floor.

Mother remained in her black traveling suit with a high-necked white blouse beneath.

When the gentlemen swung their partners, the ladies' full skirts created a polychromatic assortment of colors and patterns.

Captivated by the sight of the dark-haired captain, Sabrina intertwined her gloved fingers and laid them in her lap. He exhibited an entirely different image from the one she met earlier.

Captain Reed turned and landed his gaze on her. He nodded without smiling, and his blue eyes glinted like rays of sun on a frosty morning.

Sabrina eased her breath out between her lips. *So what if he doesn't like me?* She had never met anyone so irritating or rude and spouting nonsense about single women not being allowed at military forts. *This is no lady, soldier.*

"He's not married, you know." Vivian fluffed her hair with her right hand.

"Who?" Sabrina patted her mouth with her right hand.

"Captain Reed, of course." Vivian angled her head and fluttered her lashes.

"How do you know?" Sabrina bunched her brows and focused on her sister.

"I talk to people." Vivian smiled at a young private approaching. "Sister, medicine can't keep you warm on a cold winter's night." She accepted the soldier's hand and glided onto the dance floor.

Sabrina watched her sister swish into the crowd. "I can keep myself warm."

"Would you like to dance, ma'am?" Private Todd edged closer.

"I would, thank you." Sabrina accepted his hand.

The band struck a lively tune.

Sabrina and Private Todd joined other couples and formed a quadrille.

Captain Reed and Mrs. Hunter paired across from Sabrina and Private Todd.

The two couples stepped forward.

Sabrina dipped a curtsy to Ethan.

The captain bowed, then gave her a slow smile.

Fiddle notes rose and fell in the background.

While Sabrina quickstepped to the center, she felt a warm flutter in the pit of her stomach. With the other ladies, she formed a star with her right hand, circled, and partnered with Ethan.

"Enjoying the dance, Doc?" He widened his smile, revealing deep dimples in his freshly shaven cheeks.

"I am." She watched the frost in his blue eyes melt to a liquid blue. The man was dangerously handsome.

He tucked her against his side and guided her steps with his gloved hand on her lower back.

She bounced to the lively beat of the music, and as he swung her around, threads of excitement stitched into her stomach.

The song ended and another began.

Throughout the evening, Sabrina danced round and round the room, she promenaded, shuffled, and spun with different partners and different steps, but her mind remained on the handsome captain with the magnetic blue eyes.

When the band broke for refreshments, the crowd drifted, then formed lines at the buffet tables. The hum of conversations and laughter filled the corners of the room.

Delicious aromas rose from the platters of roasted meats, gravy boats filled with creamy sauces, and the many choices of desserts displayed over the tables.

Sabrina waited in line at the end of the buffet table, softly humming, and felt her stomach rumble. Breakfast at Sunflower Stage Station was some sort of mush under a layer of grease and some moldy bread. Not wanting to deal with the consequences, she declined and soon discovered her sister had eaten the last bite from their food stash. Around noon, the stage bounced into the settlement of Hope, Kansas, and she purchased a few apples from a vendor.

A smiling woman handed Sabrina a cup of punch.

"Thank you." She sipped, and the lemony flavor zipped over her tongue while she contemplated her first selection from the colorful array.

"Impossible," a male voice rose from behind her right shoulder.

Sabrina turned and faced the brown-haired soldier. "What is impossible, Lieutenant Hunter?" *If Graham knows about William, my charade is over.* She brushed fallen tendrils back from her face, catching his strong scent of bay rum.

He flashed a smile. "You have grown more lovely, Miss Sabrina."

"You flatter me, sir." She felt her cheeks warm.

"I only tell the truth." Graham secured her hand and lightly kissed her white-gloved knuckles. "Mother said you were here." He smoothed his thumb over the place he had kissed.

Sabrina drew her hand away and crossed her arms over her chest. "I'm simply starving."

"In that case, you must sample Cousin Coretta's

fried quail." Graham handed her a plate from the stack. "I don't know what she does, but the meat is so tender it melts from the bone."

Over the next few minutes, he made choices, filling her plate with a variety of foods and then guiding her to a couple of vacant chairs along the side of the room.

"I was just recalling the pie supper we attended." He grinned.

She unrolled the white napkin holding her fork and spoon. "You bought my pie."

"I did"—he leaned closer—"and I must say the pastry was a tad bit on the salty side."

She laughed. "You know I got the sugar and salt sacks mixed." She twisted her knees slightly away.

"The pie was awful"—he sipped his punch—"but the company was well worth it." He shifted in his chair. "I was sorry to hear about your grandfather's passing. I always admired him."

"Thank you." She sampled the potato salad, and her tongue registered the snap of dill.

"I expected you would have married by now." He forked a bite of green beans.

She dipped her gaze over the crowd. "No, medicine keeps me busy." *He doesn't know, or is he pretending?* She landed her gaze on her mother. Mother was smiling and nodding, as she chatted with Mrs. Hunter. Perhaps this trip was what Mother needed.

Across the room, Frannie grabbed her abdomen, and a flicker of pain crossed her face.

"Please excuse me. I think I might be needed." She set her plate aside and headed over to Frannie.

"Miss Sabrina?" Graham followed.

"Are you all right?" She leaned closer.

"My baby's coming." Frannie tilted forward and clutched her stomach.

"I'll get Cousin Coretta." Graham hustled away.

Sabrina put her right arm around Frannie's waist and aided the expectant mother to her feet and through the crowd. At the door, she retrieved her medical bag.

Outside, Captain Reed stepped from the shadows into the halo of a torch. "Is she okay?"

"She's in labor." Sabrina staggered, holding the woman upright. "I need to get her home."

"Allow me." Captain Reed lifted Frannie and headed toward Officers' Row. "Which way, ma'am?"

Frannie gave directions, and a few minutes later, they arrived on the stoop of a small cabin.

Ethan set Frannie on her feet and grabbed a lighted lantern hanging on a hook beside the door.

Frannie clutched her stomach, doubled over, and moaned.

"Captain, please fetch her doctor."

Ethan offered Sabrina the lantern.

She shifted her medical bag into her right hand and accepted the lantern with her left. "Everything is fine…your baby is ready to be born." As they entered the cabin, she tightened her right arm around Frannie's waist.

They staggered across the combined sitting room and kitchen, then into the bedroom.

Frannie collapsed on the side of the bed and leaned over, gripping her knees. "It hurts…"

"I know." Sabrina rummaged for a nightgown and found one in the wardrobe. "But soon, you'll have your baby, and the pain will be over." She tugged Frannie's periwinkle-blue dress off and replaced it with a white nightgown. She tucked several pillows behind Frannie's back. "Babies can't be rushed."

"Oh…" Frannie screamed, grabbing her stomach.

Sabrina clenched Frannie's hands and squeezed, watching the patient's face. "Breathe in and out."

Frannie blew air out and then slumped back against the pillows, cradling her stomach. "I want my mama."

Stepping to the commode, Sabrina poured water from a yellow pitcher into the matching basin. "Graham is bringing her." She used a bar of lye soap and washed her hands. "Some babies come quickly and others need more time." Shaking her hands dry, she approached the foot of the bed. "I'll see how far along you are."

Suddenly, the bedroom door flung open.

An overweight man, reeking of alcohol, staggered into the room. "Shoo away…my patient."

"Sir, you are drunk." Sabrina balled both her hands into fists.

The man stumbled and fell against the bed. "A man…sh…entitled to a drink…or shoo." He wobbled into an upright position and flung the sheet away from Frannie's legs.

Mrs. Young rushed into the room. "Oh, please, not tonight, Royce." She clasped her daughter's hand.

"Cor…ett, I can delivers…with my eyes shut. Out. All of you scat."

This will not end well. Sabrina locked her jaw and stuck her tongue to the roof of her mouth.

****

I need to be in there. Sabrina compressed her fists and marched back and forth, her boots firmly snapping against the floorboards.

Over in the kitchen area, Mother prepared a pot of

coffee.

The bail on the water bucket *rattled.*

The lid on the pot *clanked.*

The cover on the stove *clanged.*

"Aaaaah," Frannie's agonizing screams ripped.

Sabrina stopped in front of Mrs. Young and folded her hands. "He's drunk. Please...I can help."

Coretta Young sat at a sawbuck table, wringing her hands. "I don't know what to do."

The door opened, and warm air gusted from the outside.

Another scream shredded the air.

Colonel Young, followed by a heavyset soldier with darting eyes, entered.

Mrs. Young threw herself into her husband's arms. "Royce is drunk. Do something, Henry." She gripped the front of her husband's uniform. "Please..."

"Get a hold of yourself, Coretta." He squeezed her hands.

Sabrina approached the lieutenant. "I'm Doctor Clay. Your wife is having a difficult labor. Please allow me to help her." She clenched her hands together.

Colonel Young shoved between them. "Doctor Morgan is our physician, young woman."

Sabrina inhaled deeply. "I'm sure he is a very good doctor, but he is drunk, sir. Your daughter needs a sober physician."

Colonel Young jabbed his right index finger at Sabrina. "Not you."

The bedroom door flung open.

Doctor Morgan, his uniform covered with blood, staggered into the doorway. He propped his shoulder against the doorframe. "Baby's breech." He smeared a blood-soaked towel over his face. "Can't save."

"Oh, God. No." Mrs. Young seized her husband's military jacket, buried her face in his chest, and sobbed.

Sabrina sprinted into the bedroom.

Mother followed.

The bloody scene catapulted Sabrina into the middle of a battlefield littered with bodies. The stench of burnt gunpowder mixed with the coppery smell of blood snatched her breath. *Breathe in and out.* She closed her eyes.

Cannons fired. *Boom. Boom.*

The ground trembled.

Her heart pounded. *Kathump-kathump.* She bit her lip and tasted blood. "That damn butcher." She swiped the cold sweat beading on the top of her upper lip.

"Daughter, your language."

Mother's voice came from far away like an echo through a tunnel. Sabrina yanked her brain into the present and grabbed a scalpel from her medical bag on the table near the bed, then sloshed carbolic acid over the blade. She made an incision over the curve of Frannie's abdomen.

The lieutenant stormed into the room. "Don't touch my wife."

Mother blocked his passage. "She's trying to save your wife and baby. Heat us some water, and we'll need clean rags. Please hurry, lieutenant."

With bloody hands, Sabrina shoved the slippery newborn toward her mother.

Mother accepted the child. "He's blue."

"He isn't breathing. Sweep his mouth with your little finger." Sabrina continued to work with Frannie and tossed instructions over her shoulder. "His airway is blocked. Wipe his nose."

After smearing her hands on a bedsheet, Sabrina checked Frannie's carotid—weak, but beating. With blood-coated hands, she realigned the slipping flesh and stitched with a threaded needle she kept prepared. Focusing, she concentrated on her sutures. *Push in, pull through, whip over, repeat.*

Seconds later, the baby squeaked.

"Don't stop, Mother. Pat his back. Tap his chest. He needs more air."

The baby's cries grew louder.

Mrs. Young entered the room with her arms full of clean bedsheets.

Frannie's husband followed.

"You have a grandson, Coretta." Mother handed the towel-swaddled newborn to Mrs. Young.

Sabrina tied the last suture. "Get me some cold water, lieutenant." She clipped the silk thread. "The coldest you can find. Ice if you've got it." Snatching a sheet, she ripped.

The lieutenant stood unresponsive, staring at his wife.

Sabrina flung her right arm up into the air. "Now, lieutenant. Move." She pointed to the door.

The lieutenant bolted from the room.

The metallic scent of blood permeated the room.

Sabrina bit her lip and focused on the pain, rooting her mind in the present. When the cold water arrived, she soaked rags and packed the birth canal. As the cloths became saturated, she replaced them with fresh ones.

After several minutes, Frannie's blood clotted.

Sabrina stitched the torn flesh of the birth canal.

Mother stood beside her. "Frannie's not going to make it, is she?"

"Right now, she remains with us—but she's lost a lot of blood." Sabrina scrubbed her sticky hands on a torn sheet. "We need to get her cleaned. The family shouldn't see her like this."

"Is there anything you can do?" Mother held a corner of the bedsheet.

"During the war, Grandfather experimented with a procedure called a transfusion." Sabrina inhaled deeply, releasing some of the tension in her chest.

"So do that." Mother removed the soiled sheets.

"The procedure is not a simple one." Sabrina carried the basin of bloody water to the window and dumped the liquid. "And…they don't always work. Besides, I haven't performed one."

Mother removed Frannie's nightgown. "But you can do it?" She found a clean one and dressed the patient, then covered her with a clean sheet.

"I have Grandfather's journals." Sabrina plunged her hands into clean water and scrubbed with a bar of lye soap. "And the apparatus he used, and I did assist. But…"

"If you don't do this?" Mother smoothed Frannie's blonde hair away from her face.

The patient appeared angelic and peaceful on the clean linens.

Sabrina dried her hands on a towel. "She will die." She pushed her hair back from her face. "We might be too late." She met with the family while her mother and Captain Reed retrieved her medical trunk from the Young's home. "Frannie is dying from blood loss. I'm sorry."

Frannie's husband stood near a corner, wiping his eyes.

Colonel Young turned away with his shoulders hunched and shaking.

"Is...there anything you can do?" Mrs. Young snuggled her grandson closer and allowed him to suckle her little finger.

"My grandfather experimented with taking blood from a healthy person and giving it to another person who needed it." She folded her hands in front of her waist. "He called it a transfusion."

Mrs. Young kissed her grandson's forehead. "Is this...transfusion...our daughter's only hope?"

Sabrina glanced at the family. "I believe so."

Frannie's husband jammed his fingers into his hair. "Then do it."

Sabrina described the process and possible failure, and when the trunk with her equipment arrived, she searched her grandfather's journals.

April 28, 1864. Today I performed my fifth transfusion. The patient was a Confederate soldier. I used his brother as a donor. For this process, the transfusion should be from man to man or woman to woman. I also believe if a family member is available, this would be the wisest choice. The other four transfusions I performed failed.

The metal insertions needles were boiled in water while Mrs. Young, the donor, was positioned on a raised cot beside her daughter's bed.

When all the preliminary steps were completed, Sabrina attached the needles to the opposite ends of the hose. Next, she clamped the tubing in the middle with a pair of forceps and tied a tourniquet around Mrs.

Young's upper left arm. She cleaned the area over a vein, then injected one of the needles. When the blood rose through the needle into the hose, she inserted the other needle into the vein in the bend of Frannie's elbow and opened the clamp. Blood surged from donor into recipient.

Sabrina controlled the flow by monitoring the pressure applied to the hose with the clamp and used Grandfather's pocket watch and timed the process. *Give enough, but not too much.* After several minutes and a few silent prayers, she disconnected the needles.

Frannie's husband faltered to his wife's bedside and stroked her cheek. "Will she live?"

"I'm sorry. I wish I had the answer, but we won't know for several hours. In the meantime, lieutenant, you need to find a wet nurse to feed your son, and Mrs. Young needs to go home and rest. If anything changes, I will let you know."

Chapter 5

In the dark, Ethan absorbed the raspy *snik* of the male mating songs of the katydids, the lonely *grackle-click* of an owl, and the distant *yip-yip-hooowl* of a coyote. He traced his right eyebrow with his index knuckle, aware with every fiber of his being, trouble, in the form of a beautiful woman, had entered his life. He grazed his right thumbnail over his top lip, feeling the jagged edge of keratin.

Doctor Sabrina Clay is here, why?

He had read her letters, and he knew she was involved with Nelson. He scratched the back of his neck. Seeing her this afternoon, standing all prim and proper in the colonel's office, dressed in navy-blue and wearing a fancy little bonnet, had poured over him like rain bursting from a cloud on a sweaty summer's day, sweet and refreshing. His first impulse was to sweep her into his arms and kiss the stiffness from her, but...*she isn't here for me.*

The backdoor *creeeaked* open, and Sabrina stepped outside.

Ethan observed from the shadows, unsure if he should make his presence known.

She crossed to the washstand, and her footsteps *plunked* softly on the boards and dwindled into the night. Then the handle on the bucket *rattled*, and water *shushed* into a metal washbasin. She shoved her sleeves up and dipped her hands into the water, releasing a soft sigh.

Her letters reminded him of his mother's cross-stitched pictures. The paper was Sabrina's fabric, and her words were the threads. She looped and imbedded strands of information on every page, and in her written voice, she transported her world to him.

He knew all her favorites. For breakfast, she liked honey with her biscuits, her favorite color was purple, and her favorite flower was the white lily. She often ate her lunch in a small park near the hospital.

He eased the corners of his mouth up, but his vision had been incomplete. He hadn't known her hair would be the color of a summer's midnight or her eyes would be the shade of a lavender sunset or she would wear the soft fragrance of lilacs. He swallowed, feeling his chest squeeze. And he hadn't known she would trigger such a deep desire. This afternoon, he had done his best to intimidate her with his captain's glare and hard-edged voice.

She unflinchingly stood her ground with flashing violet eyes, then she stuck her adorable little chin out.

I wanted to gather her in my arms and kiss her. He pulled a leather cigar case from his pocket, removed a cigar, and bit off the end, then spit out the chunk. *And I still do.* Striking a match against the bottom of his boot, he held the flame to the end of his cigar and puffed.

The tobacco burned red, and the rich earthy aroma twined with the sweet honeysuckle in the air.

Was she here because she loved Nelson, or because she was involved in the Lincoln Conspiracy?

Sabrina turned and peered into the shadows while water dripped from her hands. "Who's there?"

Ethan sauntered into a wedge of moonlight.

"Spying on me, Captain?" She flipped her back and resumed washing.

Interesting choice of words. He contemplated the miracle he witnessed of blood going from one person and into another. "Will Mrs. Rice recover?"

"Nothing is certain"—she rinsed the soap from her hands—"but she has a chance."

He ambled closer. "And the baby?"

"Grows stronger by the hour." She scrubbed the blood splotches on her navy-blue dress with a washrag.

"Have you delivered a lot of babies?" He blew a cloud of smoke into the air.

Sabrina turned with a hint of a smile on her face while she rubbed the spots on her dress. "Are you asking to see my credentials, Captain?"

Ethan slid his brows up and shook his head. "No, just making conversation." He stroked his lips with his left thumb. *She should smile more often.*

"My grandfather was a physician and my mentor. When I was fourteen, I delivered my first baby." She dunked her rag into the water.

"Fourteen?" He leaned his left shoulder against the side of the house. *She hadn't been more than a child.* "Kind of young, weren't you?"

"The baby's mother was a slave on a neighboring plantation and was only thirteen." She resumed dabbing the blood spots.

"You grew up in the South?" He flicked his ashes to the ground.

"Virginia." As she released a deep breath, she used the back of her right hand to push her hair back. "When rumblings of war became a reality, we found a house in

Washington City, and Grandfather built a hospital."

He blew smoke into the air. "For which side?"

"Grandfather did not choose a side. He said he was a doctor and not a soldier." She rinsed the washrag. "Where are you from, Captain Reed?"

"Born in Missouri." The breeze toyed with her dark hair along the sides of her face, and he felt his heart flutter while his breath seized in the back of his throat. "But I spent some time out West and served back East in the war."

"And your family?" She draped the rag on a nail.

"I don't have any." The graves of his mother, wife and son flashed. "Since you lived in Washington City, you must have known President Lincoln."

"I did. Grandfather and Mr. Lincoln were good friends, and we dined often at the White House." She shook her hands, flipping the excess water before reaching for the towel, then buffed her neck and face.

He shifted his stance. "Why are you here, Doc?"

"I have a contract." She used one hand and finger-combed her hair back up and into the bun on top of her head.

"So"—he nudged his eyebrows up—"you are telling me you had no patients to treat in Washington City?"

She rested her right hand on her hip. "Captain, I'm not telling you anything."

"I can only think of two reasons a person comes into Indian Territory, Doc. One, they are running from something, or two, they are searching for something."

"Frannie's coming around," Mother called.

Sabrina moved toward the doorway, then stopped. "Which one applies to you, Captain Reed, running or searching?"

Damn. Ethan puffed his cigar. *Why is she here?*

****

After checking Frannie, Sabrina joined her mother at the kitchen table. "You didn't have to stay."

The light from a single candle cast shadows along the board wall.

"I wanted to." Mother filled two mugs with steaming coffee and then returned the pot to the stove. "I thought poor George would drop in his boots." She eased into a chair. "How is Frannie, really?"

"Better than she was an hour ago." Sabrina rested her elbows on the table and cradled the hot mug with both hands.

"If you're hungry, Millie brought some leftovers from the dance." Mother uncovered a mixed platter of fried quail and dove pieces. "When we lived at Fort Union, we ate a lot of game birds. I stewed them and made dumplings." She blew across the surface of the hot coffee. "I wonder if Vivian is in for the night."

"I wouldn't think so…with all these men around." She tasted the bitterness of the coffee slide over her tongue.

"I know you and your sister have had problems, but she is your sister. She is not the trollop you believe her to be." Mother's mug *thumped* the table.

"You do remember Mathew, don't you?" Sabrina poked her tongue against the inside of her cheek.

"Vivian was young." Mother fluttered her hands. "She didn't know what she was doing."

"She knew how to get pregnant. And trap the man I was going to marry." Sabrina selected a breast piece of quail, then bit into the meat, registering the flavor of salt and grease. She brushed her fingers along the edge of a tea towel lying on the table. "Do you remember my eighth birthday?" She dropped the quail bone onto the table.

"Of course, I do. Vivian and I traveled across the country to celebrate with you." Mother transferred the bone to the corner of the towel.

"Do you remember the porcelain doll Grandmother gave me?" She twisted her mouth, recalling the purple-gowned doll she had loved.

"You lost the doll." Mother folded the fabric over the bones.

"I didn't lose the doll, Mother." A dam broke inside, and her words flooded. "Vivian took a pair of scissors and cut my doll into bits and bashed her china head into a million pieces."

"She was only three." Mother folded the cloth again. "You have to make allowances."

"Of course, I do." Sabrina wrinkled her chin. *When horses sprout wings and fly.*

****

Returning to her patient, Sabrina used the tail of her dress and wiped the grime from the back of her neck, if only she could clean the memories away. Lifting Frannie's wrist, she monitored her pulse. *Strong and steady.*

She spied a slat-backed rocker in the corner and scooted it closer to the open window, then wilted onto the woven-tape seat, inhaling the sweet fragrance of honeysuckle blended with four o'clock blossoms. Old memories stomped.

Vivian had worn white satin, and Mathew wore a West Point gray jacket and white trousers. The couple stood side by side, pledging their undying love for one another.

A lonely *yip-yip-yowl* drifted like dandelion fluff in the Kansas night.

She closed her eyes, and the captain's words echoed.

...two reasons...one, they are running from something, or two, they are searching for something.

First and foremost, she was searching for the truth about William's death, but if she was being honest, maybe she was running, too. Earlier, the sight and smell of all the blood triggered a vision, plunging her back into a battle. She never knew what would produce the hallucinations: a spoken word, a scent, or sound, and then her brain filled with flashes of mangled arms and legs, men crying, swearing, and praying. During quiet times, the war replayed in a never-ending kaleidoscope of rotating scenes, not enough bandages, not enough medicine, and not enough time while helplessness looped over and over in her head.

During the war, her emotional survival depended on not seeing patients as people, but as injuries to be treated. Hour after hour, in order to do her job, she hardened her heart and bit back tears. She stood on blood-soaked earth hearing the soldiers' pleas...some begging to live, others begging to die, and her body begging for rest. Grandfather told her to focus on the men she was saving, but that never seemed enough. *What could I have done differently?*

****

Sabrina jerked awake to the rapid fire of "Reveille" and blinked the cobwebs of sleep away. She stood, setting the rocking chair into motion, *crick-crock-crick.*

She rotated her shoulders and stepped toward the bedside while massaging the stiffness from her lower back.

Frannie opened her eyes. "Doctor?"

"How are you feeling?" She raised the patient's wrist and monitored the pulse rate.

"Tired." Frannie licked her lips.

"Understandable and expected." Sabrina poured water from an ironstone pitcher into a tin cup and then held the rim to Frannie's lips.

The distant high-pitched cries of a baby grew louder.

"I do believe I hear the arrival of your son." Sabrina set the cup on the bedside table.

"My son?" Frannie lay back and a ghost of a smile flitted across her face. "I was so afraid."

Mrs. Young entered, carrying the newborn, and the crying intensified, bouncing off the walls. "Your little darling is ready for breakfast." She placed the baby into Frannie's arms.

"Oh, my sweet thing." Frannie kissed the baby's fuzzy head. "Where's George, Mama?"

"He's officer of the day and proud as a peacock." Mrs. Young helped Frannie lower the neck of her nightgown. "Mrs. Howard fed little Georgie last night. She delivered about two weeks ago and said if we needed, she can help out."

Frannie nuzzled and cooed nonsensical sounds to her baby while he nursed.

Witnessing the intimate scene, Sabrina felt a deep emptiness claw inside her chest. With William's death, her dreams of having a family had vanished like fog on a winter's morning.

"Isn't he the most beautiful child you've ever seen?" Frannie stroked her baby's downy cheek with her finger.

Feathers of peace blew into Sabrina's heart. "He certainly is."

Frannie lovingly cradled her baby's hand. "If you'd let me, I would like to name him George Henry Clay Rice. Clay after you, Doctor."

"I am truly honored." She wiggled her lips up and laid her right hand over her fluttering heart. "Thank you."

The colonel entered the room.

Mrs. Young looped her arm through her husband's and smiled.

Colonel Young cleared his throat. "Doctor Clay, we owe you a deep debt of gratitude which we can never repay. But I can apologize for my bullish behavior yesterday and last night, and I sincerely do so." He put his left arm around his wife's shoulders and squeezed.

Mrs. Young smiled up at her husband. "We have a little gift for you. She's waiting outside."

"She?"

A few minutes later, Sabrina stepped into the morning sunshine and held the tail of her dress down while a warm breeze threatened to send the hem over her head. Spying the captain, she nudged the corners of her mouth up.

At the edge of the yard, Captain Reed held the reins of a gray mare with a white blaze face, four white stockings, and a military saddle.

"We wanted to give you a little something to thank you, Doctor Clay." Mrs. Young clasped her husband's right arm.

Sabrina eased closer to the horse, feeling a quiver of lightness radiate into her limbs. "She's beautiful." Standing beside the horse, opposite of the captain, she passed her right hand over the horse's soft neck.

"I apologize...we do not have any ladies' saddles at the fort." The colonel covered his wife's hand with his.

Sabrina curled her lips higher. "Quite all right, sir." She fluttered her gaze to the captain and tilted her chin. "I do not require a lady's saddle."

Ethan covered his mouth with his gauntlet-protected hand while the corners of his eyes crinkled, and something between a cough and a chuckle happened.

"Do you know how to ride, Doctor?" Mrs. Young smiled.

"Yes, I do. I've been riding since I was a little girl." Sabrina stroked the horse's snow-white muzzle and then placed her cheek on the mare's forehead. She cut her gaze up at the captain. "Please tell me her name isn't Lady."

He twitched his lips into a smile and the blue in his eyes darkened. "Lily."

"Perfect." She looped an arm around the horse's neck while joy shimmied from her head to her toes. "Thank you. She is absolutely exquisite."

"The weather is lovely for a ride." Mrs. Young smiled with her gaze on Sabrina.

Vivian sashayed into the group. "With just the right amount of sunshine." She smiled at Ethan, cocked her head, and toyed with a curl on the side of her head. "I saw you at the dance last night, but I don't believe we've been properly introduced, I'm Vivian Starr."

"Ethan Reed, ma'am." He touched the brim of his black hat.

"It has been simply ages since I've had a chance to ride." Vivian smiled and batted her eyelashes. "I just wouldn't want to impose, but could you please... Captain?"

"This horse belongs to Doc." He flicked his gaze to Sabrina.

Vivian moved closer to the captain. "My sister won't mind. Will you, dear?"

"Of course not—dear—" Sabrina shoved air from her lungs—*witch.*

Chapter 6

Sabrina sat in a tin bathtub filled with warm water while twilight shadowed the corners of the bedroom. Using a washcloth, she dribbled lilac-scented water over her chest. The drops sluiced downward in tandem with her thoughts, drizzling like rain on a windowpane. She inhaled deeply while the captain's handsome face formed in her mind, then she inched her mouth upward.

This morning, when he had covered his mouth with his hand at the mention of a lady's saddle, she almost laughed out loud. The captain might have hidden his smile, but not his reaction. The corners of his blue eyes crinkled and their color shifted, indicating he was enjoying her teasing as much as she was.

Something elusive teased. At times, she thought, or maybe imagined, sparks of recognition reflected in the depths of his loadstone eyes. Their paths could have crossed during the war. She bit her lip. Too many soldiers...and too many faces...but she was fairly certain...she would have remembered him.

Sabrina dunked her head while honeyed sensations coated the inside of her stomach. Of all the names, why did he choose Lily for her horse? He could not have possibly known the lily was her favorite flower. So...it had to be a coincidence, right? Using a pitcher of clean water sitting beside the tub, she rinsed the soap from her hair, gathered the ends, and squeezed. Excess water trickled like her doubts about William.

Had William loved her, or had he only wanted to marry her to hide his identity? She respected William as a doctor, but if he was a traitor to the United States or had anything to do with President Lincoln's death, then what? Was it possible Grandfather had suspected William? Is that why he cautioned, "Marriage to the wrong person will be a disaster."

Sabrina stepped from the tub, and rivulets trickled down her legs. She brushed the drops away with a sun-scented towel. Leaning forward, she twisted the towel around her hair and tucked the end beneath the edges. After slipping into her blue cotton robe, she retrieved William's letters from her trunk.

December 1, 1865.

This has been a most trying day. One of the laundresses asked for help. I told her I would not perform such an act. We had words. She left, and by the time I was notified, she or someone had attempted to correct the problem. I got her into surgery and did everything I could. I have seen so much death.

William suffered from mood swings.

She refolded the letter. Some days, he would be laughing and joking, and nothing could get him down. Other times, he couldn't get out of bed. Following the war, his depression deepened, and he developed a frightening paranoia. If he were leading a secret life...that would explain some of his actions. She returned the letter to the bundle, balanced on the side of the bed, and braided her hair.

Could the father of the laundress' child be involved in William's death? She twisted her lips and drew her brows together. Or...and this was something she did not wish to consider, but...had William changed his mind about marrying her? Sabrina coiled the rope of hair into a bun on top of her head and anchored the topknot with hairpins.

William dabbled in oil paints and wanted to go to Paris on their honeymoon. He often said he wished he had pursued art instead of medicine. William could have killed himself for any number of reasons.

Shuffling through her trunk, Sabrina selected a high-neck cotton gown of pale lavender, with buttons down the front, and trimmed with black cording around the neck and sleeves. She slipped into the garment, and as she walked from the room, she smoothed the wrinkles with her right hand. At the bottom of the cramped staircase, she turned left into the kitchen.

The enticing aromas of roasting meats, with hints of onion, garlic, and sage, created a mouthwatering blend.

At the stove, Mother stirred a pot of chicken and dumplings.

"*Mm-mm.* Something smells good in here. What can I do?"

At a table in the middle of the room, Mrs. Young worked the lip of a drinking glass into a flat piece of dough and cut round biscuits, which she placed into a greased pan. "Not one blessed thing. You, dear, are the guest of honor this evening."

"Me? But you have already given me a horse."

"The horse was mainly from Henry, but this is a little something I can do." Mrs. Young wiped the corner of her eye with her apron. "Go on now, shoo."

Sabrina drifted across the hallway into the nicely furnished sitting room.

A medallion-back sofa, edged with dark wood and upholstered in floral burgundy, sat along the east wall. Matching side chairs with cabriole legs flanked the sofa, and in the corner, stood an upright piano. A cold fireplace occupied the west wall.

Ambling around the room, she halted in front of a gold-framed painting of Colonel Young in the full military regalia of a Union officer. She folded her arms over her chest. *Mrs. Hunter's husband and son were Union soldiers, and her cousin married a Union officer. Interesting.*

Beneath the portrait, a mahogany lowboy held a collection of figurines.

Sabrina landed her gaze on a porcelain ballerina dressed in a pink tutu, and a snippet of a sweet memory pirouetted. She and her grandparents had attended the ballet in celebration of the removal of her braces, and she had worn a bright sunshine-yellow gown. Holding the porcelain figurine in her right hand, she traced the tutu's golden ruffle with her left index finger. After the performance, they met the dancers, and Grandfather explained about the celebration.

The lead male dancer tucked her into his arms and spun her across the floor of the stage, and without the weight of the braces on her legs, she floated on air.

Vivian twitched into the room. "So...this is where you are hiding."

At the sound of her sister's shrill voice, Sabrina cringed, the figurine wobbled, and she clamped her hand around the dancer.

"I was wondering where you had gone." Vivian flounced farther into the room, wearing a gown of sky-blue satin and smelling strongly of summer roses.

Blue was the color of the captain's eyes. Sabrina inhaled. "Aren't you a tad bit overdressed?"

"I want Ethan to see what he can have. We had a lovely afternoon." Vivian turned and scanned the room. "You haven't seen a mirror, have you?"

"Ethan?" She set the porcelain figure back, feeling the needle pricks of her sister's words. "So, you are already on a first-name basis."

"We are. I have decided Captain Reed will be my new husband." Vivian swished closer to the framed mirror beside the front door and fluffed the pile of blonde curls on top of her head.

Sabrina stiffened the muscles around her mouth. "Don't you think he might have something to say?"

"The captain wants me"—Vivian thrust her bosom up and tugged her neckline to reveal a more daring glimpse of cleavage—"he just doesn't know it yet."

"Are you going to trick him like you did Mathew?" While her heart squeezed, Sabrina sauntered around the room.

"Trick is a harsh word." Vivian slid her little finger over her bottom lip. "Mathew and I made love, and a child was created."

Sabrina flipped her gaze and pointed her nose toward the ceiling. "That is certainly one explanation."

"You know, you really should stop pretending." Vivian pinched her cheeks while watching her reflection in the mirror. "Everybody knows you didn't love William."

"I was fond of William." Sabrina mashed her lips into a hard line and trailed fingers over the back rail of a rocking chair, sending the piece into motion *crick-crick-crick.*

"Fond?" Vivian pinned her gaze on Sabrina and shook her head, jiggling her blonde curls. "Really, Sabrina, don't you know anything?" She flipped back to the reflection. "When you love a man and he loves you, a fire burns between the two of you." Her voice dipped low and dreamy. "The word fond does not enter the conversation. Big Sister, your problem is you are not woman enough to go after a man."

Sabrina bit her bottom lip. *Is that why Mathew chose Vivian over me?*

****

A few minutes later, Sabrina stepped into the dining room, and introductions were made. She knew everyone except two lieutenants—Clark, a short squat man, and Smith, a red-headed man with lots of freckles.

The oval table had been extended with additional leaves, and in the middle, a centerpiece of red flowers produced a sweet scent. Candlesticks held burning white candles strategically set in a line down the middle. An assortment of side chairs lined both lengths of the table and at each end sat an armchair.

Graham held the back of a side chair.

"Thank you." Sabrina slid onto the wooden seat and adjusted her chair closer to the table.

"My pleasure." As Graham edged in beside her, he brushed her back with his body.

Sabrina leaned away.

Lieutenant Clark aided Vivian into a chair directly across from the captain.

At the head of the table, Colonel Young rose and rapped his spoon on his wine goblet. "Before we get good and started...I would like to make a toast." He lifted the long-stemmed glass into the air, glanced at his wife, then Sabrina. "To the good doctor who saved our daughter and grandson. Thank you from the bottom of our hearts."

The group raised their glasses. "Here, here."

Vivian pasted an impish smile on her face and toyed with curl dangling on the side of her head.

Sabrina felt her cheeks warm. "I am glad I was here." She sipped her wine and slanted her gaze toward Captain Reed. *Instead of being forced to return to Washington.*

He lifted his right eyebrow, tilted his head, and smiled.

Bowls of buttery corn, peas, and potatoes, platters of roasted meats, beef, venison, and turkey, passed around the table, and the well-prepared foods were transferred onto plates.

All around Sabrina, conversations hummed, and the occasional laugh created a comfortable atmosphere, but her mind clamped onto the captain's words...*two reasons a person comes into Indian Territory...one, they are running from something, or two, they are searching for something.* Was the captain here because of military orders, or something else? She peeked through her eyelashes and watched him converse with Colonel Young.

Ethan's sun-bronzed skin reflected the many hours he spent in the saddle, and his wide shoulders filled the federal-blue uniform without any room to spare. In the flickering candlelight, his blue eyes appeared calm like a sea on a summer's day. But yesterday in the colonel's office, his eyes flashed dark like a storm boiling on the horizon.

The captain leaned his left elbow on the edge of the

table, then tweaked his lips into a smile, flicking his gaze to her.

Sabrina felt heat splash over her face, and she ducked her head and locked her gaze on the painted blue ribbon winding around the edge of her plate. She swallowed. *No...he knew I was watching. What must he think?* Without lifting her head, she sneaked a peek through the corner of her eye.

"Where is your home, Captain?" Mother blotted her mouth on a white linen napkin.

Ethan redirected his attention. "I grew up on a little farm in Missouri, ma'am, but I call the army my home."

"My husband, Warren, felt the same way. God rest his soul." Mother held her wine goblet. "He's been gone about five years." She sipped. "He was firing a Parrott Rifle, and the barrel exploded."

A hush fell around the table, and condolences were expressed.

Mrs. Hunter wiped her mouth on her napkin. "One of my all-time most favorite memories is the time you and Warren married." She lifted her long-stemmed glass. "You wore a gown the color of a Virginia sunset. And Warren...land's sake...that man was as nervous as a cat on a hot tin roof."

Masculine chuckles ringed the table.

"The day was everything a bride could hope for." Mother smiled, returned her attention to her plate, and cut a slice of roast beef. "How long have you been at Fort Greer, Captain?"

Before answering, Ethan tossed Sabrina a glance. "Came out last June, ma'am."

Sabrina sipped her water, calculating the months.

He arrived shortly after William.

"When do you think we will be able to leave for Fort Greer?" Mother placed the bite of roast beef in her mouth.

"I've got the supplies loaded"—Ethan glanced at his commanding officer—"waiting on your orders, sir."

Colonel Young wiped his mouth on a napkin, then put the cloth back into his lap. "I suppose that decision rests with Doctor Clay."

"If Frannie continues improving"—Sabrina set her water glass down—"we can leave in a couple of days."

Vivian twirled a curl hanging over her shoulder. "I just can't believe our good fortune in having Captain Reed here to escort us to Fort Greer." She batted her eyelashes and flashed a flirty smile. "Do tell us about Fort Greer, Captain."

Sabrina recognized the look her sister was giving the captain, and the bite of turkey in her mouth turned to powder.

Vivian was stalking the man.

Never again. Sabrina swallowed.

"Not much to tell. Fort's small, not many civilians. Only soldiers and their families"—Ethan pinned his gaze on Sabrina and raised his brows—"until now."

She wiggled the corners of her mouth and tilted her head. *Touché.*

"I enjoyed our little ride this afternoon, Captain." Vivian daintily blotted her mouth on her napkin. "You all should have seen this creek Captain Reed showed me. Such a lovely little spot." She smiled and tipped her head slightly down.

What is she hiding? Sabrina concentrated on her sister. *Did Ethan kiss her?*

"I believe there are some fish in that stream, Miss Vivian." Graham blotted his mouth.

"Why would anyone want to do such a disgusting thing?" Vivian shuddered. "Those squirmy old worms."

Graham turned his head toward Vivian and smiled. "Fishing is more than catching fish. Time stands still while you sit there and watch the bobber dance in the wind. And just when you're about to doze off, a big fish grabs ahold, and the fight is on. Sometimes, he gets away…and sometimes, he is your supper."

Everyone laughed.

"Spoken like a true fisherman." Colonel Young forked a bite of beef.

"Do you like to fish, Miss Sabrina?" Graham stroked his lips with his index finger and leaned a bit closer.

"I do." She reached for her wine goblet and felt dots of heat on her cheeks. "When we lived in Virginia, Grandfather and I used to go to Muddy Bend."

"What kind of fish, Doctor?" The colonel set his elbows on the table.

She tilted her body closer to Mrs. Young and away from Graham. "Catfish, mostly." She sipped her wine, and the taste of plum registered along the edges of her tongue.

"We have a river near the fort." Graham focused on her. "Perhaps we can go fishing sometime?"

"Perhaps." She flitted her gaze to the captain. *Why is he scowling?*

****

Ethan moved with the group from the dining room into the parlor. Unless he was mistaken, which he wasn't, Graham Hunter had his eye on Sabrina. *Not in this lifetime, mister.*

"I understand Miss Starr is a wonderful singer." Colonel Young chose an upholstered side chair.

Vivian swished deeper into the room. "You're much too kind, Colonel." She fluttered her eyelashes.

"If you'll sing, Miss Vivian, I'll play." Graham approached the piano in the corner of the room. Sitting on the three-legged stool, he pushed back the fallboard and cracked his knuckles.

"If you all are sure you want to hear me?" Vivian cocked her head and smiled, touching her mouth with her fingers.

The group applauded and called out a few words of encouragement.

Vivian glided across the floor and conferred with Graham.

With his knees apart and his hands steepled in front of his face, Ethan observed from a hoop-back armchair in the corner. Vivian Starr reminded him of Marianne— same blonde hair and the same fake smile. Marianne Kimble was the daughter of a neighbor, and her green eyes made promises they never intended keeping.

Graham played the familiar chords of an old English ballad.

"Alas...my love...you do me wrong...." Vivian drifted around the room, smiling and flirting with the men.

Just like Marianne. Ethan rested his elbows on the chair's wooden arms. One afternoon, he had found Marianne in the barn with his friend, Cal. At first, he wanted to fight Cal, but then he learned Cal wasn't the only one who had been with Marianne. No thanks, Vivian Starr was not for him.

He stroked his left index finger along his right jawbone and inched his gaze to the tempting beauty sitting beside her mother on the sofa. From the time he read Sabrina's first letter, he had been mesmerized and fascinated by a woman he had never seen, and feeling deeply intriguing emotions he had never experienced. After meeting her, talking with her, and seeing her dedication, he had fallen deeply in love with this smart, strong—he elevated the corners of his mouth—and definitely hardheaded woman.

At supper, knowing she was watching him, he felt a tingling sensation similar to warm fingers caressing his face. And when her cheeks flashed pink, he felt his breath jam deep in his chest. He traced his lips with his fingertips. *Damn, she was intoxicating.*

****

After the other guests left, Ethan trailed Colonel Young into a cozy book-lined room at the back of the two-story house.

"Care for a drink, Captain?" The short, stubby colonel indicated the crystal decanter in his hand.

"Thank you, sir." Ethan claimed a blue-and-gold overstuffed chair and accepted the half-filled whiskey glass.

Colonel Young eased into the matching mate. "I don't know what to make of Doctor Clay being here." He sipped the liquor. "I'm glad she is, but how did a woman come to be assigned to a post in the military?"

"I don't know, sir. During the war, some civilian doctors were contracted to care for the soldiers. Maybe this is an extension."

The colonel swirled the liquid. "I received a letter from the general yesterday." He tapped his chin with his left index finger. "The commander is curious about how your investigation is going."

"More questions than answers." Ethan swallowed a mouthful of whiskey, feeling the burn glide down the back of his throat. "And the answers I do have…might not be right."

"Is the general correct in his assumption Nelson was a Confederate spy?" The colonel opened the lid on a wooden cigar box.

"Some things pointed that direction before he left Washington"—Ethan accepted a cigar—"but we didn't have any hard evidence, only circumstantial."

Snapping the lid shut, the colonel set the box on a low table in front of his knees. "And now Nelson's dead?"

"Things have become more difficult." Using his pocketknife, Ethan removed the end of the cigar and dropped the nub into a ceramic dish. He leaned forward and lit his cigar from a candle burning on the claw-footed table in front of him. He drew the smoke into his mouth tasting the leathery flavor sting his tongue.

The colonel lit his cigar. "Find anything unusual when you searched Nelson's quarters?"

"A collection of newspaper articles about the assassination." Ethan studied the amber liquid in his glass. "And a note from Mary Surratt about one of her boarders, a Mrs. Holahan."

Silver smoke blanketed the air.

Doctor Sabrina Clay's letters belong to me.

"Doesn't that connect Nelson to the conspirators?" The colonel rolled his cigar to the other side of his mouth.

"Yes…and no." Ethan scraped his left thumbnail

along his jaw. "Being a doctor, he might have been caring for a patient."

Colonel Young flicked cigar ashes into a dish on the table. "Both Booth and Nelson grew up in northern Maryland. They might have known one another."

"Might have." Ethan nodded and puffed his cigar, watching the end glow red.

"And now with Nelson's suicide, what happens?" The colonel sipped his drink.

Ethan inhaled and let the breath float out. "Nelson was murdered."

The colonel pinned his gaze on the captain and adjusted his body forward. "The report said suicide."

"Shot twice, once in the back and once in the right temple." Ethan flicked his ashes into the dish. "My theory is...whoever shot Nelson...slipped into his bedroom while he was asleep and shot him in the back at close range."

The colonel jogged both brows up. "And the other shot?"

"Someone covering up the first."

The colonel scratched the side of his head. "So, two people are involved."

"At least." Ethan knocked his ashes into the dish. "There was an incident which happened and has nothing to do with the conspiracy, but...gives another possibility for the murder." He pulled the woodsy tobacco flavor into his mouth, then blew out and wrinkled his lips. "Both Graham Hunter and Nelson were involved with the same laundress. Woman by the name of Lila Minton. She got pregnant, and rumor has it, Nelson tried to fix the situation, but the woman died."

A clock, on a shelf near the cold potbellied stove, ticked.

A soft breeze fluttered the curtains and brushed the candle flame.

Colonel Young tilted his head. "And one of them is the father?"

"Don't know." Ethan puffed his cigar. "Several people witnessed an argument between the two men. And according to what they observed...the lieutenant threatened to kill the doctor." Ethan clamped his cigar between the fingers of his right hand and reached for his drink with his left. "Graham Hunter might have been the father." He scrutinized the colonel's face for a reaction.

The colonel leaned back. "I bet James was foaming at the mouth over this." He sipped his drink. "He would do anything to protect his son." The colonel laid his cigar in the dish and emptied his glass. "Another?"

Ethan nodded and handed up his glass. The colonel had shown no surprise at the possibility of Graham being the father. Did he know something? They were family.

"So, the question we are chasing is"—the colonel refilled the glasses and returned—"not only who killed Nelson, but why?" He resumed his seat and crossed his ankles.

Ethan swirled his glass, jiggling the amber liquid and watching the motion. "Maybe someone at the fort is involved in the conspiracy, and Nelson was a threat to this person."

"You mean a fellow spy?" The colonel nodded, then lifted his glass.

"Not long after Nelson arrived, a guy by the name

of Fowler appeared, and Nelson made him the medical steward." Ethan rose and sauntered to the window on the north side of the room. "Seemed suspicious as hell. Almost like they knew one another." Pulling the curtain aside, he stared into the ebony night, feeling a light breeze on his face. "Booth had plenty of help. Some of the bastards we've caught. Some we haven't." He turned and perched on the windowsill facing the room.

"And you believe Fowler could be involved, as well?" The colonel shifted his cigar to the opposite corner of his mouth.

"Might be. He doesn't appear overly bright, but one can never tell." Ethan shoved away from the sill. "Something's been puzzling me." He scratched the back of his head. "Nelson had been at Greer almost a year, so why was he killed now?" He returned to his chair. "Everything slingshots us back to the laundress."

The colonel finished his drink. "Another thing to consider is the person who killed Nelson might have only recently arrived at the fort."

Ethan lowered his brows. "You might be on to something, Colonel." He nodded. "I'll get a list of the last recruits, and if any are from Washington City or Maryland, we might have a new lead."

Chapter 7

In the flush of the predawn, Sabrina followed her mother to the waiting ambulance. The canvas sides of the wagon were rolled up, and their trunks were stacked in the back.

Mrs. Hunter sat on the front seat with her back rigid and her face completely hidden behind the edge a black bonnet.

"Good morning, Millie." With the aid of a soldier, Mother climbed onto the second seat. "We missed you at breakfast, dear." She adjusted the green bag she was carrying to her lap.

"I was just recalling"—Millie patted her right hand on her mouth—"the time we all traveled to Rocky Gorge."

Mother fanned a horsefly away from her face. "My goodness, dear, a lot of water under that bridge." She fluffed the skirt of her black gingham dress, making the seat springs squeak.

Sabrina joined Mother on the seat and glanced toward the boardwalk where a small crowd of well-wishers were gathering.

Mrs. Hunter twisted around. "I recall the weather was spring-like and simply gorgeous. We rode in such fine carriages, and birds filled the air with their sweet songs." She cradled her cheeks between the palms of her hands. "We were a sight to behold, Sabrina. We wore summer gowns with ruffles and lace and were feeling so grown up. Mammy Florene made us a fine luncheon, and we had a picnic. So, peaceful..." She firmed her mouth and slowly shook her head. "I don't imagine anything appears the way it once did, with the war and all."

"I don't imagine it does." Mother removed an unfinished multicolored baby blanket from the large bag and began crocheting. "Why so melancholy, dear?"

"A dream I had seems to be taunting me." A ghost of a smile crossed Mrs. Hunter's lips. "Polly, I can't tell you how glad I am you and your girls are here."

"I'm glad, too." Mother glanced around. "I wonder what's keeping Vivian."

Sabrina scanned the cluster of people in front of the general store and spotted her sister smiling and sashaying through the crowd, perfectly dressed for an afternoon tea.

Vivian wore an apple-green frock with a matching large-brimmed hat and carried a frilly parasol. "I'm going to miss, you all." From beneath the edge of her umbrella, she perused the group. "You all are so kind to come and see me off."

Two soldiers rushed forward with their forage caps in their hands and silly smiles on their faces.

"Miss Vivian, I'd give my right arm if you'd marry me," one soldier said.

"She's going to marry me." The second soldier elbowed the first soldier out of the way.

"I'm very fond of you both, but..." Vivian smiled and repositioned her parasol. "My heart belongs to another." She skimmed the faces in the crowd. "Have either of you seen Captain Reed?"

"Last time I seen him, ma'am, he was checking on the horses in the corral," the first soldier said.

Vivian edged closer to the ambulance. "Mother, you know riding in the back makes my stomach all fluttery." She pooched out her bottom lip and cocked her head to one side.

"Sabrina?"

"I'll sit in the back, Mother." She pressed her lips together and placed her booted foot on the top of the wheel, and a helpful soldier rushed forward and aided her dismount.

"You are such a sweet dear." Vivian batted her eyelashes.

"Don't pretend with me." Sabrina paused in front of her sister. "I know the real you." She arrived at the rear of the ambulance and grabbed the top of the tailgate. The wood bit into her hand.

"Here, ma'am. Allow me."

Sabrina turned and recognized the kind brown eyes of Private Todd.

"Got my transfer, ma'am." He lowered the tailgate and then offered his hand. "Guess I'm coming with you."

"Congratulations." She steadied herself against his arm, climbed into the wagon, then squished her body between the trunks.

Private Todd refastened the tailgate. "See you later, ma'am." He jogged away.

Sabrina tied the ribbons on her brown bonnet and inhaled, focusing on the sunrays painting strands of pink and lavender along the edges of a blue sky.

Mrs. Young's face appeared above the tailgate. "I have a little something for y'all's luncheon." She handed up a large wicker basket. "And this is just for you." She offered Sabrina a round silver tin. "I made a batch of pecan pralines last night. The pecans are from last year's crop, but they're still good. Polly told me this was your favorite candy."

Sabrina clutched the tin to her chest. "Thank you." She tucked the treasure inside her medical bag. "Please write me about Frannie and the baby. I must know how my little namesake is growing."

Tears appeared in Mrs. Young's gray eyes. "I shall. And I'll get Frannie to write, too. Have a safe journey, Doctor." She waved, then turned away, wiping her eyes on her calico apron.

In the distance, Sabrina caught a glimpse of the captain issuing orders from the back of a sorrel gelding. His wide-brimmed hat rode low across his forehead, and last night, she mustered all she could to keep from staring at him.

Ethan and his reddish-brown horse synched as one. Every time he shifted his weight, the horse responded, leaving no doubt as to who was in charge.

Oh no, he's coming this way. She licked her lips and her heart sped, *kathump-kathump.*

"Morning, Doc." He hitched his lips upward into a half-smile, forming deep dimples in his cheeks. "Care to ride?"

She grabbed the top of the tailgate. "I would love to."

"Hold on." He dismounted. "Let me get you out of there." He unhitched the barrier, and the heavy chain *rattled*, then the board dropped.

Rising on her knees, she gripped his shoulders.

He positioned his hands around her waist and lifted

her with one arm around her back and one beneath her legs. "Sergeant, bring Doc's horse."

"Yes, sir." The bear-sized, red-bearded sergeant guided his horse closer, wearing a broad smile and leading the smoke-gray mare with four white stockings.

Ethan continued holding her.

Sabrina looped her arms around his neck while her backside settled securely in the cradle of his arms. He smelled of coffee, leather, and a hint of soap. When she was a little girl, she was carried by her grandfather like this, but never had she been carried as a woman by a man.

Ethan set her into the saddle and then handed her the reins.

"Thank you." She placed her pointed-toe boots into the stirrups, fluffed her brown skirt over her legs, and nestled her bottom into the split-seated McClellan saddle.

Ethan touched the brim of his hat. "My pleasure, Doc." He grinned.

Next to the ambulance, Vivian waved. "You-hoo, Captain, I need just a tiny boost." She handed the closed parasol to Mother and then gathered her apple-green skirt in one hand. She placed her multibutton shoe on the hub of the wheel and waited.

Ethan moved beside Vivian and offered his arm.

"Thank you…" Vivian latched on, pushed upward, and placed her mouth close to Ethan's face. "Ever so… much, Cap…tain…"

Sabrina gritted her teeth.

The captain stepped quickly away. "Sergeant, we need two scouts." He swung into the saddle and secured his hat.

"Yes, sir." The sergeant faced the men. "Privates Todd and Butterworth. Ye heard the cap'n, mount up."

As the caravan trudged westward, Sabrina angled Lily alongside the ambulance. The landscape spread outward like a giant green ocean surging toward the horizon and merging with the cerulean sky, with almost nothing in-between.

"Camptown ladies…" From the seat of one of the wagons, a soldier's singing voice rose over the sounds of the *clanging* and *rattling*.

"I declare…I can't believe this heat. The air's so thick it's like breathing through cotton." Vivian flapped a lacy fan in front of her face.

"Goin' to get worse, ma'am." The corporal flapped the reins. "Hup now. Git up there."

Ethan rode point, blazing a trail through the waving grasses.

As Sabrina watched his navy-blue back and broad shoulders, a fragment of her wanted to explore the tiny bubbles of pleasure created every time she was near him. *But…if Vivian has set her cap for the captain…what chance do I have?*

Dipping back into the past, she recalled the most magical night of her life. She felt her chest squeeze and opened her mouth, feeling the heat scorch her throat. She and Mathew had planned a spring wedding in the garden at Carter Hall. She caught her bottom lip with her teeth. In Mathew's arms, all things seemed possible…until they weren't. Father was killed. Vivian got pregnant. Mathew married Vivian. *If Vivian wants the captain…*"At least I have you, Lily." She tilted forward and patted the horse's neck.

On her fourth birthday, she had received a little

brown pony from Grandfather, and Grandmother gave her a royal-blue riding habit with a matching hat. Muffin became her legs, and when she was on her pony's back, she could run. They were always up for a race and often left the other children in the dust, something she couldn't do when she was wearing her braces. Over the years she had many horses and had loved them all, but Muffin was extra special.

Patches of yellow and blue wildflowers studded the long strands of green grasses playing a game of peek-a-boo in the occasional breeze. The sun followed an ordained path across the sky, dropping heat in waves.

Using the neck of her brown dress, Sabrina smeared the sweat from her cheek, then unscrewed the lid of her canteen and filled her mouth with water while doubts nibbled. Was going to Fort Greer the right decision?

At noon, the caravan stopped at Bluff Creek, a meandering stream with a few scraggly trees.

Sergeant O'Rourke barked orders.

Todd and Butterworth built a fire.

Two soldiers laughed and joked while they peeled potatoes.

Their driver, whom she had heard called Corporal Davis, slapped salt pork into a cast-iron skillet.

Sabrina rode to the edge of the creek and inhaled the pungent fish odor coating the brown water. She stood in the stirrup with her weight on her left leg and flung her right leg back over the saddle seat, but unsure of the distance, she dangled her right leg in the air. She could drop, or she could call for help.

From behind, unseen hands grasped her waist and swung her safely to the ground.

She swiveled and faced her rescuer and felt her knees go limp. *Ethan.*

He slanted his lips into a cocky grin, displaying deep dimples in his cheeks.

The blue in his eyes softened to a spring day, and she forgot about everything but him and finger-combed wayward strands back from her face. She tucked the locks beneath the edge of her bonnet while her heart *kathumped* against her ribcage. She swallowed.

He frowned. "Your nose is sunburnt."

Suspended in the moment, she touched the tender skin on the bridge of her nose, completely beneath his spell.

"Sister dear, aren't you going to eat?" Vivian's overly sweet voice punched through the dreamy haze.

For a second longer, Sabrina held his gaze, pushed the corners of her lips upward, then ambled away. She glanced toward her sister.

Vivian sat on a blanket and fanned her full skirt outward and formed a sea of green.

Men buzzed around the queen, wanting to be noticed.

"Miss Vivian, I brung ye a cup of water."

"Miss Vivian, can I git you anything?"

"Here, Miss Vivian, let me."

From the ladies' picnic basket, Sabrina retrieved a piece of fried chicken and a thick slice of bread. What made men act like such fools? Why couldn't a man see her sister for what she was—spoiled and conceited to high heaven? In her sister's world, Vivian was the only one who existed. Sabrina crouched onto a rock. Perhaps one of the reasons she was drawn to William was he seemed immune to Vivian. She bit into the crusty bread and sidled her gaze toward the captain.

Ethan filled his plate with salt pork, beans, and fried potatoes and then plopped a biscuit into the mix. Holding his tin plate in one hand, he squatted at the campfire, poured a cup of coffee, and then he stepped away.

Vivian flipped back her skirt and peeked from beneath the edge of her straw hat. "Captain, would you care to join little ole me?"

"No, thank you, Miss Starr."

"Captain, you promised." Vivian pushed out her bottom lip, creating a young girl's pout.

"Miss Vivian." He nodded in passing.

Sabrina bit into a piece of fried chicken and tasted salt and pepper and, as she chewed, sought the man she found fascinating.

Between bites, the commander laughed and talked with his men.

Closing her eyes, she vividly relived the quadrille and the captain holding her. A warm flush spiraled over her body. Then, the zingy scent of his shaving soap floated. She snapped her eyes open.

"Don't move, Doc." Ethan held his service revolver in his right hand and a biscuit in his left.

"What do you mean?" She stood and started to step.

Shush-shush-shush.

She stiffened, barely breathing. Cutting her gaze toward the sound, she located a coiled serpent, head raised, tail shaking, and within striking distance. Her heart pounded. *Bam! Bam! Bam!* She felt her knees quiver, and her saliva evaporated. She swallowed.

Ethan put the biscuit into his mouth.

She closed her bottom lip over her top lip and squeezed her eyes shut.

Bang!

She flinched. She peeked.

The snake's head—completely gone.

She melted.

Ethan grabbed her upper arms. "No need to go all mushy, Doc. Only an old rattler."

"I…don't like…snakes." She felt his strength holding her and preventing her body from dissolving into a puddle.

"Be careful where you sit, Doc." He grinned while he squeezed her upper arms.

"Sabrina." Mother rushed forward with others in pursuit. "What is going on?"

"Nothing to see, folks." Ethan released his hold. "Doc got a little too close to a rattler." He lifted the dead snake and tossed her a wink. "No need to waste fresh meat."

Trembling, she folded her arms across her chest and stroked his warm finger imprints. She gasped air. *Because of the snake or because of him?*

****

Sabrina maneuvered Lily alongside the ambulance and observed the burning sun dropping lower, and the blue sky exploding into fragments of orange and pink. Insects swarmed in a buzzing-biting feeding frenzy, and she slapped the stinging spots on her cheeks, then smeared the grime and sweat with the sleeve of her dress.

Lily shifted downward, locking her knees.

Sabrina counterbalanced by leaning backward and allowing her body to sync with her horse.

The ambulance lumbered and creaked into the circle with the other wagon.

"Welcome to Cimarron Creek, ladies," Corporal Davis announced. "We'll bed down here."

Around the site, soldiers laughed, and words were batted between the men.

Mules *hee-hawed,* and harnesses jangled.

Two privates unloaded the grub wagon, and pots and pans rattled.

Sergeant O'Rourke barked orders, and within minutes, the camp became a knot of activity.

Sabrina coaxed her mare to a large boulder and dismounted. Clutching the reins in her left hand, she hopped down, then led her horse to the creek. "You are such a good girl." She buffed her cheek on Lily's soft muzzle.

At the edge of the water, Butterworth held the reins of a mule. "You probably don't know this, ma'am, but Cap'n Reed picked that little lady just for you." He patted the hip of the mule he was watering. "You should've heard him and the old blacksmith go at it. The smithy tried to get the cap'n to take this old broken-down nag. But the cap'n said he wanted the best and wouldn't settle for nothing less."

Ethan wanted the best...for me? After caring for Lily, Sabrina moved into the heart of camp, inhaling the food-scented cloud hovering above the fire.

Prairie chickens, rabbits, and chunks of rattlesnake roasted on a spit above the flames, potatoes sizzled in a cast-iron skillet, and the aroma of baking biscuits rose from a Dutch oven. When everything finished cooking, the meal was served buffet style on a folding table.

Sabrina selected a piece of the prairie chicken, a

scoop of potatoes, and a biscuit, and then she eased down on the tongue of the grub wagon.

Graham joined her.

"Your mother seems a little depressed today." She balanced the tin plate in her lap.

"Mother suffers from painful headaches. When they come, her mind goes to happier times." He found a place for his tin coffee cup.

"I recall how beautiful the rose gardens were at Homewood." She sampled the dark meat and registered a flavor similar to beef.

"Grandma Oldine's rose gardens were her pride and joy. She would gather the spent blooms and make potpourri, so every room in the house smelled like her garden all year long. I can still smell them"—he sniffed the air—"fresh and sweet."

"Did your mother live at Homewood during the war?" She laid the chicken bone on the side of her plate.

"Shortly after the war began, Homewood burned. Mother went to Maryland and lived with some of our kinfolk." He took a bite of rabbit and chewed.

"The war must have been especially difficult for her with both you and your father fighting for the Union." She bit into her biscuit, tasting the tang of sourdough.

"I believe Mother has forgiven me for the part I played in the war, but she will never forgive Father." He washed the bite of rabbit down with a sip of coffee. "As far as she's concerned, he is a traitor to the South, and nothing will change that."

Did Graham spy for the Confederacy? She forked potatoes into her mouth, and as she chewed, the pepper tingled over her tongue.

"I hope when we get to Fort Greer you will allow me to call on you, Miss Sabrina." He smiled.

Should I encourage him? "I'm not sure I will have much time." She finished the last bite of her biscuit.

In the background, the clatter and scraping of tin plates indicated the meal was over, and the soldiers prepared to wash the dishes.

The first notes of "When Johnny Comes Marching Home" flowed across camp and took flight into the evening air. The ladies were quickly claimed for a lively polka.

"Shall we?" Graham offered his hand.

Sabrina started with Graham but soon twirled with Private Todd and then spun with Private Butterworth. She laughed, and as she bounced, hairpins dropped from her thick bun.

The song ended, and the dancers broke apart, laughing and clapping.

Private Johnson flipped a musical switch and played the sad lingering notes of a slow song, reflecting the heartbreak of war.

"Dearest love, do you remember..." Vivian's bell-like voice blended with the mouth organ's raspy sounds, as she sauntered closer to the private and put her right hand on his left shoulder.

Ethan claimed Sabrina.

Using her left hand, she shoved her lopsided bun back up and the roll fell again.

"Let it go."

"But..." She felt him squeeze her right hand.

"I like it." He smiled. "Just like that."

Dimples bracketed his lips and his eyes turned a

soft liquid blue, sending tiny dots of heat fluttering in her stomach, and she inhaled in stutter-breaths.

"Did you sample the rattlesnake?" He veered her in another direction.

She leaned back, noticing the playful glint sparking in the blue pools, and elevated the corners of her mouth. "I did not."

"Some say an old rattler can taste like chicken." He applied gentle pressure to the small of her back.

Pebbles shifted beneath her feet. "The only thing that tastes like chicken is chicken."

"You might be right, Doc." He chuckled, the sound vibrating deep in his chest.

She angled her nose closer to his left shoulder and inhaled the primal merging of masculine scents. On her lower back, through the fabric of her brown dress, she felt the warm tips of each of his fingers. *No matter what, I can't forget my purpose for being here.*

The song ended, and Vivian smiled and curtseyed to the group.

"More. More." The soldiers cheered and whistled.

Vivian conferred with Private Johnson, then smiled at the soldiers. "I hope you like this one." She smoothed the front of her gown, waiting for the beginning brassy note. "In scarlet town…where I was born…" She called the group into the haunting ballad of love gone wrong.

Soldiers stood mesmerized while Vivian wove between them and around them, teasing and seducing.

Sabrina focused on her sister's performance. *Now or never.* "Captain, did you know the post surgeon I'm replacing?"

"Why would you ask about him?"

"Just curious." She felt the heat from his gaze but

continued watching Vivian.

"You know what they say about curiosity killing the cat, don't you, Doc?"

"Was he discharged?" She swayed her body to the beat of the song.

He let out a hard breath. "Lieutenant Post Surgeon Nelson died."

"How dreadful." She turned and made eye contact, then flattened her right hand on her chest. "What happened?"

"You don't quit, do you?" He formed his lips in a hard straight line. "Suicide."

"Suicide? How dreadful."

The music stopped.

Ethan scrunched his lips, and the tiny muscle on his left temple moved in and out. "All right, people." He faced the group and raised his hands. "Time to turn in. Sergeant, assign sentry duty.

"Yes, sir. Corporal Davis, first watch."

Why do I get the feeling he knows I'm faking?

Chapter 8

A stub of a candle lit the inside of the tent Sabrina shared with the other women. Wearing a white cotton nightgown, she sat cross-legged on her pallet and listened to the soft snores of her mother and Mrs. Hunter. Why had Captain Reed been reluctant to talk about William? She sprinkled lilac perfume on her comb. *Is he hiding something?*

"I do wish I could take a bath." Vivian dipped a large sponge into a basin.

"How did you get the water?" Sabrina leaned forward and scraped the teeth of the comb through her hair. "Too clean for creek water."

"A friend got it." Vivian dabbed the grime from her face and neck, releasing a faint hint of roses.

"Captain Reed would not be happy knowing you are bathing in our drinking water." She watched her sister between strands of dark hair.

"Who's going to tell him?" After completing her toilette, Vivian raised the side of the tent and tossed the water.

Sabrina blew out the candle and retrieved a piece of candy from her medical bag. Lying on her back, she felt the hard ground poke through the folds of her pallet.

Outside, the soldiers spoke in hushed tones and secured the camp.

The sweet pecan praline lump melted over her tongue, and she drifted into a light sleep, floating deeper into the misty shadows.

The sweet syrupy scent of ether filled her nostrils, and she plummeted into the middle of a battlefield. Cannons fired. *Boom-boom-boom.* Layers of mangled bodies rose higher. Men screamed, and blood coated everything.

She flipped upright and grabbed her head while pain radiated outward from the center of her chest. Her heart hammered. *Air. I need air.* She shoved her right fist into her diaphragm and inhaled through the stone-hard muscles. Like the tide waving back into the sea, the stiffness ebbed from her body. Gradually, her vision cleared, and she could see the walls of the tent angling upward. She felt her ears pop open.

Mother's soft snores grew louder.

Sabrina pushed her feet into her boots, then stepped outside into the steamy night air. Embers glowed from the campfire in the center of the circled conveyances. She bent her head backward and inhaled deeply while she focused on the surrounding sounds—snores from the soldiers, *clicks-clacks* of crickets, and in the distance, the deep mournful howl of some animal—she released her breath in short bursts. *The war...is...over.*

****

Unable to sleep, Ethan dismissed the sentry and assumed guard duty. After checking the picket line, he stopped at the edge of the moonlit creek and inhaled the fishy scent, swimming his thoughts into the past. The hot July day remained crystal clear. He and his younger brothers had been checking trawl lines. He was fifteen, and since the age of twelve, he had been the man of the family. *That day, I failed.*

John slipped and skidded into the water.

Vincent ran for help.

Ethan dove into the muddy creek, and beneath the surface, he hit a whirlpool. He swirled round and round trapped in a spinning vortex, flopping over and under, his lungs burning for air. The force, like a hungry beast, threatened to devour him, sucking his legs, gripping his arms, and tying his body into knots. He kicked and flipped, then with one final punch, he broke free and propelled upward, shooting from the water, gasping and coughing.

Two days later, John's body washed up three miles downstream.

Ma never blamed him.

But he carried the guilt, always playing a game of *if only.* He leaned his left hip against a boulder and scraped a match head on the rough surface. The match flared, and he lit his cigar, puffing until the end glowed. He tossed the match into the air, and like a falling star, the flame arched, then vanished into the water. He blew out a cloud of smoke while guilt continued stampeding.

During the war, he had been wounded, but by some unknown miracle, survived. *Better men than me died. Why did I live?* Returning home after the war, he found his mother, son, and wife had died in a cholera epidemic. Alice pleaded with him not to enlist, but…he hadn't listened. He lay across her grave, sobbing and begging for forgiveness. How long he stayed there, he couldn't say. Eventually, he walked away, dead inside. *If only.*

He tried to wash the memories away by staying drunk, but the inside of a bottle was no place to find peace or forgiveness. When he received the general's offer to join a special investigation force, he jumped at the opportunity.

He had found Sabrina's letters in Nelson's quarters and read them, hoping to learn more about Nelson's activities, but instead, he discovered the charming Doctor Clay. As he read her letters, he imagined her sweet voice reciting her daily frustrations and fell deeply in love. But his imagination had not come close to reality.

His wife reminded him of a newly opened rose, dainty and fragile. But Doc reminded him of a lily, delicate on the surface, but strong at her roots. As the image of a dark-haired enchantress, with lilac-tinted eyes spilled into his brain like sunshine from an azure sky on a winter's day, he stroked his mouth with his left index finger and recalled her exit from the colonel's office. He chuckled.

Stiff-backed, she had walked away with her anger reflected in every stomp of her dainty feet and every wiggle of her backside.

He filled his mouth with the earthy flavor of tobacco. Doc was beauty and strength wrapped in a ruffled petticoat. His cigar tip burned red. A petticoat had to be under her dress somewhere, and he would certainly enjoy searching for the ruffles. Tracing the thin scar curving at the edge of his right eyebrow, he held the smoke in his mouth and inhaled through his nose.

Did she know the bastard she was planning to marry was a damn Confederate spy? Was she a co-conspirator? Nothing in her letters indicated she was involved, but…he blew a cloud of silver smoke into the air. What he didn't understand was how she had gotten hired by the Secretary of War and assigned to an army post. And incidentally, the same post Nelson had been assigned. This could not be a coincidence. *Somebody pulled strings.*

Behind him, leaves rustled.

He bolted upright, clamped his cigar between his teeth, and pulled his gun.

A twig snapped.

Gripping the handle of his service revolver, he held his breath, scanning dark shadows.

Sabrina floated into a puddle of milky moonlight. Moonbeams shimmered through her thin nightgown, outlining every curve of her body in a halo of white. The breeze teased and lifted the hem of her gown, revealing a shapely calf above the top of her boot.

What was she doing away from camp? He exhaled, holstered his gun, and removed his cigar from his mouth.

She dropped onto a nearby rock, starred into the darkness, then her head fell into her hands, and she cried. Her mournful sobs rippled through the darkness.

"You all right, Doc?" He approached, unsure of what to say or do, so he put his cigar back into his mouth and chewed.

She jumped up, faced him, and dashed tears away with the heels of her hands. "Spying again, Captain?"

He jerked the cigar from his mouth. "I'm on guard duty. What the hell are you doing out here?"

"Leave me alone." She spun her back toward him.

"I can do that." He tossed his cigar stub into the water and marched away.

"Ethan...please stay."

Hearing the anguish in her voice, he stopped. "If you've got something on your mind, Doc"—*she called me Ethan*—"I can listen." He retraced his steps.

"The nightmares never stop." In a wedge of bright moonlight, she folded her arms across her chest and stroked her upper arms. "Do they?"

He stuffed his hands into his trouser pockets and sauntered closer.

"I never knew their names—but I see their faces—and I hear their voices." She licked the corner of her mouth. "Over. And over. Again."

He understood and mashed his lips together. There were no words.

She scraped her fingernails down the backs of her upper arms. "I remember one spring day." As though she were telling a bedtime story to a child, she softened her voice. "White clouds striped across a blue sky. We arrived at a meadow with lovely wildflowers bursting from their buds. I recall the black and blue dragonflies with lacy wings, dipping and bobbing between the blades of green grass. So beautiful."

He felt his heart seize. He wanted to hold her, and he wanted to tell her she wasn't alone. But if he did, what would she do? He edged closer, hoping to absorb some of her pain.

"We pitched the medical tent and waited." She pressed the palms of her hands on her cheeks. "After the cold winter, the sun was bright and felt so warm. In the center of the beautiful meadow, American soldiers, some wearing blue and some wearing gray, marched forward. The drummers were young boys…only eight or nine—children in war." She covered her ears. "*Rump-pa-pa-pump…rump-pa-pa-pump.* We waited for the killing to start." She laughed without humor while tears sluiced down her face. "Civilized people waiting for the killing to start. Isn't that a joke?"

He untied the yellow bandana around his neck and offered her the fabric.

She accepted the scarf and brushed his hand with her fingers.

He felt his breath snatch, and his lungs refused to fill. He swiped his right hand over his mouth, while an overwhelming desire to protect her hurled straight into his heart. He firmed his jaw, grinding his teeth.

"An hour later"—she blotted her tears—"the battle was over."

He heard the quiver in her voice and balled his fists. How could he help her? What could he do?

"I could no longer smell the flowers...only the stinking sulfur odor of the gunpowder and the coppery scent of blood." She crumpled his bandana. "The birds no longer sang...only the men crying out. All the beauty was gone, buried beneath a layer of bodies. Some men were dead and some were dying, and the blood soaked into the ground like a summer's rain."

He wanted to say something, but what? She carried the scars of a battle-hardened soldier, she had witnessed the horrors of war, and she was fighting visions she could never un-see, *just like me.*

"For two days, we worked—in the heat—with the mosquitos and the flies—and the putrid stench of rotting bodies. The wounded just kept coming...without arms...without legs...and without faces." She scrubbed the bandana over her face.

He helplessly listened.

"At night, I peeled off my shoes and socks because

they were stuck on from the blood." She scrubbed her hands with his bandana. "There are times I feel I shall never be clean again."

He couldn't afford to become involved with her. Hell, she could be as guilty as Nelson. "Sometimes, war is the only way to solve a situation."

"Not a very good one." She sniffed.

"No, maybe not." *Damn my investigation.* He drew her against his chest and folded his arms around her. He wanted to confess he was in love with her, but this was not the time. *God help me.* This was the moment he had dreamed, and for now, she was his. He leaned back, focusing on her beautiful eyes, and seeing nothing but trust. He lowered his head, and when his lips touched hers, he discovered her mouth soft and yielding. She smelled faintly of summer lilacs and tasted like sugar. As her sweetness coated the inside of his mouth, he deepened the kiss and moaned. Frozen in a single moment with no past or future, he sensed her surrender.

Suddenly, high-pitched screams of the mules ripped the air.

Terror-stricken whinnies of the horses shredded the dark.

Gunshots blasted. *Bam! Bam! Bam!*

"What the hell?"

****

"Who was the daft pup on guard duty?" Sergeant O'Rourke stomped around the campsite.

"I was, Sergeant." Ethan strode past a wagon and into a section of lantern light.

"Sorry, sir," the sergeant mumbled with his head bowed.

"What happened?" Ethan glanced around at the

soldiers in various stages of dress.

"Wolves, sir." Private Todd pulled his suspenders over his shoulders.

"Damn." Ethan jerked off his black hat. "How many did we lose?" He slapped the hat against his thigh.

"None, sir."

"Good." He put his hat back on and wiped his right hand across his mouth.

"Cap'n, over here," Corporal Davis called from somewhere near the picket line. "I shot one, and the creature's still alive. Want me to finish him off?"

"Stop. Please don't." Sabrina rushed between the wagons with her hands up.

"Doc"—Ethan rubbed the back of his neck—"this is a wolf."

"I know, but he was only hungry." She gripped Ethan's bandana in her left hand.

"The poor animal is suffering. Wouldn't it be more humane to put him down?"

"Maybe I can help him." She crushed the yellow fabric in a fist and glued her gaze on Ethan.

"Doc." He exhaled deeply.

"Please, let me try." She clasped her hands in front of her chest. "Please."

He scrubbed his right hand over his face, grabbed a lantern, and stepped off the distance to the furry body crumpled on the ground.

Sabrina shadowed him.

In the rays of light, the wolf's eyes beamed golden, and blood soaked the silver fur around the right shoulder. He lifted his head and emitted a guttural growl from between barred teeth.

"Easy, fellow." She stepped around Ethan. "I want to help you." She held her hands out.

Grrrr.

Ethan jerked her back and slid in front. "You can't get close enough, Doc." He fixed his gaze on the wolf. "He's going to eat you alive."

"I have to try."

"If the wolf makes a move"—Ethan wiped his right hand over his mouth—"any move—he will be killed." He faced her. "Do...you...understand?" He crossed his arms over his chest.

She nodded. "Thank you."

"Corporal Davis, you keep your gun drawn and aimed." Ethan let out a hard breath. "If the wolf moves, shoot." He mashed his lips into a hard line.

"Yes, sir."

The horses and mules quieted, while the soldiers formed a semi-circle around Sabrina.

"I'll need a long pole or something." She glanced around.

"Butterworth, get Doc a stick." Ethan shook his head. "I must be a daft pup, after all."

"Seems to me"—the sergeant stepped closer—"it won't be making a bit of difference if this here creature lives or dies."

"You're wrong, Sergeant"—Sabrina shook her head—"it will make a difference to him...and me."

Ethan watched her head toward her tent. *What is she thinking?*

****

Sabrina crossed the camp and entered the women's tent. She peeled her nightgown up and over her head.

"What is happening?" Mother sat on her pallet with

strips of white fabric tied around her brown-gray locks.

"Wolves attacked the stock. One of them was shot, and I'm tending the wound." She floated her brown dress over her body and then folded Ethan's bandana into a triangle and tied it over her hair.

"A wolf? Daughter, that is insane."

"I have to try." Clutching her medical bag, she headed back to the canine patient and was intercepted by Graham.

"Miss Sabrina, why would you want to save a mangy old wolf?"

"Because he is hurt." She zigzagged through the circle of men.

"Is this long enough, ma'am?" Private Butterworth handed her a long stick.

"Perfect." She set her bag on a barrel. "Now I need a rag."

"Will this work, ma'am?" Private Todd handed over his bandana.

"It will. Thank you." She doused chloroform onto the fabric, then tied the cloth to the end of the stick. "Keep your fingers crossed, gentlemen."

The animal snapped and bit at the waving flag.

"Easy, boy. I'm not going to hurt you." She held the fabric near the wolf's nose and mouth. "Just…take it easy.

The beam from a lantern spotlighted the wild canine's face, and he slowly blinked his eyes.

Seeing the wolf's eyes shut, Sabrina crept closer and examined his shoulder. Blood matted the silver fur and covered her hands. "No exit wound." Turning around, she scanned the area. "We have to get him into the center of the wagons, and I'll need a board for a surgery platform and plenty of light."

"Sergeant." Ethan massaged the muscles between his eyes. "Do your best."

"All right, laddies, ye be a hearing the cap'n. Some of ye bring a couple barrels from one of the supply wagons, and a couple of ye, get the seat from the ambulance. The rest of ye, light some more lanterns and hang them over near the campfire, so the doctor lassie can see."

Two soldiers positioned the animal on a board and prepared to transport him.

Sabrina directed the men, and the board was laid between two barrels, creating a makeshift surgery table.

"Daughter." Mother approached, wearing her black-checked dress over her nightgown. "Are you sure about this?"

"Yes." Sabrina glanced at the patient. "I am." She adjusted the lanterns and watched a cloud of fluttering moths scatter into the night. Taking a swallow of air, she opened her bag and removed a razor.

"Very well...what can I do?" Mother straightened her shoulders.

"Monitor his condition." Sabrina handed Mother the bottle of chloroform and the rag she had used. "I can't have him waking before I'm finished."

Mother examined the amber bottle. "How much do I give him?"

Pouring water from a canteen, Sabrina flooded the wound. "Every time he moves, give him a sniff." She flipped open the straight-edged razor, then shaved the silver fur, exposing a hole filling with blood. She grabbed a roll of bandages and slapped them onto the wound. "Mother, hold these."

Men clustered around.

"I ain't never seen nothing like this."

"Don't it just take the cake?"

Sabrina opened the clean towel surrounding her surgical instruments and poured carbolic acid over them. From the assortment, she selected a pencil-like tool. She heard the mosquitoes whining in her ears. She felt their bites sting her cheeks. *Please let this work.* "More light."

A lantern beam haloed over the patient.

Mother pulled the compress away.

Sabrina traced the path of the bullet from the outer skin and into the muscle. As blood filled the wound, she sopped. "I don't see any fragments. Looks like a clean shot." She pressed her instrument deeper into the animal's right shoulder, then scraped the edge of something hard. She inched her gaze upward to the person holding the closest lantern.

Ethan elevated his brows and smiled.

Concentrating, Sabrina bit her bottom lip and plunged the needle-nose pincers through the thick tissue. "If I can just...get a good hold...on it." She held her breath, twisted her hand, and latched onto the slug, then guided the metal ball free. She dropped the lead into the basin.

Clang.

"Don't that just beat all?"

"Dang. I ain't never seen nothing like this."

The soldiers chattered their disbelief.

"How's our patient, Mother?" With bloody hands, Sabrina reached for a canteen of water and flushed the wound.

Mother put her fingertips in front of the wolf's

nose. "Breathing."

"Good." Sabrina wiped her hands on a towel. "I need to cauterize." Holding a thin metal rod with a pair of forceps, she made eye contact with Ethan.

He opened the glass side of his lantern.

She stabbed the rod into the flame. Seeing the iron glow hot, she pulled it from the flame and jammed the point into the wound, creating a foul odor of burning hair and searing skin.

The wolf jerked and moaned, sounding almost human, but he remained sedated.

"I declare"—Vivian pranced into the group—"a body can't get any sleep around here with all of this racket." She wore a green satin nightgown with a matching bed jacket edged with dyed-to-match feathers. "What's happening, anyway?"

Corporal Davis and Private Butterworth began talking at once, describing what they had witnessed.

"What's that disgusting animal"—Vivian wrinkled her nose—"doing here?"

"The doctor lassie just saved the poor creature's life." Sergeant O'Rourke smiled.

"That's my sister"—Vivian fluffed the feathers on her jacket—"saving the world."

Ethan scraped his right jawline with his thumb. "When will your patient be well enough to go home, Doc?"

"Maybe in a few days." She poured water from the canteen over her hands.

"Days?" Ethan widened his eyes. "Are you kidding me?" He held his hands out, palm sides up. "What in blazes are we going to do with him?"

The wolf's back legs twitched.

"I don't know, but it had better be fast." Sabrina monitored the wolf's breathing. "He's coming around."

Ethan threw his hands higher. "Sergeant."

"Get me a couple of ropes from the tool kit, lads." The sergeant hobbled the wolf's hind legs together with one rope and looped another rope around the wolf's neck and circled a nearby cottonwood tree.

As he regained consciousness, the wolf wobbled, keeping his gaze on Sabrina. He collapsed onto his stomach and crawled closer to the trunk of the tree.

"Doc, you can't keep him." Ethan stood behind her left shoulder.

"I know." She couldn't explain her feelings, but by rescuing the animal, she had salvaged a tiny bit of herself.

Mrs. Hunter clutched a red shawl over her yellow nightgown. "I cannot believe my ears. A wild creature being kept here among us womenfolk. Ridiculous."

Sabrina held her hands out. "I just couldn't let him die."

"Who are you to decide life is better than death?"

Nobody and sometimes, I fail.

Chapter 9

The following day, Sabrina tossed bones from the previous night's supper to the silver-haired wolf, observing his hairless wound which remained closed and healing. "Eat up, fellow. You'll be leaving soon."

The wolf crouched while crunching the bones with his powerful jaws and keeping his gaze sealed on her.

Like the sun burning through an early morning mist, the captain's kind and strong face emerged. He had granted her one day to care for the animal, and although he hadn't understood her need to save the wolf, he supported her. She was beginning to see things from Private Todd's point of view. She jiggled the corners of her mouth up. *Captain Reed is a good man.*

Last night, for the first time, she had spoken of the horrors she witnessed, and he had listened. She always thought if she voiced the scenes, they would destroy her. But safely tucked in his arms, she felt her heart burst open like a milkweed pod releasing seeds, and her haunting memories took flight. *Then, he kissed me.*

Sergeant O'Rourke approached. "Ye know, Doctor Lass, this here being a wild creature, he won't be none too happy 'til he's free to roam again."

"I know." She squeezed her chin between her thumb and index finger. "For some reason, I needed to help him."

"I'm sure this fellow is glad ye did." The big man

held out some hard biscuits. "When I was a young lad, I had me a dog. I couldn't have loved old Booze more if he had been human." Chuckling, the sergeant ambled away. "And at times, I could swear the old boy was."

She tossed a biscuit. "We need a name for you." On her hands and knees, she crawled deeper into the animal's territory. "How about I call you Wolf?"

****

Purple twilight lit the evening sky while Ethan observed the camp from the tongue of the grub wagon. The ladies sat in rope-bottom chairs, eating supper while the soldiers sat on the ground or squatted on their haunches. The sounds of eating utensils scraping the tin plates intertwined with the humming of conversations and insect serenades. He landed his gaze on the one who flittered in and out of his dreams every night like an elusive butterfly, just out of reach but with each passing day, drawing closer. Reading her letters, he learned about her heart and soul, and he often speculated about the woman behind the pen.

Sabrina revealed a picture of the poverty and the malnutrition of Washington's women and children resulting from the war. She wrote about battling infections and colleagues who said medicine was no place for a woman. After her grandfather died, men had petitioned to have his hospital closed, but she ignored them and kept the hospital open.

He stroked his mouth with his right index finger, reliving the moment his lips had touched hers and wisps of contentment floated into his heart. Ambling to the campfire, he refilled his cup. "How's your patient, Doc?" He dropped into the empty chair in front of her and felt his heart kick into a gallop. Holding his tin cup with both hands, he glided his left thumb along the rim.

"No complaints." She playfully raised her shoulder and cocked the corners of her mouth.

"So…you can turn him loose tomorrow?" He blew on his coffee, being close to her generated nothing but pleasure in his body and mind.

"I'm not sure he's ready." She bit into a biscuit and chewed. "After all, he is recovering from a gunshot." She shifted her lips into a sassy grin.

"Ah, Doc." He chuckled, enjoying her wordplay and her smile. "He can't go with us." He sipped his coffee, and like his desire bubbling beneath the surface, the heat floated over his tongue. He wrinkled his chin while his thoughts flowed unrestrained and uninhibited. He craved the feel of her warm, lovely body like a winter day needed a slice of sunshine. He wanted to enclose her in his arms and tell her he loved her, and above all, he wanted her for his wife. But…

"Is it because unmarried wolves are not allowed at Fort Greer?" She grinned and batted her eyelashes.

He laughed and shook his head. *She is perfect.*

Vivian flounced between the couple with her supper plate in her right hand and wearing a blue dress printed with miniature yellow flowers.

The conversation stopped.

"Mind if I join you all?" Not waiting for an answer, she pulled an empty chair forward and perched.

Sabrina rose. "If you'll excuse me." She glanced at her sister, then Ethan. "I'll feed my leftovers to Wolf."

He watched the seductive sway of her womanly hips and shifted in his chair while flashes of different scenarios entered his brain. All of them involved her being naked. But a question nibbled. Was she an innocent, or had Nelson crossed the line?

Vivian fluffed her skirt. "You haven't heard a word I've said, Ethan."

"My apologies." He rubbed the back of his neck. "I have a lot on my mind."

"I'm sure you do...with my sister bringing a wild animal into camp." She shuddered. "We might all catch some sort of deadly disease from the creature."

"If you don't mind my asking...what's going on between you two? Seems you're always fighting." He sipped his coffee.

"Long story and quite boring." Vivian shrugged.

"Humor me." Ethan leaned back and widened his knees.

"Sabrina was engaged to Mathew Stark, and he decided he would rather marry me." She fluffed the white-blonde curls on the side of her head.

Ethan arched his left eyebrow, speculating on what man would choose Vivian over Doc. He knew he sure as hell wouldn't.

"Mathew died tragically, and my sister has never forgiven me. I'm the one who has suffered the great loss of my husband, and I lost our child." She tilted her head. "But...life must go on."

"How did you get the name Starr?" He swallowed the last of his lukewarm coffee.

"When I became an actress, I decided I liked Starr better than Stark." She leaned forward, and the neckline of her dress gaped open.

Seeing the white lacy edge of an undergarment, he averted his gaze. "Did you ever perform at Ford's Theater?"

"Sometimes." She rested her right hand on her

chest. "As a matter of fact, when poor Mr. Lincoln was shot, I was there."

"Now, I find that very interesting, Miss Vivian." He removed his cigar case from his trouser pocket, then selected a cigar.

"You do?" She smiled and cocked her head to one side.

"Did you know Booth?" He recalled a newspaper article. The reporter had commented on a mysterious beautiful woman who had been seen in the company of Booth and his associates on numerous occasions.

"I knew Johnny quite well." Vivian half-closed her eyelids and peeked through her eyelashes.

The unknown woman could have been Vivian, or God help me, Sabrina. "Mind if I smoke?"

Vivian shook her head, jiggling the ringlets framing her face. "Even though Johnny was married, I think he was a little sweet on me. Once we visited his sister, Asia, in Philadelphia."

He bit off the end of the cigar and spat the tip out. "Did you ever meet any of Booth's friends?"

"Sure. I knew Mikey and Sam. They and Johnny grew up together."

He struck his match on the bottom of his boot and lit his cigar. Michael O'Laughlin and Sam Arnold were two of Booth's cohorts involved in the conspiracy.

"I can't imagine Johnny meant to kill the president. You know actors, always playing a part." She cocked her head to one side and batted her eyelashes.

While the evening sky darkened, Ethan puffed his cigar, tasting the smoky tang. How could they be sisters?

"Johnny told me he only wanted to kidnap the

president and use him in exchange for some prisoners or something." Tilting her head, she tapped an index finger on her chin. "Now, why would little ole you be so interested in all this water under the bridge?"

"Morbid curiosity, I suppose." He needed to keep her interested. "Or maybe I just like having an excuse to be with you."

"Excuse me." Sabrina nudged into sight. "I hope I'm not intruding." She kept her gaze down and avoided any eye contact. "I need water for my patient."

Damn. Ethan scrubbed a hand over his mouth. *Did she hear me?*

****

The following morning, Ethan rested his booted left foot on a spoke in the grub wagon's wheel. Last night's dreams of the sable-haired beauty, with flashing violet eyes, reminded him of a summer storm building on the horizon, dark clouds rolling and dipping with unpredictable energy, exciting and uncontrollable. Conversations with Doc were never boring. He elevated the corners of his mouth up. *Unmarried wolves.* He chuckled and soul-touching joy vibrated in his chest.

Sergeant O'Rourke snapped orders to break camp and load the wagons.

Private Todd rattled pots and pans into wooden boxes.

"More coffee, Cap'n," Butterworth held the soot-covered pot.

"Don't mind if I do." Ethan raised his tin cup.

The sandy-haired private poured the coffee.

Ethan replayed last night's conversation with Vivian and blew on the brown liquid. If he was a betting man, and sometimes he was, he would put his money on the actress being involved. He filled his mouth with coffee, and suddenly, Doc's face flashed in his mind, and he swallowed. The liquid burned a trail to his stomach while guilt burned in his heart. *I have a job to do.* Leaning against the wheel of the wagon, he spotted Doc at the edge of camp.

"I have to let you go." Sabrina's voice *shushed* across the camp like a spring rain washing the tree leaves after a long drought. She knelt in a clearing with her right arm looped around the wolf. "You deserve your freedom." She brushed her cheek against the wolf's muzzle. "I love you, but I can't make you stay. It wouldn't be right."

The gray wolf took a couple of steps, stopped, and glanced back.

"Go on, shoo." She waved her hands.

Ethan scratched the back of his neck and watched the animal lope westward toward the distant red potato-shaped hills. Would she ever say the words *I love you* to him?

****

All day, a vision of Antelope Springs and the promise of a swim kept Ethan pushing the company after sunset. Overhead, stars twinkled in a charcoal sky, and cool, clear water gurgled from an underground source. Feeling his stomach rumble, he dismounted. The only thing he wanted was a bath, something to eat, and his bed—all in that order. He released the saddle girth, and the leather strap dropped free beneath the horse's belly. An unmistakable prickle crawled up the back of Ethan's neck, shifting his body into high alert. He scanned the area. They were crossing Comanche hunting grounds, and a night assault would be rare but not unheard of with a full moon. Over the seat of the saddle, he landed his gaze on the source of his uneasiness.

Doc's wolf observed and waited.

Sabrina rushed forward and dropped on her knees in the thick layer of grasses, her brown skirt billowing like a flag on a windy day. "Wolfie, come."

The animal wagged his tail, then crouched and crept into her open arms.

She hugged his neck. "I hoped you would come back."

The wolf licked the end of her nose.

She squealed with childish delight while her hair tumbled like a waterfall, wild and free. Over her shoulder, she glanced at Ethan. "Can I keep him?"

For the first time in a long time, Ethan felt pure bliss breeze into his heart. Without a doubt, he would grant *his* Sabrina anything.

"Captain." Mrs. Hunter stomped closer. "Are you seriously considering allowing that…wolf to remain?"

"I am." He slid the saddle off the horse's back.

"Have you taken complete leave of your senses?" Mrs. Hunter wagged her index finger in the air.

"Quite possibly, ma'am." He laid the saddle on the ground and returned for the blanket.

Mrs. Hunter's round face flamed red. "I shall speak to the colonel about this." She drew her mouth into a straight line.

"You do that, ma'am. Until I have orders to do otherwise"—he connected his gaze with Sabrina's—"the wolf stays." Colonel Hunter would give him hell over this. *But…worth any reprimand.*

Chapter 10

Two days later, in the middle of the afternoon, Sabrina glanced up from the saddle. The sun vanished behind thick dark clouds, and the sky glowed with a peculiar light. Familiar objects appeared strange and unreal. She tilted forward and patted Lily's neck while studying Ethan. Since breakfast, he had driven them harder into the Southwest, the scowl he wore deepened, and his orders snapped sharper and more clipped.

Suddenly, gusts of wind hammered the ground with powerful surges, ripping dried weeds from their roots and tossing them into the rust-colored air. Dust devils pirouetted over the flat ground.

Sabrina sucked oxygen through the thick blanket of humid air, and in her head, alarm bells jangled. *What is happening?* She locked her body into hyperalert with taut muscles and shallow breaths.

Lily frantically danced, tossing her head, jerking the reins, and giving high whinnies as debris whipped into her legs.

Ethan rode in the dirty haze and jerked his yellow bandana over his mouth and nose. "Sergeant." He pointed to a gorge splitting the red ground. "There."

Following orders, the sergeant led the caravan down into the opening.

Sabrina directed her horse behind a supply wagon and clutched the front edge of her saddle with her left hand.

Lily moved stiff-legged down a narrow shelf road which had been carved, over time, into the side of a clay wall. The horse lost her footing, and her hooves scooted on the loose rocks.

Sabrina bobbed in the saddle. The farther down she traveled, the higher the red walls climbed, and claustrophobic sensations sprinted deeper into her chest. Dirt granules blasted between her lips, and she jerked the neckline of her charcoal-gray dress up and covered her mouth.

At the bottom of the gorge, sounds crammed the gritty air.

Mules squealed.

Men shouted.

Thunder rumbled. Wind battered and the squall intensified, restricting visibility to inches.

Soldiers jacked into action and threw blankets over the animals' heads.

The wind morphed into a living breathing monster, snatching her bonnet and clawing and pelting her body with cutting grains of sand.

Ethan grabbed Lily's reins and pointed to the nearest supply wagon. "Go."

Sabrina kicked free from the stirrups, and lowered her head, bending into the force. The gale plastered her clothes, and grit blasted into her mouth, eyes, and nose. She grabbed the top of the tailgate and dug her fingernails into the wood. She shoved the toe of her right boot into the crack at the bottom and pitched her body over into the wagon, banging her knee. Pain shot along her shinbone, and she scrambled deeper into the shuttering wagon.

Wolf vaulted in beside her.

She crammed her body between the animal and some wooden crates, then flung her gray skirt over their heads. She clamped her fist in Wolf's fur and buried her face in his thick coarse hair, finding comfort in his oily scent and steady heartbeat.

The wind bellowed.

Sand whirred.

Grit sliced.

The wagon vibrated.

Canvas flapped.

The rage of the storm blasted like a train.

The wagon capsized. Barrels rolled. Crates flipped.

Sabrina somersaulted over and over, and pain splintered into her skull, behind her eyes, into her knees and through her elbows. Feeling pain pound and pump into every nook and cranny of her body, she surveyed the mountain-high jumbled mess between her and the vertical tailgate.

Wolf licked her face.

"Wolfie—" she smoothed her hand over his back, then checked her palm for blood. She wiggled, and her right leg was pinned.

Outside, the raging tempest exhaled, and an uncomfortable quiet developed.

Within seconds, Ethan appeared. "Doc," his voice muffled through his bandana.

"Ethan?" She felt her body sag, and something hard gouged into her back.

He shoved a crate of army bread with his left foot. "Are you all right?" He lugged a barrel of vinegar to one side, sloshing the liquid and releasing a zingy odor.

Wolf lowered his head and growled deep in his

throat.

"Wolfie." She elbowed the wolf's body. "Out—my foot"—she yanked her right leg, and pain shot to her knee—"is caught."

Ethan stepped closer, and the wagon shifted. "What's holding you?"

"This"—she slapped a small keg wedged between two larger barrels—"I think."

"Hold on." He rolled the container.

The lid clunked off, and nails spilled out.

"Is it broken?"

"I don't"—she untangled her leg and massaged her ankle—"think so."

He scooped her up.

Sabrina clamped her arms around his neck and touched her nose to his skin, inhaling the masculine sweat, with an underlying hint of spicy shaving soap. She bit her bottom lip and tucked the moment into her heart for safekeeping.

Ethan carried her toward the canvas opening and shoved, rolled, and pushed obstacles with his right foot, creating a cacophony of sounds. Outside, he took a deep breath.

Feeling the pressure beneath her legs lessen, she latched her gaze on his face and held his shoulders for support. She skidded downward, and her gray skirt and petticoat tangled together, bunching at her waist. As her left hip scraped his body, she felt every male indentation whisper through her thin cotton pantalets.

He caught his breath and widened his eyes.

Breathing through her mouth, she planted her feet between his and wiggled her hips, freeing her skirt and petticoat. She eased his dirt-crusted bandana down, and using her fingertips, she brushed the grime from his brows and explored the soft lines of his lips while the blue in his magnetic eyes shifted lighter.

He smiled, and his dimples deepened.

Dangling like a single drop of water suspended on a spider's silken threads, she held her breath.

Ethan bracketed her cheeks with his gauntlet-covered hands and dipped his head closer.

She felt the worn-smooth surface of his gloves and smelled a whiff of horse, leather, and shaving soap.

He covered her lips with his.

The bold, stimulating scent of *him* slammed full force into her body. She felt her knees weaken and her senses scatter like colorful beads breaking free from a string. Buttery warmth surged. She wanted to laugh. She wanted to cry. She never wanted the kiss to end.

He plunged his tongue into her mouth.

She tasted his coffee, his cigars, and him. A creamy sensation began at her lips and flowed downward, luring her into an unknown world, but one she willingly wanted. She would follow him anywhere.

Ethan broke the kiss. "Ah, darling"—he pressed his forehead against hers—"you don't know what you do to me."

Darling. She curved her lips.

"Daughter, we need some help over here."

The dark skies opened, and rain poured.

Sabrina pulled away from Ethan and dashed to the ambulance. Cold water saturated her clothing, and as she climbed into the front seat, she felt the weight of her dress hang like an anchor.

"I've cut my arm." Mrs. Hunter held up her blood-soaked sleeve.

She scrambled over the front seat and crawled to Mrs. Hunter, who was wedged against the floor of the second seat. As she rolled Mrs. Hunter's sleeve, she flitted her gaze to the back of the conveyance.

Ethan dropped the tailgate.

Vivian launched into his arms. "Captain, I've never been so terrified in all my born days." She wound her arms around his neck. "Thank goodness, you've come to rescue poor little ole me."

Over Vivian's shoulder, Sabrina slammed her gaze into Ethan's, and she recalled the words she wasn't meant to hear, *maybe I just like being with you.*

****

The following day, Ethan rode point in the mid-morning darkness. Rain peppered his hat and dripped. He scrunched his neck deeper into his black poncho while rivulets ran down the back of his neck. Yesterday, when the supply wagon toppled, he had forgotten to breathe. He ran as hard as he could, but his legs felt heavy and clumsy. His brain tortured him with visions of what he would find. He released a hard breath, blowing water from his lips. *Someday, darling, you and me. Together.*

Around noon, the caravan slopped through the gates of Buffalo Mail Station, a small redoubt with vertically lined log walls.

Lightning snaked across the sky. Thunder *boomed*. The ground trembled.

"Take cover." Ethan pointed toward a lean-to, with a sheet iron roof and three sides, running along the north wall. "Hold your positions." He drew his brows together and swiped a gloved hand over his face. Last month, five privates and one lieutenant were stationed here. *Where are they?* He licked his lips and listened.

The travelers spoke in hushed tones. Rain *pinged* on the metal roof. Horses *nickered* and *snorted*.

He skimmed the area.

No lights. No movement. Nothing.

Mules shook their heads and harnesses *jangled*. Wind whistled between the upright logs.

By all indications, the mail station was abandoned.

Ethan dismounted, then tied his horse to the wheel of the ambulance. As he footslogged across the middle of the redoubt, he scrunched his neck deeper into his poncho and covered his ears. Rain pummeled his hat and shoulders while uncertainty pounded in his brain. Eerie goose bumps skated along his neck. He hammered his fist on the cedar plank door of the commander's cabin. "Lieutenant Jeffers." He jerked the leather strap and lifted the inside bar.

The door creaked open.

"Permission to enter." Not hearing any movement, Ethan stepped inside and scanned the shadowy room. A thick layer of dust coated everything; otherwise, nothing appeared out of order. He whacked his soggy hat on his thigh, flinging droplets of water into the air. He shook his head and returned to the others. "Mister, get the ladies into the cabin. Sergeant, see to the stock." He scratched the back of his neck. "What in the hell is going on?" He started toward the tents along the west wall. Different scenarios flipped through his head and none of them good.

****

Sabrina slogged behind the others to the cabin, lugging her saturated hem with one hand and carrying her medical bag in the other.

Wolf trotted inside, shook water from his silver fur, and curled against the wood box on the east wall.

"Sabrina"—Vivian wiped her face with a hand—"I can't believe you've gotten us into such a mess. If you had stayed home, I could be clean and dry in the safety of Carter Hall." She tossed her poncho onto the wooden floor.

"No one forced you to come"—Sabrina draped her dripping poncho over the back of a chair—"actually no one invited you."

A mounted deer head, with black glassy, unseeing eyes and a spreading antler rack, hung above the double bed. The cabin's floor space was compact with only about ten steps from one side to the other. A rectangular table, with legs made from tree saplings, sat near a two-burner, cast-iron stove on the east side of the room. Four rope-bottom chairs, with peeling red paint, provided the only seating in the room. A rickety washstand, with a bucket and a basin, paralleled the west wall and completed the furnishings.

Graham squatted in front of a stone fireplace and coaxed a sputtering flame into a warm ball of fire.

"I'm tired and hungry." Vivian flopped on the bed, creating a multitude of *screeches* from the wrought iron bedstead.

"I declare"—Mrs. Hunter dropped her soggy black bonnet onto the table—"I'd give my eyeteeth for a cup of Lovey's mint tea." She slumped into a chair, wringing the hem of her blue-checked dress and dribbling water onto the board floor.

Mother scrounged the kitchen area, creating sounds of *scraping, scooting,* and *squeaking.* "Give Grace to the Lord. I found a coffeepot and a bag of beans."

Mrs. Hunter blotted water from her face with the back of her hand. "I suppose, I could keep my eyeteeth and settle for a cup of coffee."

"I'll fetch the food basket." Graham rose from the floor and brushed his hands on the seat of his pants.

"You are my knight in shining armor, Graham Hunter." Vivian lifted her right hand. "And if I wasn't so plumb tuckered out, I would rise from this bed and bestow a kiss of gratitude."

"Miss Vivian"—Graham crossed to the door and ducked his head—"you do know how to make a grown man blush." He disappeared into the storm.

Sabrina found a dry match in a box near the fireplace, lit a lamp, then set it in the center of the table. "Mrs. Hunter, I need to check your arm." She retrieved her bag from the floor near the door.

"A hot bath is what I want." Vivian unhooked her shoes.

"We have been in the rain for two days"—Sabrina released a hard breath—"and we are soaked to the bone—and you want a bath?"

"Hot." As Vivian dropped her left shoe on the floor, she flipped her gaze.

Sabrina removed the old bandage from Mrs. Hunter's arm and touched the edges of the gash. In the flickering light, she smeared a layer of ointment over the cut and then applied a fresh bandage.

Graham returned and set the wicker basket in the middle of the square-topped table.

Mother opened the wooden lid. "I packed some leftover biscuits and with Coretta's apple butter and a cup of hot coffee, I do believe that will do nicely." She pulled a tin container from the basket.

"Nothing else?" Vivian wrinkled her nose.

"You can eat or go without." Mother slapped the round tin box on the table creating a *thwack* which vibrated the air. "Those are your choices, young lady."

Holding a lantern, Ethan appeared in the doorway. "Doc, come with me. Bring your bag."

She galumphed behind him toward the tents lining the west wall. *This can't be good.* Mud sucked her boots and squished beneath the soles. Wind whipped her skirt around her legs, and rain sluiced down her face.

Outside the first tent, Ethan struck a match and lit the candle inside the lantern. "Prepare yourself." He covered his mouth and nose with his waterlogged bandana.

Sabrina licked the rain from her lips and stepped inside the tent. A stomach-turning, putrid stench of rotting bodies slapped from her past, and she jerked a handkerchief from the sleeve of her gray dress. Tying the fabric over her nose and mouth, she was able to block some of the odors, but not the memories.

The light haloed over the area and illuminated six cots, three on each side of the tent.

"This tent will need to be burned." Sabrina approached the first cot and covered the corpse with a blanket, and then she stepped to the next bed and repeated the process.

A faint groan came from the last cot.

Ethan hoisted the lantern higher.

The beam hit a man's face.

His pus-filled sores left no doubt. "He's in the final stages." She felt her stomach knot.

"Smallpox?" Ethan flattened his lips into a straight

line.

"Smallpox."

Minutes later, Sabrina met with the others in the cabin. As she paced in front of the stove, she made the announcement.

Mother folded her arms across her chest. "Are you certain, Daughter?"

"I am." Sabrina firmed her mouth. "If you have not been vaccinated, you will need to be inoculated. During the war, Grandfather and I set up inoculation tents. We weren't able to stop the disease, but we did control the spread."

"We've already been exposed." Ethan scraped his right thumbnail along his whiskery jaw. "How will this work?"

"After exposure, the disease takes about ten days to develop." She tapped her right finger on her lips. "Inoculations run their course in about seven or less."

Ethan raised his brows. "Cutting it kind of close, Doc."

"Close is all we have, Captain." Sabrina blew out a hard breath.

"Do you have some of this...vaccine?" Mother tapped her left elbow with her right hand.

"No"—Sabrina opened her medical bag—"what I do have...is some of the toxin from the one survivor." She held a small glass bottle with a whitish material inside. "I can put this in your system. Your body will build up a defense against smallpox, then you will be immune to the disease."

Mrs. Hunter wrung her hands. "This is the most ridiculous thing I believe I have ever heard of. Our best chance is to leave."

"Mother, please." Graham put his right hand on his mother's shoulder. "Go ahead, Miss Sabrina."

"What I expect to see"—she held her hands out and made eye contact with each person— "within the seven-day period…a local inflammation will appear on your arm. Sometimes, a fever occurs, but should break in a day or two. When the fever is over, you will be protected." She massaged the back of her neck. "Have any of you been vaccinated or have you had cowpox?"

Corporal Davis held up his left hand, and Sergeant O'Rourke raised his right."

"Anyone else?" She connected her gaze with Ethan and lifted her brows.

He firmed his lips and shook his head.

She swallowed. "Every hour we delay increases the risk." She felt her heart thud beneath her breastbone. *This has to work.*

"All right, Doc." Ethan tossed his dripping poncho over the back of the chair and rolled up his sleeve. "I'll go first." He dropped into a chair and rested his elbow on the corner of the table.

From her bag, she retrieved a small bottle filled with whiskey, several clean white handkerchiefs, and a folded towel. She flipped the towel open, and several silver-bladed scalpels gleamed in the lamplight. *What if this fails and Ethan dies?* She dabbed whiskey on his arm, selected a scalpel with her right hand, and paused, watching the blade tremble.

"Steady, Doc." He grinned. "Don't go all mushy on me now."

She pressed her lips into a line. "I'm not that kind of a woman."

He elevated his brows. "You do remember the old

rattler, don't you, Doc?"

"I do." *And you...holding me.* "This might hurt."

"I'm tough." He quirked his mouth and formed a playful grin.

"Sure you are." She briefly made eye contact and then cut two parallel marks into the skin on the outside of his upper arm. When the blood appeared, she pinched the wounds open, and using a second scalpel, she smeared smallpox toxin into the cuts. "This will need time to seep into your system. Leave your sleeve up. Keep the area dry. And do not rub."

"Got it." Ethan pushed the chair back, causing the legs to *rub-rupt* over the floor. "Butterworth, you're up."

Over the next hour, she inoculated everyone, but her sister. "Vivian, you're the last one."

"I won't do it." Vivian crossed her arms over her chest. "And you can't make me."

"Why would I want to make you?" Sabrina inhaled deeply, then fixed her gaze on her sister. "When you get smallpox, and if you survive, your face will be pockmarked with scars. Your entire body will be one large crater. If you don't believe me, go and examine the one man who has survived, or maybe you would rather view the five rotting bodies?"

"All right. You don't have to be so mean about it." Vivian flounced across the room and flopped into a chair. "If I get sick, I swear I will never forgive you." She shoved her sleeve up.

You won't forgive me? Sabrina clenched her jaw. *And why should I care?*

Chapter 11

Three days after the inoculations, Sabrina surveyed the inside of a tent she had transformed into a hospital. She had supervised the scrubbing and sanitizing and hung a privacy curtain, created from a blanket, in the middle of the room separating the men from the women. As the travelers developed fevers, she put them in here. The infected tent, with the deceased, was sealed and, when the weather cleared, would be burned. She washed her hands in a basin of clean water and prepared for morning rounds. Wiping her hands on a towel, she approached the sandy-haired patient. "Good morning, Private Butterworth. How are you feeling this morning?" She held his wrist and monitored his pulse.

"My appetite is stampeding like a herd of wild steers this morning, ma'am."

She nudged the corners of her mouth up. "We'll have to see if we can fix that." She darted her gaze to the doorway.

Ethan swayed into the opening, carrying a black kettle of breakfast mush. He set the pot into the seat of a chair and leaned his forearms on the crest.

No... She strode across the floor. "Ethan?"

He edged his gaze up and attempted a smile, but he shook his head and slumped against the chair.

She laid her right palm on his forehead, and heat radiated into her hand. "Give me your arm." She detected air wheezing into his lungs. *This is bad.*

Breathing through his mouth, he shifted his weight and attempted a chuckle. "Didn't expect this, Doc."

She unbuttoned his shirt sleeve and examined the inoculation mark. Pustules marked the ends of the cut and were enclosed in a bright fiery ring.

"Can't...put me...here."

She flicked her gaze around the tent for Corporal Davis. The dark-haired corporal was handing Graham a cup of water. "Corporal, please serve breakfast."

"Yes, ma'am."

"Ethan, why didn't you tell me?" She circled her right arm around the back of his waist and hooked her fingers into the top of his trousers.

He leaned against her. "Thought...would...get better." He labored for a deep breath. "Cabin...can't let others...know."

They wobbled outside into the gloomy darkness. Low dark clouds evolved, threatening more rain.

She locked her hold around his waist and footslogged across the open area, staggering and swaying beneath his weight. She felt the muscles in her chest knot and squeeze while her heart crashed against the underside of her sternum. *Please, God, not Ethan.*

When they arrived at the cabin, he faltered on the stoop. "You're one...hell of a lady...Doc."

She shoved the door with her hip. "If you'll recall, Captain, I'm no lady. I'm a doctor." She maneuvered him through the opening and zigzagged closer to the bed.

"Thank the Lord"—he fell onto the bed in a dead heap—"I don't need a lady right now."

She heaved him over onto his back. At the sight of

his beard-darkened jaw, she gulped a mouthful of air and stepped to the foot of the bed. *Please don't die.* She grasped the heel of his left boot and pulled up, wriggling the footwear back and forth, then up and down.

His foot slipped free.

She set the boot on the floor and repeated the process with his right boot. When the boot came off, she landed her gaze on a hole in his black sock. With a few stitches, she could repair the opening, but...*can I save his life?*

Sabrina crossed to the washstand and ladled water from a bucket into a metal washbasin and added a dollop of whiskey, then carried the basin to the bedside and set it on the floor. She submerged a rag, then wrung the excess back into the basin. "You are not going to die." Balancing on the edge of the mattress, she opened the top button of his shirt and examined his neck for a rash while she bathed. She made a fresh compress and laid the folded fabric on his forehead, then she scrounged the room for quilts and blankets.

The door opened, and Sergeant O'Rourke ducked his head beneath the door frame and entered. "Davis told me about the cap'n."

She slumped on the edge of the bed.

"Is there a rash, lass?" The gentle giant's words were soft.

"I don't think so." She shook her head and pushed her fingertips against her burning eyelids. "A high fever but there's nothing to give him. I'm out of quinine." She hurriedly swiped the tears seeping around her fingers. "My apologies, Sergeant." She swallowed and forced air out. "I don't mean to lose control."

The sergeant lightly touched her shoulder. "Lass, 'tis a fine doctor ye are. One who has worked night and day and yer tired." In front of the fireplace, he hunkered on his heels and added buffalo chips to the dwindling flame. "We need the room as hot as ye can stand." He glanced at her. "If there's one thing I can tell ye about our cap'n, lass"—the sergeant tossed another chip into the twirling flames—"he's as hardheaded and...as stubborn as an old mule." The sergeant chuckled. "He won't be going nowhere unless it's on his own terms." Rising, he brushed his hands on the seat of his trousers. "I'll be back, lass."

She rooted through the cedar chest next to the bed and found a man's nightshirt and sniffed the light woodsy scent. *Help me, God. Please don't let him die.* She leaned over and unbuttoned the leather flap securing his service revolver in the black holster. Using both hands, she freed the firearm and laid the gun on the kitchen table. She stared at the long, steel-gray barrel.

No—she felt her chest constrict and sucked air, forcing her diaphragm to inflate her lungs. *Kathump-kathump* her heart hammered. *Not now.* She swiped icy beads of sweat from her upper lip with her fingertips. *Oh, not now, not now.* Flashes of light filled the room, and the sickening stench of rotten eggs jammed her nose.

The battlefield appeared.

She felt her body jangle from the inside out. *Bam-bam-bam.* She clamped her hands over her ears and slammed her eyes shut. A winter sweat drenched her body. She gasped for a pocket of air around the icy fingers clutching her throat. The blood in her feet chilled, and the cold rose upward like water, higher, higher, and higher. *Breathe, in, out.* Her stomach swooped, and the room spun faster and faster. She sensed her body drop in a free fall. No sound. No sight. Nothing.

****

In a murky dark fog, the acrid odor of fire reached Sabrina's nostrils. *Breathe.* Something pressed hard against her back. She ran her tongue over her lips and tasted salt. *Relax. Breathe. Relax.* The sound of a whining animal registered in her brain while a weight squished down on her chest. Something wet and rough swiped her cheek. She turned her head and a stiff cloud of fur pricked her face, and something wet nudged her chin. She opened her eyes. "Wolfie?" She clamped her arms around her life preserver and pulled from the dark abyss.

Wolf lay on her chest with his golden gaze locked on her face.

She touched her nose to his black one. "Get off, fellow."

He didn't move.

She wiggled and squeezed from beneath the canine's four legs, then crawled to the bed. Reaching up, she gripped the edge of the mattress and heaved her body from the floor. Twisting around, she perched on the side of the bed while pain danced from her head to her toes. She rubbed the back of her skull. *How long have I been unconscious?* She shoved her hair back from her face.

Wolf whimpered and dropped his head into her lap.

"Good boy." She scratched his ears, and like molasses oozing on a snowy day, she felt the artic numbness in her legs shift into hot, stinging pinpricks. She jiggled her right foot, then her left.

"Sniper"—Ethan moaned and tossed his head—"General, get down." He hit the mattress with his fist. "God, no—hang on, General—I've got you." He grabbed her hand and jerked her forward over his chest. "Now, you listen to me, you son-of-a-bitch…you patch him up, or I'll blow your bloody head off. Do you hear me?"

His voice registered calm, cold, and deadly. "I do." She lifted her body away, feeling his torment with every breath. "I've got him, soldier. You can rest now."

Ethan groaned and fell into a deep sleep.

She unfastened his military gun belt, with *US* imprinted on the buckle, and slipped her hands inside the front band of his trousers, unhooked his suspenders, and freed his shirt. She unbuttoned the last four buttons of his navy-blue blouse and revealed a broad chest with well-defined muscles, covered with a mat of curly dark hair, and no signs of a rash. She caught her breath at the sight of a scar, slashed across his left side, then stroked the thick, puckered mark. "Oh, Ethan." She unfastened the top button of his trousers and freed the tab on the waistband, then undid three more buttons, and halted. She swept the front of her teeth with her tongue and dipped her gaze down the line of dark hair beneath his navel to the top of his drawers and blinked. In her duties as a physician, she had seen and studied the male anatomy, but this…was different.

"Alice." He moaned. "Forgive me."

Sabrina felt an internal heat wave up from her core and over her face. Vivian said he wasn't married, but…*who is Alice?*

The door opened, and Sergeant O'Rourke strode inside. "Doctor Lassie." He handed her a tin cup filled to the brim with a dark liquid. "When I was a wee lad and got a fever, me dear mam would boil up a cup of willow bark tea."

"And you found some willows?" She peered into the murky brew.

"This morning...out back."

"And this will stop the fever?" Sabrina sniffed the scent of wet tree bark.

"Ye have my word on it, lass." The sergeant crossed to the fireplace, his boots thumping the board floor.

"My grandfather had a friend named Granny Birch. People called her a witch, but she knew a lot about plants and how to make healing potions and salves." Sabrina found a spoon and sat on the side of the bed. "Some Grandfather used, and some he avoided, but he always listened."

"Me mam was a lot like yer Granny Birch." The sergeant added more fuel to the fire. "She grew an herb garden and made all kinds of special teas and such."

Sabrina pushed the spoon against Ethan's mouth.

He locked his jaw and flattened his lips.

She pinched his nose and shut his airway, a technique she used with children.

He opened his mouth and gulped air.

She shoved a spoonful of tea inside.

The sergeant brushed his hands on his thighs. "Not many people know this, but me and the cap'n grew up in Texas County, Missouri. Mustered in together and got sent to Tennessee." After the fire blazed, he sat in a slat-backed chair and rested his forearms on his knees.

"I was there when him and Alice married."

"He's married?" Her hand trembled, jiggling the liquid in the spoon, and her heart pumped faster.

"Was." The sergeant took a plug of tobacco out of his pants pocket. "All he talked about during the war was getting home to Alice and his boy."

"He has a son?" Sabrina blotted the dribble from Ethan's beard with a cloth.

"Had." Sergeant O'Rourke bit a chunk and chewed. "Lost them to cholera. And his mam, too." He spat a brown line of juice into the fireplace, and the flames hissed. "I lost track of the cap'n. Then we both ended up at Fort Greer."

Over the next few minutes, she listened to the sergeant reminisce about his boyhood, but her thoughts lingered on Ethan and the devastating pain of losing his family. She administered all the tea, then handed the sergeant the empty cup.

"I'll fetch ye another cup, lass." The red-headed giant prepared to leave. "The more we can get down him, the better his chances."

"Sergeant, before you go." She lifted the nightshirt from the foot of the bed. "I think he would be more comfortable in this."

"Yes, ma'am."

Sabrina sat on the stoop with her left arm circling Wolf and studied the afternoon sky. Gunmetal-gray clouds boiled away, painting the fortress with a dreary light. On top of the upright logs, bastions pointed outward. With a little imagination, Buffalo Mail Station resembled a small castle in a fairy tale.

"Wolfie, when I was a little girl, my favorite bedtime story was about a handsome prince who fell in

136

love with a beautiful princess. She was being held prisoner in a tower by an evil sorcerer, and the prince fought the evil one and saved his ladylove. And…they lived happily ever after." She jiggled her chin on Wolf's head. *My handsome prince lies ill.* She wilted against Wolf, buried her face in his thick fur, and sobbed. "I love him. Please don't let him die."

****

Lying beside Ethan, Sabrina watched dust motes dance in a splinter of new-morning light. She had lost track of time. The last few days merged like dye in a vat of water, mixing and blending until they became one. She massaged the stiffness from her right shoulder, then laid her hand on his chest and monitored the rise and fall of his ribs and the steady thrumming of his heart. Another night survived. She cupped his cheek, feeling the soft strands of his thick beard. He reminded her of a rugged mountain man, all grizzled and bear-like in his appearance.

In the fireplace, droplets of water popped from an iron kettle and sizzled on the stone hearth.

Sergeant O'Rourke kept the pot full and steaming into the room. He said Indians often put their sick in sweat lodges to chase away evil spirits which they believed caused the illnesses. At this point…who was she to argue?

Heading into a new day, she heaved herself up and kneaded the muscles in her lower back. Using the tail of her black-plaid dress, she wiped the sweat from her face and slogged to the washstand, scraping strands of hair back into a lopsided bun at the nape of her neck. She grabbed the empty bucket, making the bail rattle, and then crossed to the door. Outside on the stoop, she exchanged her empty bucket for the waiting full one.

Soldiers' voices and laughter drifted from the cook shack.

The inoculations were successful, and no one had died. *Yet.*

Back at Ethan's bedside, she prepared a fresh compress and laid the cloth across his brow. When her fingers touched his skin, she felt her heart lurch, and her breathing increased. She swiped her hand over his cheeks and neck. Jerking the covers back, she stroked his chest, shoulders, and upper arms and all were cool to the touch. She firmed her chin, her eyes burned and tears fell. "Thank you, God." She crawled onto the bed and collapsed into a deep sleep beside him.

Like a heavy fog, a lovely dream waft. Her handsome prince carried her in his arms to an enchanted castle high in the clouds. He whispered her name and lightly brushed his lips against hers.

Sometime later, Sabrina climbed slowly from the depths of sleep and found Wolf lying beside her. "Good morning." She snuggled with the furry canine.

Wolf licked her nose.

Ethan's nightshirt lay crumpled on the pillow.

She gathered the fabric and inhaled his scent, manly and stimulating. Tingling sensations churned over her body. Her prince was alive, but...he was not well enough to be walking around. She scooted from the bed and scrambled to her feet.

The door opened, and Ethan ducked his head beneath the door frame and stepped into the room. He carried a plate with biscuits in one hand and, in the other, a cup of steaming coffee.

"What in the world do you think you're doing?"

She shoved her hair back, and her heart quickened, while bubbles of joy jostled over her body.

"Trying to serve you breakfast in bed." He set the plate and cup on the table and tossed Wolf a biscuit.

Wolf caught the treat in midair.

"Outside, old boy." Ethan kicked the barrier closed behind the animal and faced her. "Back to bed." He sauntered closer and flashed a grin.

"I can't. I have work." She attempted to pin her hair. "And you shouldn't be out of bed."

"I said"—he twitched his mouth higher into a smile—"get back into bed."

She caught his playful tone and put her hands on her hips. "Captain, you have no authority over me."

He stepped closer and inched both eyebrows up. "Oh, yes I do."

The light in his blue eyes shifted, and she felt bonded to the spot by an invisible force. Ripples of relief eased the stiffness from her body, and she ducked her head.

Using his right index finger, he elevated her chin. "You're exhausted." He traced the area beneath her left eye with his right thumb. "I know you saved my life." He slid the pad across her bottom lip.

"S-Sergeant O'Rourke made some willow bark tea."

He crinkled his mouth. "I know all about the tea." He lowered his head.

"I believe the tea is what saved you." Completely beneath his spell, lovely sensations cascaded over her body.

"I know you remained with me." He dipped his lips closer, hovering over her face.

She swallowed, feeling his warm breath whisper over the sensitive area beneath her nose. "I-I was only doing my duty."

"Is that right?" He created a slow smile and cocked a brow.

She locked her gaze on his mouth. *Oh, his heart-stopping dimples are hidden in his beard.*

He brushed a kiss on the tip of her nose, then floated his lips to the right corner of her mouth.

Kiss me. Now...Please. She felt the strength in her knees evaporate and leaned into his embrace.

He pressed his lips against hers while sliding his hands down her back and cupping her hips.

She felt the softness of his beard brush against her face as she tucked her arms beneath his, and her world tilted. She plummeted into a sensuous net, suspended by threads of desire, and held in a magic moment where all things are possible.

He drew back his head, breaking contact with her mouth. "Bed." He rested his forehead against hers.

She whimpered. "I have things to do." She refilled her lungs with tiny bursts of air.

"Not today, Doc." He chuckled, then swept her into his arms and lifted her from the floor.

"Put me down." She kicked air. "What do you think you're doing?"

"You want down?" He cocked his left eyebrow. "You want me to put you down?"

"Yes, right now."

He dropped her into the center of the bed, then trapped her beneath his weight. "Happy now, Doc?"

She squirmed. "Ethan, stop this nonsense and let me up." She shoved his left shoulder.

He popped his thick brows up. "Since you've seen mine"—he eased his finger around the neckline of her black-plaid dress—"maybe you would like to show me yours." He wiggled his eyebrows.

A playfully wicked gleam sparkled in his eyes. "I didn't"—she swatted his hands away—"I never—Sergeant O'Rourke."

"Doc"—he chuckled and tucked one of her hairpins in his hand—"this cabin is quarantined." He removed his weight, and the bedstead creaked. "Until I say it isn't. No one in or out."

She crab-crawled to the edge of the bed. "Am I a prisoner?"

"Not hardly, darling. You need your rest, and I'm going to make it happen. Enjoy your breakfast, biscuits and honey." He chuckled, heading to the door. "Your favorite, I believe."

She halted. "How did you know?"

He glanced over his shoulder. "I'm in charge, I know everything."

Do you know about William and me?

Chapter 12

A week later, dressed in a brown riding skirt and a blue-and-green-plaid blouse, Sabrina rode Lily beside the ambulance. The churning wheels stirred red dirt into the air. She blinked the grit from her eyes and swished her tongue over her teeth while her mind drifted. During her quarantine, she had made medical notes in her journal and described the inoculation process. She commented on the success of the willow bark tea, but mostly, she slept.

Private Todd delivered her meals and scraps and bones for Wolf. And for some odd reason—she lifted her lips—she always had honey with her morning biscuits. She eased her brows together. How could Ethan have possibly known her favorite breakfast? Mother must have told him. Vivian certainly wouldn't have.

One evening, Butterworth and Davis presented her with a wooden washtub filled with warm water and said it was with compliments from the cap'n.

Ahead, Ethan rode point.

She watched his well-formed body sway in rhythm with his reddish-brown gelding. His considerate order probably meant nothing more than him being thankful for her care but—she felt the muscles at the corners of her mouth curve up—whatever his reason, she had certainly enjoyed the soak. She crinkled her brow and massaged her left shoulder with her right hand. She had hoped he would visit, but he hadn't. Did his kiss mean nothing more than gratitude? Being the highest-ranking officer, he was responsible for seeing the death tent burned and arrangements made for the one survivor. His words to Vivian *bonged. Maybe I just like having an excuse to be with you.* The sour taste of betrayal hit her tongue. *Again.*

"Welcome to the north fork of the Red River, ladies." Corporal Davis rocked the conveyance into the muddy water, mixing up a gooey glob and stirring up the mosquitos.

Bzzzz-mmmm, a dark swarming cloud of biting insects shrouded her and Lily. "Shoo." She fanned the air near her ear. "Go away." She slapped the stinging dots on her face.

Lily splashed into the mucky-red water.

Sabrina felt her body shift and tightened her hold on the front of the saddle.

Ethan suddenly appeared beside her. "Doc, be careful. There are lines of quicksand running along the river bed."

"Quicksand?" She felt her throat tighten.

Lily waded deeper into the stirrup-high water.

"You'll be fine." He chuckled. "Stay close to the wagons."

Outlined against the southern sky, Fort Greer appeared in the distance. Adobe clay bricks created terra-cotta walls, and bands of sunshine highlighted the watch towers at the four corners. The fort grew larger and more daunting. She swiped her right-gloved hand over her mouth and glanced around at the limited vegetation, a few shrubs, with zigzagging branches, and wadded clumps of weeds.

Martha's words boomeranged. "Sometimes, there ain't no way to tell if something's wrong until you've already done it."

A soldier, small in stature, stepped into view and saluted. "Good to have you back, Cap'n."

"Thank you, Bailey." Standing in his stirrups, Ethan returned the salute. "Is the colonel in his office?"

"No, sir." The smooth-faced soldier flattened his lips while shaking his head. "Took some men out this morning and ain't come back." He pushed the gate wider, making the hinges *screech*. "Had reports of Cheyenne dog soldiers over at Quartz Mountain."

The wagons lumbered inside.

"Polly, you and the girls shall stay with us, and I won't take *no* for an answer." Mrs. Hunter released a deep breath and smiled. "We have plenty of room, and besides, we Virginians must stick together."

Ethan rotated in the saddle. "Corporal Davis, see the ladies to the colonel's quarters."

"Yes, sir." Davis jiggled the reins over the team of mules and whistled between his teeth. "Hup. Gid-up there."

Sabrina followed the *rattling* ambulance past two rows of cabin-like houses and across the parade ground. They stopped in front of a white two-story house with curved arches forming a shaded porch. Clusters of yellow and orange honeysuckle vines twined along the front and scented the air with whiffs of sweetness. Several large clay pots of red geraniums hinted at civilization. She glanced around. *In the middle of nowhere.*

"Miz Millie, lands sake, I'm surely glad you're

home." A buxom woman, with her head wrapped in a turban of red-and-green floral fabric, rushed from the house, wiping her hands on a bright-yellow apron layered over a tan dress.

"I am ready to sleep in my own bed, Lovey." Mrs. Hunter gathered the skirt of her peach-colored gown, placed her ankle-high black shoe on the top of the wagon wheel, and prepared to step down with Corporal Davis' help.

Sabrina swung from the saddle and handed her reins to Private Todd. She brushed the dirt from her tan skirt and watched Wolf flop into a curl near a white wicker chair on the porch. *I can't give him up.* As she drifted behind the others, she tucked her gloves into the waistband of her skirt and crossed the porch into a small foyer.

A staircase angled upward along the west wall and on the east, a parlor. Family-type portraits adorned the walls, and a circle-topped, tripod table held a grouping of porcelain figurines. Appetizing food aromas scented the air.

Sabrina laid her bonnet on a cherrywood table near the door and felt her empty stomach rumble.

"When them scouts come in"—Lovey brushed her hand over her apron—"I put on a fresh pot of coffee. And I have a big roast of venison in the oven for supper."

"Lovey, these are my friends. You remember Mrs. Clay, and these are her daughters, Sabrina and Vivian."

"It's been a mighty long time, Miz Clay." A wide-smile split the woman's friendly face. "I remember you as Miz Polly, Doctor and Miz Carter's daughter." Lovey swiped her chin with the bottom of her apron.

"Go on now, and sit yourselves down while I show this here gentleman where to put y'all's things."

"Before the war got good and started"—Mrs. Hunter dropped into a rust-colored upholstered chair with doilies over the arms—"we put some of our things in a cave not far from the house. You remember the cave, Polly. We used to go there on picnics in the summertime." She laced her fingers together and rested her hands in her lap. "Long before the war."

Sabrina skirted a wing chair and stepped to the east window. With her back to the room, she watched Ethan between the edges of the lace curtains.

He sat military straight in the saddle with his wide-brimmed hat low on his brow. He waved his arms, directing the supply wagons to the buildings on the south side of the fort.

Sabrina trailed her right thumb across her lips and floated her fingertips over her left cheek, recalling the soft sensation of his beard and the warmth of his lips. She was sorry to see his beard go, but—she did like seeing his dimples. *No.* Her true purpose was finding answers about William's death, and falling in love with the handsome captain was not part of the plan. She leaned her forehead against the warm pane, and a little voice tweeted inside her head—*too late, too late.*

Suddenly, Ethan snapped his head toward the window and honed his gaze on her. He flashed a broad smile, tipped his hat, then rode away.

She jerked back into the shadows, and heat radiated up her neck, then spread across her cheeks. She forced out tiny bursts of air. "Mrs. Hunter, can I see the hospital from here?"

Mrs. Hunter joined her at the window. "No, dear.

The building is over yonder on the other side of the mess hall, and in complete disrepair. You'll certainly have your work cut out for you."

"Has anyone been treating the soldiers?" Using her fingers, Sabrina combed strands of hair back to the snood-covered chignon at the nape of her neck, then turned from the window.

"Mr. Fowler fills in as best he can, but…he's no doctor." Mrs. Hunter returned to the cushioned chair in front of the cold cast-iron stove. "He's the hospital steward."

"Why isn't he treating people in the hospital?" Sabrina sank down beside her mother on the cream-and-brown-striped settee.

Vivian held the skirt of her lilac-and-green-floral dress outward as she sat in the rose-colored wing chair with a faint smile.

"Because…" Lovey *clunked* a silver tray, with a pot of coffee and cups, on the low table in front of the sofa, rattling the china. "When a body goes and kilts itself somewheres, that place ain't fit for nothin'."

"Lovey, please." Mrs. Hunter reached for the pot and filled the delicate gold-rimmed cups with dark coffee. "After the unpleasant incident, the colonel ordered the hospital closed. I'm surprised he's allowed another doctor to come here."

He doesn't know. Sabrina accepted a cup and watched her sister through her eyelashes.

Vivian tilted her head and gave a smug smile.

"Not a very good foot for you to start off on." Mrs. Hunter added sugar to her coffee, then stirred.

Over the brim of her cup, Vivian darted her gaze to Sabrina. "How did he do it?"

Don't you dare! She mashed her lips inward and leveled her glare on her sister.

"Poor man shot himself." Holding the handle of her cup, Mrs. Hunter sipped.

Lovey set a platter, with painted roses decorating the edge and layered with slices of buttered bread, on the table. "After that poor girl died, he started drinkin'." She shook her head and jiggled her double chin. "*Uh-uh.* Ain't nothing good ever come from drinkin'."

"Lovey, enough. I'll not stand for gossip in this house." Mrs. Hunter blotted her mouth with a lace-edged napkin.

"After what girl died?" Vivian bit into her bread, then dabbed the butter from her lip with her pinkie finger.

"One of the laundresses, who washed for Doctor Nelson, got with child." Mrs. Hunter's cup *clinked* against its saucer. "I suppose she serviced him in other ways, too. Men have their needs." Her face pinkened. "Doctor Nelson tried to fix the problem, and the poor girl died."

Was William hiding another secret? Sabrina stared straight ahead and gripped the delicate cup handle, feeling the heat of her mother's glare while pinpricks poked into her stomach.

"I imagine we could all use a little rest before supper." Mrs. Hunter stood and fluffed the skirt of her dress. "I'll show you your rooms. I'm sorry, I only have two."

"Sabrina and I can share a room." Mother brushed breadcrumbs from the bodice of her black waist. "And after sleeping on a pallet, I will welcome any kind of a bed."

Vivian reached for another piece of bread and flaunted a cat-in-the-cream-pitcher smile.

What is she up to? Sabrina watched her sister out of the corner of her eye.

On the landing of the narrow staircase, Mrs. Hunter indicated Vivian's room on the right, then led Sabrina and Mother into the larger bedroom on the left.

Two double beds were butted against the east wall, and on the opposite side, a wardrobe and a commode. Two ladder-back chairs, with flaking white paint, flanked the window on the south. On the north wall, left of the door, a large tapestry hung. Hundreds of stitches and knots created an image of a white house with four stately columns stretching three stories high. Large wings extended outward in opposite directions. Trees, with large green canopies, formed parallel lines along the driveway in front of the house. Colorful threads, representing a flower garden beside the wraparound porch, fanned on the right.

Mrs. Hunter drifted to the tapestry. "Granny Elgin worked several years on this and finished right before she died." She stroked the canvas. "This is the only picture I have of my Homewood."

Mother joined her friend. "It's lovely, Millie."

"I expected the sounds of laughter and happiness to go on forever"—Mrs. Hunter blotted the moisture from her eyes with the tail of her dress—"but that old war destroyed everything I loved."

"You're tired, dear"—Mother gave her friend a hug—"you need some rest."

"I suppose—none of us can change—the past." Mrs. Hunter left the room, and her words faded behind the closed door.

"I told you Nelson wasn't to be trusted"—Mother flung her right arm in the air, her tone a harsh whisper—"carrying on behind your back with a laundress."

"We don't have all the facts." Sabrina folded her arms across her chest and sauntered closer to the tapestry.

"Daughter, you had better start facing some of the facts we do have."

Had William been unfaithful? Sabrina massaged her temple. Was he a Confederate spy?

Peck-tap-peck-tap. A trapped fly hit the inside of the windowpane.

Mother released a deep breath. "Homewood was beautiful, especially in the summertime. See that?" She pointed to the oval-shaped green stitches at the corner of the house. "Those are the magnolia trees. I swear to this day, I can still smell the citrus-vanilla scent. And my goodness, the honeybees would latch onto those blossoms." She tilted her head. "Miss Oldine could plant a stick, and it would grow. Millie's mother was a lovely, genteel lady." Mother moved to the pile of luggage and retrieved her carpetbag. "Did Father ever take you to Homewood?"

"I went a couple of times. I don't think Mr. Elgin approved of me helping Grandfather." Sabrina eased her right index finger over the pink, red, and violet threads, feeling the tiny dots press into her skin.

"Millie's daddy liked having lots of folks around, and he was always inviting us over for dances and barbeques and such." Mother rattled the buckle apart on her much-used floral bag. She removed her nightgown, shook the article, then hung it on a nail inside the wardrobe. "I met your father at a party there." With her hairbrush in her hand, she marched to the bed, farthest from the door, and kicked off her shoes. Sitting on the edge, she pulled the hairpins from her silver-streaked brown hair, and her long locks fell. "From the first time I met Warren, I knew I wanted to marry him. But Warren had feelings for Sarah Jackson."

Sabrina approached the other bed. "What happened to Sarah?" She toed off her right boot, then rolled down her stocking, and repeated the process with her left.

Mother stood and jerked her black blouse tail from her skirt band. "She married Millie's brother, Hansford." Balancing on the side of the bed, Mother leaned forward. "Poor dear died in childbirth. I wasn't Warren's first choice"—she brushed—"but sometimes, that's the way life is."

"It must have been difficult knowing Father loved someone else." Sabrina ambled over to the small dormer window, feeling the cool polished floor slide over the bottoms of her bare feet.

"He loved me, too, Sabrina. Warren and I had a good marriage. And we have three very fine children. Soon, Robert and Carolina will have a child, and our family will continue. Which reminds me"—she twisted her hair into a long rope—"I must write Robert and let him know we have arrived."

"Was Colonel Hunter one of Father's friends?" Below, Sabrina observed Lovey tossing Wolf a bone. *I won't give him up.*

"Millie and me were good friends, still are, but Warren and James never took to one another." Tucking her hair beneath a ruffled cap, Mother bounced on the side of the bed.

Scritch-screech creaked from the leather straps beneath the mattress.

"Tell me more about the colonel." Sabrina opened the window, closed her eyes, and put her face into a warm breeze, feeling the kiss trickle over her skin.

"When James was young, he suffered the death of both his parents. Millie's folks took him in and raised him. When Warren and I married, we left for Fort Smith. Millie and I wrote letters back and forth. James didn't join the army at first, and when he did, he learned Millie was expecting. She stayed behind until after Graham was born. For a few years, I lost track of Millie and James until we arrived at Fort Union. When the war started, I know Millie returned to Homewood, and not long after, the place was destroyed." Mother stacked the two feather pillows and laid back. "Aren't you going to unpack?"

"Not now." Sabrina claimed her carpetbag and carried the case to her bed. "As soon as I can, I shall have my quarters."

"Of course, dear. When everything settles, we will have our own place." Mother fluffed her top pillow.

"I shall be living at the hospital." She located her hairbrush and perched on the side of the bed. "Alone."

Mother wrinkled her chin and narrowed her gaze. She locked her fingers together over her chest. "Did you know William had a drinking problem?"

"I was aware William took a drink now and then"—she unpinned her hair—"but an occasional drink doesn't constitute a problem."

"No matter how hard I try…" Mother rotated her right thumb around her left. "I still can't figure out why William didn't stay in Washington. Father left you the hospital, and as your husband, he would have benefited. Greatly, I might add."

Sabrina jammed her fingers into her hair and fluffed, recalling Uncle Nathan's information. William leaving Washington, when he did, made perfect sense. She bent forward and brushed from the nape of her neck to the ends of her hair. First, she needed her letters. If William saved them, they would be in his quarters. She braided her locks and tied the ends with a strip of cloth. She lay back onto the bed and folded her hands over her waist. *I have to get into the hospital.*

A breeze ruffled the curtain, and Mother's snores created a lullaby of sorts.

Sabrina dropped into a fitful sleep, always fighting the shadowy faces and the coppery scent of blood. When she awakened, evening darkness invaded the corners of the bedroom and she was alone. Crossing to the commode, she poured water from a pitcher into a china basin, scooped the tepid water into her hands, and submerged her face. The liquid flowed over her nose and mouth, washing the residue of sweat and sleep away. She dried with a stiff towel and returned to the bedside.

Lovey's frantic voice osmosed through the door. "Miz Sabrina, the colonel's done come home. Please hurry. Lordy, we don't want him in one of his ugly moods."

Ugly moods?

Minutes later, Sabrina entered the parlor.

"Colonel, this is Polly and Warren's other daughter, Sabrina." Mrs. Hunter made the introduction.

The commander did not stand but remained seated in the wing chair. A scraggly salt-and-pepper beard covered the lower half of his face, and deep furrows permanently creased his forehead. He refilled his glass from the crystal decanter on the knee-level table, sloshing the liquid onto the cherrywood surface.

Sabrina felt her cheeks warm, and sweat beads formed along her upper lip while her hands turned icy. She swallowed. *I must not make him angry.* She chose the straight-back chair near the end of the cream-and-brown-striped settee.

Mrs. Hunter glared at her husband, then smiled at Sabrina. "May I offer you some wine, dear?"

The colonel smirked. "The wolf goes." He sipped his whiskey and leaned back into his chair.

No... Sabrina felt her heart stutter and struggled for air. *I can't give him up.* "Colonel..."

"The wolf stays." Stone-faced, Mrs. Hunter lifted the crystal wine decanter, and her gray eyes darkened to the color of steel. She half-filled the short-stemmed glass with dark burgundy wine. "Colonel, I, for one, am grateful we had Sabrina with us, or we would all be dead from smallpox. She can keep her wolf."

What is going on? Sabrina swung her gaze like a pendulum between the couple.

The colonel's face blasted red. The tiny muscle at his temple pulsated in, then out.

Mrs. Hunter handed Sabrina the glass. A tiny muscle quivered at the left edge of her mouth.

The atmosphere throbbed, and no one spoke.

The soft rattles of pots and pans floated from the kitchen.

Somewhere in the room, a clock marked time, *tick-tock-tick-tock.*

Sabrina gripped her glass, feeling the hard crystal

indentions. She filled her dry mouth with the wine, tasting the fruity-tart flavor, and shifted her weight on the seat of her chair. *What is happening?*

The colonel smiled, raised his brows, and toasted his wife. Over the edge of his glass, he pinned his glare on Sabrina. "The army is no place for a woman, and I have no idea how you got this assignment. But please tell me, Doctor Clay, why would you come here to practice?"

"No great mystery, sir." She held her left palm out. "General Callison said your post surgeon had died and asked if I would take the assignment."

"Ah, family connections." The colonel lowered his caterpillar brows and pursed his lip. "Old Natty made general...isn't that nice?" He knocked back the last of his drink. "I must write and congratulate him." He poured another drink. "Perhaps, he can tell me...how I might get a...promos...tion." He emptied his glass and poured another.

Lovey appeared in the doorway. "Miz Millie, supper's on the table."

Mrs. Hunter climbed her gaze heavenward. "Thank the Lord." She rose and fluffed the skirt of her brown-and-gray dimity gown.

As the colonel hoisted himself up, he tilted to the left. "I am indeed a slucky man tonight—feasting with so many handsome—womeeen." He stumbled to his wife and tucked her hand into the crook of his right elbow, keeping his glass in his left hand.

Mrs. Hunter turned her face away from her husband, showing no emotion.

"And may I say"—Vivian slipped her hand around the colonel's left elbow—"we are lucky as well, dining with such a smart and courageous man." She smiled and batted her eyelids.

Another conquest for Vivian. Sabrina followed.

A yellow crocheted tablecloth covered a formally set dining table, and red roses, in a white vase, formed a centerpiece. Unadorned white china bowls held an array of colorful vegetables—green peas, yellow corn, and purple beets. The dinner plates were stacked at the head of the table.

Sabrina unfolded her napkin and draped the fabric across her lap, then shot her gaze across the table to Vivian.

Vivian licked her lips.

What is she planning?

Lovey carried a blue-and-white platter, with a roasted rump of venison and ringed with red-jacketed potatoes, to the head of the table and placed the food in front of the colonel.

"I hope thisss is seasoned to my taste." The colonel grabbed the wide-bladed knife in one hand, a long-handled fork in the other, and butchered the meat. "Can't ssstand overly seasoned meat." He forked the first slice onto a gold-rimmed plate, then passed to his left.

Vivian accepted the plate. "Captain Reed took me on a tour this afternoon, Colonel." She handed the plate to Mother and flounced her gaze to Sabrina. "And I must say, you have a well-run fort, sir." She curled her lips into a smug smile.

Sabrina stopped breathing. The muscles in her chest constricted, and air refused to push into her lungs. *No. Not with Ethan.*

Colonel Hunter gave Sabrina a plate.

Air. She set the plate on the table. *I have to breathe.* She drew a tiny bubble into her lungs.

"It must be terribly hard work"—Vivian cocked her head and fluttered her eyelashes—"to run such a large fortress."

Sabrina covered her mouth with her napkin and gasped oxygen into her tight lungs.

"Sooo good to have someone notice my accomp...lish...ments." The colonel seized his whiskey glass.

"How many soldiers do you have here, James?" Mother sliced her potato in half.

"Mrs. Clay"—the colonel *thumped* his glass on the table, jostling the whiskey—"I must insissst...on being properly...addresssed by my title."

Mother continued eating while her face bloomed into a bright-red shade matching the roses in the center of the table.

"We've one hundred and twenty me...n, and I...twenty are married." The colonel grabbed the slice of bread on the saucer sitting at the top of his plate, folded it, then shoved a bite into his mouth. Beads of sweat dotted the colonel's forehead while a tiny muscle twitched at the corner of his eye.

Sabrina forked a chunk of potato and observed the man through her eyelashes. *Was the colonel merely drunk, or was he coming unhinged, or maybe both?*

"Colonel, has Reverend Jones been here recently?" Mrs. Hunter sampled her salad.

"Arrived yes...ter...day." Colonel Hunter sawed his venison, scraping the knife on the surface of his plate.

"Dear Reverend Jones travels from post to post,

performing marriages and recording births and deaths." Mrs. Hunter listed the reverend's duties, and then she arched her brows and addressed her husband. "How many lucky couples do we have getting married tomorrow, Colonel?"

"One."

Mrs. Hunter inhaled deeply and let the air float out. "Hansford and Sarah's wedding was such a beautiful affair."

The colonel stopped eating and planted his elbows on the table, keeping his blood-shot gaze on his wife. A shadow of a crimson flush started at the base of his throat and migrated upward while a faint smile hovered around his mouth.

"My brother was so handsome in his black suit, and Sarah was a beauty in her ivory gown." Mrs. Hunter rested her knife on the top of her plate. "Papa threw a big, big party, and we celebrated for days." She sipped her wine, watching her husband over the edge of her glass. "Then my home was burned to the ground." She rested her elbows on the edge of the table. "And my sweet brother died in a Yankee prison."

An undercurrent arced between the couple, and tension crackled in the air while hostility clouded over the table.

Mrs. Hunter hates her husband. Sabrina rubbed the sensations creeping along the back of her neck.

The colonel tipped his head and toasted his wife with his almost-empty glass. He knocked back the last drop and heaved himself up. "La...diesss." He tossed his napkin beside his plate, turned, and stumbled from the room.

Mrs. Hunter dangled a silver bell.

Lovey appeared.

"Please serve our dessert." Mrs. Hunter smiled, and a light sparked in her gray eyes.

Sabrina scraped her tongue along the edge of her front teeth. Was Mrs. Hunter angry because her husband fought for the Union, or was the reason more complicated and sinister?

Chapter 13

The following morning, Sabrina sat on a wooden bench between Mother and Vivian in the fort's mess hall which had been converted for church services.

Officers and their families congregated on one side of the room, and on the other side, enlisted men and their families gathered. Some soldiers stood at the back of the hall, leaning against the wall. Voices droned in conversations with the occasional high-pitched squeal of a child and the intermittent cries of a baby.

A dining table, covered by a white linen cloth, represented the altar. The flickering flames of several white candles highlighted the makeshift pulpit with a spiritual glow. On the floor, in front of the table, red, blue, and yellow blossoms emitted a wild-floral scent from a woven basket.

Graham played the chords of a tender hymn on an upright piano in the corner, the notes rising and falling.

Vivian twisted and glanced toward the back.

"Expecting the captain?" Sabrina folded her arms cross her chest while hot needles of betrayal stabbed.

"I am. And if you want some advice from your little sister…"

Sabrina brushed imaginary wrinkles from the lap of her black skirt and locked her ankles. "I don't."

"I'll give you some anyway." Vivian swiveled her gaze. "Men are like honeybees. They're attracted to the prettiest flowers." Vivian fingered the lacy ruffle along the revealing neckline of her pink-and-white-gingham gown. "Graham is interested in you, but if you don't start fixing yourself up, even he will find another pond to fish in."

"We are only friends." She tugged the left cuff on her black-and-gray pinstriped blouse and shoved air into her lungs.

Graham struck the first chords of an old hymn, and like the waves of an ocean reaching the shore, conversations stopped.

In unison, the congregation rose. "Rock of ages...cleft for me..."

The preacher, dressed in black, approached the altar and opened his Bible, and when the last note was sung, he raised his arms, like a giant bird preparing for flight, and preached about hell and damnation.

Sabrina recalled attending the little valley church in Virginia, near her home, with her grandmother. When she asked Grandfather why he didn't go, he said he preferred talking to God himself, not through an interpreter.

At the end of the sermon, Graham played a few marching chords, signaling the beginning of the wedding.

The brown-haired bride wore a cornet of yellow wildflowers and smiled at the guests from the arm of an older gentleman. She floated down the aisle, and the hem of her lavender bridal gown whispered over the puncheon floor. At the altar, she took her groom's hand.

Sabrina stuck her tongue to the roof of her mouth. *Vivian and Ethan. Together. Did he kiss her and call her darling?* She felt her eyes burn. *I will not cry.*

****

Leaning against the back wall, Ethan perused the crowd. Yesterday, after giving the colonel his report, he had an interesting conversation with Vivian. Shortly following the president's assassination, Nelson left Washington. No one could understand his reasons, because if he had married Sabrina, he would have become part owner of the City Hospital. *The coward was running.*

According to Vivian, when their little theater group had congregated at the Surratt's Boarding House, Nelson was often present. And then, Vivian dropped another nugget of information. She bragged about how she and Sabrina often attended functions at Mrs. Greenhow's Washington residence. Greenhow's name was on a watch list of people sympathetic to the Confederacy.

He clenched his jaw and massaged the muscles in the back of his neck. What was the possibility both sisters worked as spies for the Confederacy?

****

Sabrina waited in the shade of the mess hall between her mother and Graham while the yeasty aroma of baking bread circled from outdoor ovens. *Maybe with everyone at the picnic, I can search for my letters.*

The soldiers formed two navy-blue parallel lines and held their swords high.

The bridal couple dashed beneath the silver arch while the crowd tossed handfuls of rice and cheered. The groom helped his smiling bride onto the seat of a buckboard and when the wagon rolled away, tin cans, tied to the rear axle, *clanged.*

Sabrina adjusted the bow on her black bonnet and faced Graham. "I was wondering if you would show me the hospital."

"I'm sorry"—he frowned and pursed his lips—"but the colonel had the building boarded up."

"Please...just a teeny-tiny peek." She indicated the amount with her thumb and index finger.

He grinned. "I swear, Miss Sabrina, you could wrap me around your little finger." He broadened his smile. "But I wouldn't mind at all."

Guilt, over the game she was playing, left a sour taste in her mouth. "You are such a good friend." She linked her right arm with his left.

He guided her over the dirt-crusted ground and smiled, while patting her hand. "The schoolhouse is over yonder." He pointed to a small square building near the east gate. "We don't have a lot of children, but the few we have are being educated."

She halted, staring at the black cannon, mounted on two large wooden wheels, with its barrel pointed into the air, goose bumps skittered over her shoulders and upper arms. *Father was killed by a Parrott Rifle.* She skirted the pyramid of cannon balls.

Graham pointed to a cube-shaped building. "And this little office is where you can post a letter."

"I do need to send a letter to my uncle and let him know we have arrived safely." She craned her neck for a better view. "And...I need to send one to the hospital and check on things with my friend, Drew."

"No sweetheart or anything?" With his free hand, he covered her fingers resting at his elbow.

"No." She breathed a sigh of relief. *He doesn't know about William and me.* Rounding the corner, she startled a flock of chickens.

The birds *squawked*.

"*Yip…*" She tightened her hold on Graham's arm, staring into the fluttering frenzy of flapping wings and flying feathers.

"Not to worry, Miss Sabrina…" He patted her hand. "I'll take good care of you."

"Yes, chickens are such dangerous birds." She laughed.

Graham led her to a roofed well with a wooden bucket sitting on the edge and a chain running over a pulley. "This is our new water source. Our last doctor and the colonel had quite a row over the placement."

They ambled closer to another building. Upright posts formed the walls, and boards crisscrossed the windows. A sagging sign, hanging by one nail, creaked in the warm breeze.

"And this…is our hospital." Graham climbed onto the porch, then turned and offered his hand.

Sabrina pulled herself up. "Can we go inside?" She cut her gaze toward him and fluttered her eyelashes. "I can't wait to get started."

"Sorry, not today." He wrinkled his forehead and mashed his mouth into a thin line. "When the colonel closed everything, he issued strict orders against anyone going inside."

She cupped her hands around her eyes and peered between the slats into the shadows. "Your mother said Doctor Nelson committed suicide. Why would he do such a thing?"

Graham shrugged. "I don't know. Tomorrow…I'll speak with Captain Reed"—he drew her from the window—"but not today. Besides"—he tucked her right hand into the crook of his left arm—"if we don't get to the picnic, there won't be any of Lovey's fried chicken left."

They exited through the east gate and joined the others hiking along the path toward the river. Adults introduced themselves, and children played a game of chase, running between the sand dunes and boulders.

Caught in the net of merriment, Sabrina dashed to the nearest dune. "Catch me if you can." She slogged higher, expecting to become unshod any moment while the deep sand sucked at her boots. She laughed and removed her bonnet, feeling the warm sunrays coat her face. Arriving at the top, she leaned forward and gasped air into her burning lungs.

Below, billowing canvases, attached to poles, flapped and filled with air. Beneath the shading, the women unpacked food-filled washtubs and baskets, setting the items on long tables while a gaggle of happy children played a game of tag, darting in and out and laughing and singing. Along the river, older children flew kites on the sandy beach. The cheerful ribbon tails bobbed and dipped, creating streaks of color in a blue-and-white sky.

Sabrina replaced her bonnet, leaving the ties loose.

Graham arrived, sucking air into his lungs. "I'm too old...for this..." He folded forward and rested his hands on his knees.

"All the canvases remind me of the time Grandfather took me to the circus to see the elephants, and I got to feed one. I held out a wad of hay"—she demonstrated with her hands—"the fellow took it in his trunk, then carried the bundle to his mouth and chomped."

"Miss Sabrina, you are amazing. I can't believe you can feed a wolf from your hand." He pulled her left hand and kissed the palm. "But then, I would gladly eat from your hand, too."

"Graham, please." She drew away and trudged downward, feeling her face flush hot. When she arrived at the bottom, she excused herself and found a knee-high granite rock and perched. She wiggled off her right boot, dumped the sand, then brushed her stocking. A puff of wind whirled the powder into a tiny dust storm, and Ethan's grit-embedded face flashed. She brushed her fingers together, recalling the bumpy texture of the sand in the creases of his forehead. Then, the blue in his eyes migrated to liquid silver, and he kissed her and called her darling. She stroked her lips while warm creamy sensations spread into the pit of her stomach. She stomped her right boot back in place, then removed her left and repeated the process. As she ambled toward the dinner tables, she swept the sand from the lap of her skirt. Rows and rows of colorful bowls, plates, platters, and tin pans were filled with an assortment of mouth-watering foods. She lifted a plate from the stack.

Hearing her sister's laughter, Sabrina flipped her head, feeling her breath slam into the back of her throat.

Vivian sat with Ethan, and as though they were a couple, she was touching his arm. She locked her gaze on Sabrina and edged her lips into a half-smile.

Big Sister, your problem is you are not woman enough to go after a man. Was Vivian right? Using her fingers, Sabrina dropped a fried chicken leg into the center of her plate. *Never again.* She forked a couple of dill pickles. Her only purpose was to find the truth about William's death. She shoved the briny cucumbers onto her plate and added a piece of cornbread. *I have to find my letters.* She grabbed a mug of apple cider and joined Graham on a blanket beneath a tarpaulin shade.

"I've been waiting." He lifted his mug and sipped.

"I had sand in my boots." She wedged her cup into the silt at the edge of the blanket.

"I must warn you about shades." He bit into a piece of cornbread.

"Shades?" She brushed her fingertips over her skirt.

Graham smiled. "Rattlesnakes like to curl up and escape the heat."

Sabrina laughed. "Yes, I know." The sensation of Ethan's warm hands on her upper arms dotted her skin. *No…* She clenched her jaw.

As everyone enjoyed their meal, the air whirred with comradely conversations.

"I do believe the entire fort is here." She sampled a pickle, and the strong flavor of dill nipped her palate.

"Most are, but there are a few sentries left on duty." He held a chicken leg. "I was hoping, you would do me the honor of riding with me sometime."

She squeezed the corners of her eyes into a squint. "Ummm." *Something about him makes me uneasy.* She took a deep breath and cleaned her fingertips on her white napkin.

A tall soldier, wearing a forage cap, approached. "Graham." The soldier wore wire-rimmed spectacles. "You haven't forgotten, have you?" He removed his cap. "Ma'am."

"Joe." Graham pushed to his feet and brushed his hands on the seat of his trousers. "Let me introduce you. This is Doctor Clay, our new post surgeon. Miss

Sabrina, this is Lieutenant Joe Baker."

"Nice to meet you." She extended her right hand. "Have you been at Fort Greer long?"

"No, ma'am." The ruddy complexioned soldier shook her hand and created a thin line with his lips.

"Have we met before, sir?" She wrinkled her brow and studied the man's long nose, brown hair, and brown eyes.

He smiled and shook his head. "I don't believe so, ma'am." He glanced at Graham. "Spikes are all set up."

"You don't mind, do you? I promised Joe I'd be his partner in a game of horseshoes."

"No, not at all. I need to check on Wolf." Sabrina stacked her dishes and with Graham's assistance, she stood. "He's locked in a storage house, and with this heat, he might need more water."

"Shall I come with you?"

"No. You go and enjoy yourself. I won't be gone long." She carried her dishes to a washtub and flipped through faces and names from the past, too many to remember, but the name Baker did not match the face.

A few minutes later, Sabrina arrived at the wall of the compound. She stuck her head through the north door and surveyed the grounds. Not seeing anyone, she crept forward.

The soles of her boots *scrunched and crunched* on the ground.

She froze. Rising on her tiptoes, she slunk deeper into the fort and listened for any sounds and scanned for any movement.

Suddenly, a sentry, near the colonel's office, edged into view, lighting his pipe.

Her heart lurched, and the inside of her mouth

blasted dry. She crouched, tucked her arms closer to her body, and tiptoed to the shaded area under the northeast tower. Concealed behind a cedar post, she breathed through her mouth and felt her heart jab into her ribs.

"Come on, Samson, let's eat." A male voice floated from the direction of the mess hall.

The sentry glanced around before sauntering toward his friend.

When she could no longer see him, she eased closer to the schoolhouse.

The mess hall door *banged*.

She sprinted to the rear of the hospital and ducked behind a large rain barrel. Panting, she heard the blood rushing into her ears. *Whoosh-whoosh-whoosh*. After a couple of minutes, she stooped and dashed across to the hospital steps and turned the doorknob.

The barrier refused to budge.

Using more force, she tried again. The bottom edge moved but the top corner remained stuck. She wrinkled her chin, then rammed the door with her right shoulder.

The portal flew open.

She lost her balance and propelled headfirst into the room, landing flat on her stomach, *oomph,* the air squished from her lungs, and she lay in the middle of the grubby floor. "Ouch." She rubbed her forehead and blinked, feeling pain slash from ear to ear while her nose burned. *"Ahchoo"*. She sniffed and scanned the floor for her missing bonnet.

Sunlight filtered through a grime-streaked window revealing a wrought iron bedstead, several cobweb-covered chairs without seats, and a stack of dusty, empty crates leaning precariously in a corner.

She heaved from the floor and brushed the dirt

from her clothing, then wiped her dripping nose on the bottom of her skirt. She found her bonnet under a three-legged stool, securely tied it, then slipped to the inside door.

The door hinges *squawked*, echoing through the building.

She scrunched her face and crept into the shadowy hallway.

A scrap of sunlight, filled with jiggling dust motes, nudged between the wooden window slats. A slab-board table, coated with grime, sat below.

On the table, she found a candle stub and a box of matches. She lit the candle and tilted the flame, preventing the hot wax from dripping on her hand, then crossed the hall into the kitchen. She smelled the musty-scent of rodent droppings. *Nasty creatures.*

The kitchen table lay upside down. On the east wall, next to the outside door, was a cast-iron stove, with its vent pipe disconnected. Along the north wall, boards used as shelves, drooped and leaned. Cooking pots and pans hung on nails near the stove and an assortment of dishes and utensils cluttered the floor.

A larger room, left of the kitchen, appeared to be the main ward. Ten wooden cots jutted outward from the south wall, and ten matching cots perpendicularly lined the north wall. A slender pathway between the foot ends of the cots allowed limited walking space. A granite fireplace, built cattycornered, joined the west and south walls.

As Sabrina crossed the hall, she snapped her boots on the wooden floor. She entered a narrow room and skirted the slim table and trailed her fingers over the leather straps, *William's surgical table*. During the war, some doctors took pride in being fast with limb amputations, but William anesthetized his patients with chloroform. If he could, he saved the appendage. Many times, though, gangrene infected the limb, and in order to save the life, removal was necessary. She stopped in front of a glass-door cabinet and used her fingertips to clean an area, peeked inside, then swung open the door.

The hinges *creeeaked.*

An assortment of bottles—some with long-necks, some with short; some green, and some blue—lined the top shelf. Below, three white ceramic jars, used for salves and ointments, rested bottom-side up. A large bundle of fat white candles, tied with a string, lay beside several wax-crusted holders. On the bottom shelf, two medical books, *Plain Concise Practical Remarks on the Treatment of Wounds and Fractures* and *Gray's Anatomy.*

She ran her right index finger down the spine of *Gray's Anatomy,* then pulled the book from the shelf and flipped the pages, recalling her grandfather's excitement when he had shown her his purchase. She eased the reference back into place and shut the door, then with her hands on her hips, she rotated. A ladder, built onto the back wall, caught her eye. She squinted and gingerly moved closer. *Storage room?* Holding the candle in her left hand, she closed her right over a chest-high rung and climbed. Ten steps above the main floor, she paused, her eyes level with the wooden floor of a bedroom. She set her candle down and rose fully into the room, then wiped her sweaty face on the tail of her skirt. *This is William's quarters.*

An iron bedstead leaned against the back wall in two sections, the footboard and the headboard, but no mattress. Drawers, from a crudely constructed chest, were dumped, and William's personal belongings lay scattered over the floor. *If William saved my letters, then someone found them.* She reclaimed the candle and crossed the room, searching the floor for any bloody-brown splotches, then the beam of candlelight struck something stuck between the floorboards. Kneeling, she discovered a silver hairpin.

Squeeak-creeeak shimmied from below.

She halted, her heart pounded. *Hide.* She tiptoed to the armoire, blew out the flame, and wriggled inside.

The rungs on the ladder *creaked* followed by a firm *thump-thump* of boot steps.

She scrunched into a ball, breathing small bubbles of air and wrinkled her tingling nose. Internal pressure built. *No...not now.* She pinched her nostrils, squeezed her eyes shut and held the sneeze inside, then peered through a slit in the closet and watched black knee boots enter her view.

The man's face remained in the shadows while he shuffled through the contents on the floor, then he glanced toward the closet.

No... She pressed her back into the wall of the wardrobe and squeezed her eyes shut. Pressure built. *Not again.* She pinched her nostrils and clamped every muscle in her body and released tiny bursts of air out her mouth. *Silence.* Scrunching her face, she placed her right eye over the crack. *Where is he?* Then, below she heard the footsteps diminish. *Who is he, and why is he searching William's room?*

Chapter 14

The following morning, the hospital reopened, and Sabrina made her way across the parade grounds with Wolf on her heels.

"Ring around the roses…" Children's voices carried from the direction of the schoolhouse. "Pockets full of posies…ashes…ashes…we all fall down."

A pang hit her chest, and she bit her bottom lip. She wanted to be a mother and have children, but… She marched closer to the hospital, and the construction sounds grew louder, *bam-bam-bam, ping-ping-ping, scrip-scrap-scrip.* She stepped onto the hospital porch. "Stay, Wolfie." She pointed to a corner.

Private Todd slopped a vinegar-water mixture on the board-free windows. "Mighty fine morning, ain't it, Doctor?" The pickling aroma floated from the liquid dripping from the wad of rags in the private's left hand, and he tipped his forage cap with his right.

"The morning is lovely, and you have been hard at work."

"Orders." Private Todd smiled broadly, revealing the gap between his two front teeth. "Cap'n's, ma'am."

"Carry on then." She drew her brows together. Could Ethan have been the soldier in William's room yesterday? She shoved open the door, and a small bell mounted at the top *tingled. But why?*

As they cleaned, soldiers created large, billowing

clouds of dirt.

Sabrina fanned her hand in front of her face, chasing the dust away, and sneezed. "*Ah choo.*" Jerking her handkerchief from the sleeve of her faded-blue work dress, she rapidly blinked and blew her nose.

Private Butterworth swept with a bundle of weeds, bound together with a string, whirling dust across the wooden puncheon floor.

"Private, hold up." She sniffed and marched toward him.

"Ma'am?" Butterworth wore a yellow bandana over his nose and mouth.

"Sprinkle water on the floor before you sweep, then the dust won't fly when you do. You only need a little. If you use too much, you'll have mud."

"I'll git me some water, ma'am."

"Thank you." She scanned the room, blotting her nose.

A plump man, dressed in a white duster, gave instructions to a couple of soldiers near the cold granite fireplace. "Take these cots out in the sun and scour them with strong vinegar. Make sure you get down between those cracks. Those boards had better be clean, gentlemen, and I mean spotless."

She approached the curly-haired man. "You must be the hospital steward, Mr. Fowler. I'm Doctor Clay." She held out her right hand.

"You don't remember me, do you, Doctor?" As he shook her hand, the egg-shaped man gave a friendly smile.

"No. I'm sorry…I don't." Sabrina shook her head, studying his long nose and close-set eyes.

"At the little skirmish of Rain Creek, I took a bullet

in my leg. I asked for some water, and you gave me a mixture of whiskey and milk."

"Did I?" Faces flitted in her mind. She stroked her temple.

"As I was loaded into the ambulance, I made a deal with God. If he would let me live, then I would devote my life to helping people. I learned everything I could while I recuperated at City Hospital."

"Wait a minute"—she snapped her fingers and pointed—"your name is Thomas, but we called you Taddie." She eased her lips up.

He dipped his head. "Doctor Nelson stuck me with the name Tadpole, and you shortened it to Taddie."

"It has been three..." She floated the fingers of her right hand across her mouth. "Maybe...four years?"

"It was the summer of sixty-three." He smiled, revealing crooked-yellow teeth. "Would you care for a cup of coffee?"

She compressed the muscles between her brows. "You have coffee?"

"I do. Doctor Nelson wanted a cup first thing in the morning," He led the way into the corridor. "I always made sure a pot was waiting."

Sabrina ambled behind the waddling man into a room she missed during her earlier visit. The laboratory was sandwiched between the surgical area and a storage room at the back of the hospital. "Everything is clean." She trailed her fingers along the rough wooden counter and inhaled the scent of fresh-boiled coffee. "You must have been in here before dawn." She noticed a line of glass bottles, holding various colorful stains and potions on a shelf above a dry sink.

Taddie pulled a rag from his pocket. "After the

hospital closed, I came and covered everything." He swiped the counter. "I recall what Doctor Carter said about cleanliness keeping diseases away. I have always done my best to follow his advice."

"Grandfather would be proud." Sabrina opened a glass-fronted cabinet and touched the brass plates of a balance scale and watched the rocking motion.

"How is the great patriarch doing these days?" Taddie traversed to another cabinet and removed a couple of stoneware mugs.

"I'm sorry to say, Grandfather has passed." She sauntered, continuing her inspection. "Heart attack."

"My deepest condolences." He dropped his smile. "I believe Doctor Carter was ahead of his time. And the things he was practicing will someday be the standard of medicine." He moved to a coffeepot steaming on a rack over a burning candle.

In the center of the room, a flame gyrated beneath a covered vat, with a maze of copper tubing twisting a pathway to a glass jug, where drops of clear liquid gathered, emitting the strong odor of alcohol.

"I believe coffee is not all you have brewing." She examined the fluid.

Taddie laughed. "Doctor Nelson thought we should ferment a purer form of alcohol for medicinal purposes, spirits without tobacco and gunpowder." He poured coffee into the mugs. "The laboratory was his favorite room. He worked at his old desk"—Taddie indicated the battered roll-top in the corner with his head—"often late into the night, documenting his experiments."

She stopped at a binocular microscope. "William was so excited when he purchased this scope. He and Grandfather spent weeks perfecting a staining technique to show the different blood cells. Grandfather's theory was…diseases would show changes in the blood."

Several purple-stained blood smears, on glass slides, lay beside the scope.

Sabrina scooted a high stool from beneath the counter edge and balanced. After positioning a slide beneath the lens, she twisted the knob and pulled the field into focus. "Do you know what William was studying?"

"Malaria. We have a couple of soldiers who were infected during the war." Taddie set her mug on the counter. "I saw you at the picnic yesterday, but then I lost sight of you." He tugged a spindly-legged chair from the corner. "I did speak briefly with your sister. I was smitten with Miss Vivian from the first time I laid eyes on her." He settled into the chair and reached for his mug.

"Most men are." Sabrina sipped, and the hot liquid coated her tongue with the deep flavor of roasted beans. "What happened after you left the hospital?"

"I joined General Sherman. And because of my training at City Hospital, he made me a hospital steward." He sipped, then rested the bottom of the mug on the top bend of his stomach.

"How did you know William was here?" Was Taddie a spy, as well?

"We kept in touch." He glanced around and took a deep breath. "Feels good to have the old hospital open again."

Sabrina rotated the bottom of her mug on the counter. "Tell me about William's death."

Taddie mashed his lips. "Suicide." He dipped his head. "So sad."

"I never expected such a thing from William." Feelings of somehow being responsible whispered. "Could he have accidentally shot himself? Maybe while cleaning his gun or something. William never was good with a gun."

Taddie inhaled deeply, then let the air float out. "I found him."

She tightened the muscles between her brows. "Oh, how awful."

Taddie focused his gaze on the floor. "I arrived early. We were expecting to be busy because of all the New Year's celebrating. Doctor Nelson wasn't up, so I climbed the ladder calling, but he didn't answer." Taddie set his cup aside and stood. "I found him in his bed with his service revolver in his hand." The steward strode toward the coffeepot.

"Is it possible someone wanted his death to appear to be a suicide, and he was murdered?" She wrinkled her chin.

"I don't believe so." He raised the pot, offering her a refill.

Sabrina declined. *Did I come all this way and discover I already know the truth?*

Doctor Nelson changed those last few weeks." Taddie refilled his mug. "You wouldn't have known him. He wasn't sleeping or eating right. And…he was either drunk or had too much of a hangover to care for his patients." He extinguished the flame.

"Mrs. Hunter mentioned a laundress." She tapped the lip of her mug with her right index finger.

"Lila Minton. Her hair was blonde, just like your sister's."

The hairpin I found…Lila Minton's?

178

Taddie swirled the liquid in his cup and resumed his seat. "Doctor Nelson performed an abortion, and the poor woman died."

"Were there complications?"

"All I know is…when I arrived, Doctor Nelson was in surgery." Taddie shrugged. "I stuck my head in and asked if he needed assistance, and he told me to stay out. An hour later, he called me in and said a burial detail was needed."

"Couldn't William have been trying to save her?" She finished her lukewarm coffee.

"At first, I thought so"—he scrunched his mouth—"but then the rumors."

She drew her brows together. "What rumors?"

"Pardon my bluntness, Doctor. Some said Lila was going to have Graham Hunter's baby, and others said…the baby belonged to Doctor Nelson." He slanted his head. "He wasn't the same."

Had Lila been in William's room? If Graham and William were both involved with Lila, whose baby was Lila having?

"Of course, they were only rumors, but still…as my dear ma used to say, where there's smoke, there's fire."

"I should visit William's grave and see to a proper marker." She twisted her empty cup on the counter. *I am no closer to solving the mystery of William's death. If anything, I have more questions.*

"The cemetery is south in a grove of cedar trees." He pointed behind him.

"Taddie, no one here knows my connection to William." She bit her lip. "I'd like to keep it that way."

"Your secret is safe with me." He drained his cup.

"And now"—she edged off the stool—"I need to start earning my pay."

Taddie led the way into the hall. "The supply closet is here." He swung open a door, revealing an organized hospital cupboard. "I have stocked the shelves with clean bandages, bottles of whiskey, and some bottles of quinine and laudanum. Probably need to order more."

"Private, I'm searching for my daughter." Mother's voice rang over the cacophony of carpentry sounds.

Sabrina stepped into the wide doorway, connecting the ward and the hallway, and waved. "Over here."

"There she is." Mother marched closer, her heels clicking away the distance.

Sabrina fluttered her hands over her mouth. "I thought you were at the hospital auxiliary meeting."

"I was." Mother straightened her back. "And...I'm happy to report several women have joined and, when necessary, will provide meals and whatever for the patients." She squinted at the hospital steward. "Don't I know you, young man?"

"This is Taddie, Mother. He was an orderly at City Hospital."

"I remember." Mother narrowed her gaze on the steward. "You were always tagging after Vivian like a little puppy dog."

He laughed. "Me, along with many others."

Mother glanced around. "Where are your quarters, Sabrina?"

"Upstairs, I suppose." She wrinkled her brows.

"Sorry, Doctor. Captain Reed closed the upstairs. Might I suggest the little storage room near the end of the hall?"

Sabrina smoothed her hair back from her face. *Why*

did Ethan seal William's room?

****

Ethan leaned his left shoulder against the side of the mess hall, talking with a couple of men while the sun hovered on the western horizon.

Sabrina marched toward the south gate, carrying a bouquet of wildflowers in her right hand.

Wolf dogged her footsteps.

"Damn it." *She is headed to the cemetery.*

"Cap'n?" Butterworth frowned. "Somethin' wrong, sir?"

"No." Ethan tossed his cigar away. "Carry on." He strode toward the portal. Yesterday, he had followed her to the hospital without a plan. When he realized he couldn't tell her he had her letters, he left. Circling toward the east, he stayed out of sight and hunkered behind a mesquite bush. Visions of his wife's and son's graves formed.

The graveyard lay in a cluster of red cedars. Granite hills shadowed the eastern horizon, and a fence, of sorts, surrounded the collection of graves. Wooden crosses marked a few resting places, but others only a few stones.

Sabrina placed the flowers and bowed her head.

Ethan recalled her accusations about him always spying, and feelings of guilt trickled. But, damn it, he had no choice. Nelson might have been a good doctor, but he sure as hell wasn't a good man. He wanted to tell her what he thought about the son-of-a-bitch traitor and how many Union soldiers died because of him, but the words stuck in his throat. She loved the man, and the last thing he ever wanted to do was hurt her. One thing he found interesting was…never once…in all those letters…had she written *I love you* to Nelson.

Chapter 15

The first week of October, Sabrina lounged outside, feeling the kiss of a warm breeze on her face. She rested her stockinged feet on Wolf's back while he dozed. The lazy afternoon sun smiled from a liquid blue sky. She tilted her face toward the sunbeams, and the warmth dribbled across her nose and chin.

In autumn, the Virginia mountainsides blazed with shades of red, yellow, and orange. The vibrant colors reminded her of dabs of paint thrown haphazardly in sort of a hit-and-miss pattern. She loved walking in the woods and hearing the acorns *crack* and *snap* beneath her boots, and the smell of burning wood in the fireplaces felt comforting on a chilly morning.

"Sabrina." Mother's voice floated. "I have tea."

"Out here." She moved and held the door.

With a large, green bag hanging from her left arm, Mother carried mugs in one hand and a teapot, painted with yellow butterflies, in the other. She skirted the two hoop-back chairs and set the pot and cups on the tripod table. "This is a lovely sitting area."

"I think so. Taddie helped me paint the chairs, and Mrs. Bailey brought over the flowers." Sabrina indicated two clay pots of red geraniums.

"Lovey sent over a pair of yellow curtains for your window." Mother poured the tea. "When they're hung, I think your room will have a more feminine touch."

"I've always liked yellow. Please thank Lovey for me." Sabrina melted into a chair and accepted the cup her mother offered. "She and Mrs. Hunter are quite close, aren't they?"

"Grew up like sisters." Mother sipped her tea. "During the war, they leaned on one another. After Homewood was destroyed, they went to Maryland and lived with some relatives. Some cousin of Millie's, I believe."

"Speaking of sisters..." Sabrina sipped her tea, holding the warm, fruit-flavored liquid in her mouth before swallowing. "How is mine these days?"

"She and Lieutenant Baker are keeping company. He seems quite smitten."

"I think I've met the lieutenant before. But..." She wiggled her feet on Wolf's back. "Do you recall him?"

"No, can't say I do." Mother set her teacup on the table and pulled her crochet from her bag.

Sabrina scrunched her toes in Wolf's thick fur. "Do you think Vivian has found her one and only?" *Maybe she is no longer interested in Ethan.*

"One can never be sure about your sister." Mother worked the thread through a loop, creating a three-stitch chain. "We had an auxiliary meeting today. The gossip is...the laundress was expecting William's child."

Sabrina fingered her lips. "Interesting." *The baby could have been Graham's.*

"Is that all you have to say?" Mother jabbed the crochet hook through another loop.

"I ordered a tombstone for William's grave." She continued massaging Wolf's back with her toes.

"Are you listening?" Mother stopped her hands and glared.

She leaned forward and scratched behind Wolf's ears. "I am. William was a good doctor."

Mother tightened the muscles around her lips. "You know how I felt about him, so spare me the man's credentials."

Sabrina sipped her tea. William had a secret life. How could she have not seen? Had her admiration of his medical abilities blinded her to his faults?

Suddenly, horses galloped through the fort's south gate, creating whirls of dust and dirt.

Men shouted.

Sabrina shot to her feet.

Mother tossed her project aside.

Both women rushed to the back door and met Taddie.

"What is it?" Sabrina felt her stomach drop.

"Wounded." He handed her a white apron.

Breathe. She ran through the corridor, putting on the garment.

Ethan supported the first patient into the ward.

A group of soldiers' wives and mothers followed, all talking at the same time.

"Is my husband here?"

"I can't find my son."

Taddie physically blocked the women with his body and held up his hands. "Please, ladies, allow us to do our jobs." He guided them back to the front porch. "Wait here, and as soon as I know something, I will inform you."

Sabrina glanced around. "Mother?"

"I'm here." Mother stepped closer. "What do you need?"

Sabrina stood, in front of the soldier, watching

blood ooze from around an arrow sticking through his upper left arm. "Bandages and whiskey from the supply closet in the hallway and my bag from my room."

The smooth-cheeked soldier clenched his teeth. "Forgive me for not standing, ma'am." He gave a weak smile.

"Private Bailey, is the arrow part of your uniform, or would you like me to remove it?"

The blood-crusted private chuckled, then winced. "My gift to you, ma'am."

Mother returned with a basket of rolled bandages, three large bottles of amber-colored whiskey, shot glasses, and Sabrina's medical bag.

Sabrina popped the bottle's cork, and as she poured, the rim of the shot glass *clinked* against the lip of the bottle. She pressed the glass into Bailey's right hand. "Drink."

Private Bailey tilted the glass back and swallowed.

Using a pair of scissors, she clipped the tear in his blouse, then ripped the sleeve, exposing the wound.

Ethan observed from the foot of the cot. "What happened?"

"The colonel took us into an ambush, Cap'n"— Bailey coughed—"Cheyenne dog soldiers, sir."

Sabrina refilled Bailey's glass. "Drink up. This will hurt."

"I reckon it ain't goin' to hurt any more than it already does." The private downed the second glass and closed his eyes. "Ready whenever you are, ma'am."

She removed a surgical saw from her bag and poured alcohol over the blade. Standing behind the private, she lined the blade across the shaft, near the head, and sawed. The tip dropped, and she caught the hard projectile with her left hand and scraped her bloody thumb along the serrated edge of the triangular tip, feeling the sharp grooves. "What is this?"

"Flint"—the captain jerked the shank from the private's arm—"a type of rock and when it hits, slices through layers."

She handed the head to Ethan, then stuffed a wad of bandages over the dripping wound.

Ethan flipped the arrowhead over in his right hand. "Some are made from bone and others from deer antlers, but this one is flint."

"You're lucky, Private Bailey, this rock missed your artery." Sabrina spied her mother giving water to the soldier in the next bunk. "Mother, I need you to keep hard pressure on this arm." She replaced the blood-soaked bandages. "If we can get this stopped, I won't have to cauterize."

Taddie provided a clean basin of water.

She washed her sticky hands before moving to the next patient.

Ethan trailed.

A soldier lay on his back, staring at the ceiling. Blood saturated his left upper pant leg. "Ma'am." He bit his lip.

"What's your name, soldier?" She reached for her scissors.

"Mason, ma'am." He flinched.

She snipped the fabric of his pants leg and revealed a bullet hole. She wrinkled her brow and cut her gaze to Ethan. "Gunshot?" She continued separating the fabric from the injury.

"Someone's running guns, Doc."

Sabrina placed her hands on Mason's shoulder.

"Help me roll him, Captain. I need to see the back of his leg."

Ethan pulled Mason forward and positioned him on his right side.

Sabrina stepped behind the cot and scrutinized the back of the patient's leg. "No exit wound."

The private moaned. "Am I gonna lose my leg, ma'am?"

"Not today, soldier." She turned to Taddie. "I need to irrigate."

The hospital steward left, then returned with a bucket of clean water.

She filled the metal dipper and saturated the soldier's leg, the cot, the floor, and her stockinged feet. "Mr. Fowler, please sterilize my forceps and probe." She anesthetized the patient with several shots of whiskey, then flushed his thigh with alcohol and shoved the needle-nose instrument into the bloody hole and located the slug. Using her left hand, she grasped her forceps, retracted the bullet, and examined the edges before dropping the slug into a metal basin.

Taddie heated a knife in a candle flame.

Sabrina sealed the blood vessels with the hot blade. A nauseating and sweet odor rose in a wisp of white smoke. She ran her tongue around her mouth, tasting the putrid smell. "Mr. Fowler, bandage." She returned to Private Bailey, examined his wound, decided not to cauterize, then she approached the next patient. "Where are you injured, corporal?"

"My hand, ma'am. Hurts like a son-of-a-gun." Dirt filled the wrinkles on the corporal's face. "Blamin' horse fell on me."

Carefully holding his right hand, she examined the

black and swollen digits, jutting in abnormal directions. "Three of your fingers are broken." Into his left hand, she tucked a shot glass filled with whiskey. "Drink up." She turned to Taddie, who stood at her elbow. "Mr. Fowler, I'll need a short board to immobilize his hand."

"Yes, Doctor."

She reached for the patient's hand. "I have to realign the bones. Deep breath."

Hours later, she drifted from patient to patient and, with each step, scrunched her shoulders and massaged her lower back.

Taddie served bowls of rabbit stew to the soldiers requiring in-hospital care.

This afternoon, another war entered her life. She exited the main ward, traversed the hallway, and crossed her room. Sensing Wolf on her heels, she stepped out into the cool twilight and heaved a sigh of relief. In the western sky, a crescent moon hung on a blanket of indigo surrounded by twinkling stars. Taking a deep breath, she inhaled the smoky scent of frying meat.

Grrrrr.

"What is it, boy?" She stroked Wolf's head.

The animal jutted his ears horizontally outward, lowered his head, and snarled, glaring forward.

Keeping her hand on his head, she peered into the dark pockets. "Is someone there?"

Graham appeared in a wedge of light created by a burning torch at the corner of the hospital. "Only me, Miss Sabrina."

"My goodness, you gave me a start." She held her hand over her chest.

"I thought you might like some company."

189

She tucked wayward strands of her hair into the crocheted snood at the nape of her neck. "The day has been a long one."

"I know you haven't eaten, so…" Graham held the picnic basket in his right hand higher. "Would you like to dine inside or out?"

Sabrina lifted her tired facial muscles. "Outside." She followed him into the sitting area and moved the tea things off the garden table while appetizing aromas radiated.

Graham lit a white candle, and from the basket, he produced a plate of sandwiches, which were cut into triangles, two long-stemmed goblets, a bottle of wine, and a bread basket of half-moon-shaped fried pastries. Next, he set two white dinner plates on the table.

"My goodness, I'm dining elegantly tonight." She untied her blood-splattered apron and wrinkled her brow as she draped her apron across the crest of the hoop-back chair. "I'm not exactly gowned for a special occasion."

"Miss Sabrina, you always appear beautiful to me. And…we are celebrating." He held her chair.

She melted onto the hard seat. "We are?" She felt an ominous vibration slither down her spine. *What does he want?*

He eased into place across from her. "You and me…finding one another again." Smiling, he popped the cork on the bottle of wine, then filled the goblets.

"If I hadn't had Mr. Fowler and Mother helping me this afternoon, I don't know what I would have done." She reached for a white napkin.

Graham set the bottle down. "Please be careful of Mr. Fowler." He placed a sandwich on her plate.

"I know he's a little eccentric"—she unfolded the square of fabric—"but I believe him to be harmless."

He added a couple of sliced pickles and a wedge of cheese to her plate.

Sabrina bit into the sandwich, and her taste buds registered onion, boiled eggs, and roasted turkey. "This is delicious, but I'm afraid the onion is giving me bad breath." Laughing, she covered her mouth with her napkin.

"Your breath will always smell sweet to me, dearest." He floated his right hand over the rim of his wine glass.

His slender fingers appeared feminine with long nails. She shivered while his syrupy words and slimy smile chilled her to the bone. But...if he was in a good mood...maybe she could get some answers. She sampled the wine, savoring the spiciness along the edges of her tongue. "If you don't mind my asking...why didn't you and your father join the Confederacy?"

Graham formed deep creases between his eyes and confined his gaze on her, while his smile remained stiff.

"I...mean...your mother is a strong Southerner...I would have thought..." She observed him through her eyelashes while wiggling her right stockinged foot beneath her chair.

Graham broke his sandwich into smaller pieces and lined the bread across the center of his plate. "Mother wanted me to join with Uncle Hansford, but Father was joining the Union." He pinched a bite of bread between his right index finger and his thumb. "I wanted...my father...to be proud of me." He popped the piece into his mouth and chewed.

Is he holding something back? Sabrina stuck her tongue against the roof of her mouth.

"I hope to rebuild Homewood someday"—Graham released a hard breath—"and raise a family." He rested his gaze on her. "Do you like children, Miss Sabrina?"

"I do." She squirmed in her chair.

He snaked his right hand over the table and covered her left one.

Cold and clammy. She caught her breath. Goose bumps skated down her spine. *Was Lila's baby his or William's?* "Before we can have a relationship"—she drew her hand away—"I heard a disturbing rumor about a laundress."

"Miss Sabrina." He crushed his lips together and squinted. "People say lots of things, and most aren't true."

"Some people say…" *Here goes nothin*g. "Lila Minton was carrying your child." Beneath the edge of the table, she pinched the fleshy part of the back of her left hand.

"This is something a gentleman does not speak of with a lady." Graham leaned back and folded his arms across his chest and puckered his mouth.

He didn't deny the accusation. "I'm a physician, Graham."

"Yes, you are—but I am not your patient." He thinned his mouth into a straight line while flecks of ice glittered in his brown eyes.

Sabrina felt her face flush hot and her cheeks sting. She twisted her fingers together in her lap.

Graham shifted his weight and leaned forward. "Please forgive me, Miss Sabrina. I had no intention of upsetting you." He flashed a ghost of a smile, but his eyes remained frigid. "All this ugliness is in the past. I'm ready to settle down with a wife and have a family."

She licked her lips and swallowed. "You are a dear friend, Graham."

"I was hoping for something more." He pinned his gaze on her while he chewed another bite.

I need to know. "Perhaps in time…" She rotated her goblet. *Did you kill William?*

"Dare I hope…" Graham cocked his eyebrow. "We can have an understanding?"

She flipped her gaze to him, then darted it away. "If you like"—she locked her ankles and scrunched her toes—"but please, let's keep this between us."

"You make me a happy man." He refilled their glasses. "A toast."

She lifted her wineglass. *One wrong step and my charade will end in disaster.*

"To our future." He *clinked* his glass to hers and drew his lips into a flat smile.

She swirled the burgundy liquid and then pretended a sip. She bobbled her thoughts. *If Lila's baby was his, and William couldn't save her, then Graham could have blamed William for Lila's death. And…he could have killed William.*

"If I couldn't see you across the table, I'd swear you were a million miles away." Graham placed a fried apple pie on her plate and then served himself.

"I was remembering the last time you visited Washington." She forced the corners of her mouth up. "You came for a visit a couple of weeks before President Lincoln was assassinated." If Graham were a Confederate spy, and if he helped Booth, then Mrs.

Hunter wouldn't blame her son for the destruction of her home.

Graham broke his pastry in half. "Lincoln was about as popular as a rattlesnake at a picnic." He used his tongue and scooped the apple filling into his mouth.

Watching him from the corner of her eye, she felt her stomach muscles seize. *Ooowah.* She broke open the apple pocket on her plate. "Grandfather and I often dined with the Lincoln family. President Lincoln was kind, and Mrs. Lincoln devoted to her husband and children."

"I'm sure they were very nice people." He sealed his gaze on her. "I do not wish to talk politics." He drew a crumpled letter from his pants pocket. "Mail arrived earlier." He fanned the envelope.

"Is that for me?" She shimmed her lips up.

"Is Martha Jenkins a friend?" He handed her the correspondence.

A rush of adrenalin shot through her body. "Have you read my letter?" Her heart pounded.

"Of course not. I read the outside." He tapped the table with his right index finger.

She licked her lips. "Martha is a dear friend whose husband died in the war. Grandfather helped her build Fair Meadows Orphanage."

"Sounds lovely." He laid his napkin on the table and bounced his knee.

Sabrina stood. "At this time, we can only provide for twenty children, but I hope we can expand." She repacked the basket, and the dishes *rattled.* "When I return to Washington, I'm planning some changes."

"When we marry"—he trapped her hand in his—"we shall live at Homewood, and our children will keep you busy."

"Of course." She tossed a triangle-shaped sandwich to Wolf and avoided eye contact with Graham. "Please forgive me, but I am rather tired. As a physician, my day starts early."

"After we marry…you will no longer be a physician."

She handed him the basket and felt her stomach curl. *I am a doctor. I will not change. What if Ethan asks?*

Graham leaned forward and attempted a kiss.

"Really, Graham." Sabrina sidestepped. "You go too far." She threw up her hands and blocked another try.

"In my mind…I have not gone far enough…but soon." He stepped away and blew a kiss.

She watched the darkness swallow him, then turned and walked inside, rubbing the iciness from her arms. *Oh, what webs we weave, when we practice to deceive.* She settled in a straight-back chair and fingered the resealed wax on the letter. *The man is a liar. I am playing a dangerous game with a dangerous man.*

Wolf dropped to the wooden floor near her feet.

She took a deep breath and unfolded her letter. "Listen, Wolfie. *Dorie is running and playing. Doctor Anderson is wonderful and has been out every week since you left.*" She patted Wolf's head. "What do you say we write Martha and tell her about you?"

Sabrina scrounged the contents of her flat-topped trunk for a sheet of writing paper but without success. Cradling Wolf's head between her hands, she gazed into his golden eyes and touched her nose to his. "Shall we check William's desk?" Carrying a globed lamp, she led the way down the wide hallway, listening to Wolf's nails clicking the wooden floor behind her. She peeked into the main ward and Grandfather's words bounced in her head...*care for the ones you can, and pray for the ones you cannot.*

Snores from the sleeping men identified the day's successes.

Taddie emerged from the shadows. "Do you need something, Doctor?"

"Writing paper."

"Doctor Nelson's desk. Top drawer on the left."

In the laboratory, Sabrina identified the chemical scents of turpentine, alcohol, and soap. She set her green-globed lamp on the desk and jiggled open the top drawer. Sheets of notepaper were neatly aligned and beside the stack, a closed bottle of ink. *Maybe my letters are here.* She removed the paper and rummaged through another drawer, then another. Opening the bottom drawer, she discovered a small diary. Flipping open the journal, she read.

Treated, Harriett Shoemaker, age ten—wad of chewing tobacco on a wasp sting.

She closed the journal and rested her chin on the edge. "Wolfie, I've searched everywhere. They aren't here."

Chapter 16

A week later, after supper, Ethan yanked the wooden evidence box from beneath his bunk. The chest *shushed* over the plank floor, then he placed the box on the table in the center of his room and flipped off the lid. Reaching inside, he fingered the purple ribbon tying Sabrina's letters in a bundle. Over these last few months, he had read her letters nightly before sleeping and dreaming of her. He glided the ends of the purple ribbon between his right thumb and forefinger, and like the bow in this ribbon, Doc kept him tied in knots. One minute, he was certain she wasn't involved in the conspiracy, and then the next, she would do something stirring doubts. But if he found she was somehow involved, and her letters turned into evidence against her, he would destroy them. He laid the bundle aside and dropped into a chair, making the joints *creak*.

He popped the cork from a full bottle of whiskey and splashed a dollop into the bottom of his tin cup. Sabrina had given him the promise of a new beginning. He wiped his right hand over his mouth, and sweet memories of the mail station nudged. Waking in bed, beside the woman he loved, all curled beneath his arm, was as natural as breathing. He savored the taste of the whiskey burning over his tongue while Sabrina's image sharpened—her smile and kissable lips, her compassion and intelligence, her sparking lilac eyes—he chuckled and felt his chest vibrate—and her stubborn little chin.

He would always love Alice and Rowdy, but they were gone, and nothing would bring them back. He slanted his lips upward. Sabrina was his future. This beautiful and determined woman had saved him in more ways than one. *Someday, when this investigation is over, maybe…she will marry me.*

He pulled his leather cigar case from his trouser pocket and removed her hairpin, then traced the thin metal waves with his right index finger, releasing a kaleidoscope of manly sensations. A man could bury himself in her long, dark hair and die happy. He raised the corners of his lips while scenes from the cabin flashed. Recalling her lovely face turning a delightful pink at his suggestion of peeking beneath her dress, he chuckled. He wanted to believe she was untouched, but if he were engaged to her—he edged his lips up—it would be damn near impossible to keep his hands off until the wedding night. Returning her hairpin to the case, he massaged the back of his neck. *Did Nelson cross the line?*

Last week after leaving the hospital, he had formed a detail and recovered the dead soldiers, then gathered with their families in the cemetery. Scouts reported Cheyenne dog soldiers in the area, so why did the colonel go into the canyon? All during the service, he felt his gut coil. Afterwards, he headed to the colonel's office.

The crazed colonel was drunk and claiming a victory. "You should have been there, Captain. A glorious battle."

Ethan held the fiery whiskey in his mouth. *Glorious, my ass.* Something needed to be said, and he would say it in a report to Washington. For now, his focus must remain on this assignment, uncovering the murderer or murderers of Doctor William Nelson.

His first theory, Nelson and Graham were both Confederate spies. Both knew Sabrina and her family, and their paths could have intersected many times in Washington. After Lincoln was killed, the authorities were searching for Booth and rounding up everyone suspected of treason. Nelson escaped and scurried to Fort Greer and found Graham Hunter. The lieutenant could have been afraid Nelson would break and confess their secrets, so he killed him. Ethan stroked his chin.

He shifted the facts. The doctor had been murdered sometime during the night on New Year's Eve. Fowler found the body the next morning and contacted the sentry on duty, Private Ben Mason…who, in turn, notified him. Shuffling through the contents of the box, Ethan retrieved his crime-scene notebook and flipped open the pages.

Arrived a little after six. Body dressed in nightshirt. Blood splatters on the bed and wall above. Stiffening of the body around the face and neck. Eyes closed. Top of head blown away. Service revolver in right hand.

Suicide?

Blood concentrated in chest area. Flipped body. Small caliber bullet hole in back. Star-like pattern with burnt spots in direct line with heart.

Not suicide.

On bedside table, wallet with money and an empty whiskey bottle.

Not a robbery.

Ethan swirled the liquid in the bottom of his cup and watched the whirlpool while he recalled his actions.

After the hospital was boarded up, he searched every square inch of Nelson's quarters. The mattress was missing, probably burned, so if something had been stuffed inside…gone. Ambling around the room, he had tapped every board along the wall, searching for a hidden compartment, and then something beneath the bedstead caught his attention. He shoved the metal bed frame and discovered a loose floorboard.

He used his pocketknife and pried up the board, finding a locked metal box. After breaking the lock, he discovered Sabrina's letters, a few newspaper articles about the assassination, and a couple of scribbled notes with dates and the name Gray Hounds. Rooting through the box, he retrieved the slips of paper and laid them on the table. He furrowed his brow and scratched his head. What or who were the Gray Hounds? The puzzling note from Mary Surratt appeared innocent. But was it?

Doctor-Mrs. Holahan is getting better. M. Surratt.

Ethan rubbed his earlobe. Fact. Mrs. Holahan lived at the boarding house. He held the note to the light. Maybe the name was code for someone else. The note connected Nelson to Mary Surratt and circumstantially to Booth. He tossed the notes back into the box and continued dissecting information.

In front of witnesses, Graham Hunter threatened Nelson over Minton and because of the celebrations, the lieutenant had the opportunity. Even if Graham shot Nelson in the back, who fired the second shot?

The colonel had proclaimed the death a suicide, ordered the body to be removed, and closed the hospital. Was the colonel covering for his son or himself? A vision of the sisters flashed. Ethan raked his right hand through his hair. Vivian knew Booth, but she couldn't have killed Nelson. If Nelson's death had something to do with him being a Confederate spy, then she could be here to do something about the person who killed him. He rotated his cup and studied the sloshing liquid. He didn't sense Sabrina was involved, but...

A trapped horsefly batted its body against the shutter. *Peck-peck-peck.*

What am I missing? He downed the last of his drink.

A strong rap on the doorjamb interrupted.

Sergeant O'Rourke stood in the doorway. "You wantin' to see me, Cap'n?" He scooped off his forage cap.

"Sit down, Angus." Ethan offered the bottle. "Drink?"

"Perhaps a wee bit, sir." The sergeant untied the battered tin cup swinging on his belt.

Ethan poured. "There could be more to Doctor Nelson's death than we know."

Sergeant O'Rourke touched the bundle of letters. "From a darlin' or sweetheart, by chance?"

"Sister." Ethan dropped the letters back inside the evidence box. "Not important."

"By all appearances, the man blew his bloody brains out"—the sergeant sipped his drink—"end of tale."

"Except for one small detail, Angus."

"And that would be, sir?" The sergeant smeared his mouth on the back of his hand.

Ethan scraped his right thumb across his mouth. "He was shot twice. Once in the back, and once in the side of the head."

"Twice?" The sergeant tasted his drink, then shook

his head. "Sweet Jesus, Joseph, and Mary."

"Did you check on Fowler's alibi?" Ethan lifted the longneck bottle.

"He was delivering a babe over at the Shoemaker's place."

"So, he's telling the truth." Ethan poured, trying to fit the pieces together. "Or at least some of it."

Private Todd arrived in the doorway. "Pardon me, sirs"—the private saluted—"permission to enter, sir."

"Granted." Ethan nodded. "At ease, Private. Pull up a chair."

Todd scooped off his forage cap and tucked it under his arm. "I hate to bother you, sir, but somethin's been gnawin' on me like a dog on an old bone." He scooted a spindle-backed armchair from the corner, and the legs *rump-rubbed* over the wooden floor.

"Drink?" Ethan held up an empty mug.

"Much obliged, sir." The private sat at the small wobbly table and bounced his knee.

"Speak freely." Ethan scooted the half-filled mug across the table.

"Lieutenant Baker, sir." The private cradled the cup in both hands. "I don't rightly know where to start."

"The beginning is always a good place, Private." Leaning back, Ethan held his cup and studied the soldier. *What is going on?*

"I served with Lieutenant Baker in Tennessee, sir." The private sipped his whiskey and grimaced.

"And?" Ethan adjusted his eyebrows.

"I helped bury him, sir." Todd took another sip.

Ethan stiffened his body and slanted forward. "What exactly...are you saying, Private?"

"I don't rightly know who this man is...but he ain't

Lieutenant Joe Baker." Todd shook his head and rotated his mouth into a knot.

Sergeant O'Rourke rested his elbows on the edge of the table. "Could this be another Lieutenant Baker by chance, laddie?"

"Could be"—Private Todd twisted his mouth and thumped his mug on the table—"but ain't." He swiped his lips with his shirt sleeve.

"Let's hear it." Ethan pulled his brows together.

"When you're out in the field, and ain't nothing much happening, you talk about your family." Todd bounced his knee faster. "This egg-suckin' dog claims the same folks and all. He ain't up to no good, Cap'n." The private drained his cup.

"Nobody who uses a dead man's name ever is." Ethan offered the bottle to Private Todd. "Another?"

"No, sir." Todd pushed back from the table and stood. "I want to thank you kindly for letting me get here from Fort Hex, sir. Means a lot to me." The private ambled toward the door, then stopped, and returned to the table. He removed a slip of paper from his pants pocket. "I almost forgot, sir. I got the information you wanted." He handed over a folded note with the names of the latest recruits. "First name is Lieutenant Baker, the yellow-bellied liar from Washington." Todd left.

A new clue in the puzzle had dropped into his lap. Ethan offered the sergeant a cigar. *But how does it fit?* The last of the summer's gray moths fluttered around the lamp while a balanced blend of earth, wood, and spice merged over his tongue.

"'Tis a kettle of trouble ye've got brewin', Cap'n."

"Angus, old friend"—Ethan shifted the cigar in his mouth—"we need a poker game. If we play our cards right, we might get some much-needed answers."

****

A few nights later, Ethan met with Private Todd behind the fort stables. "What have you got for me?"

"I've been dogging Baker liked you told me, sir. And he ain't been getting no letters. He did send one to Washington, but I wasn't able to see the name."

"Anything else?"

"Just he and Miss Vivian attended a pie supper together last Sunday night, and some folks say he's spending time over at the colonel's." Private Todd spat a line of tobacco juice onto the ground.

"Is he now?" Ethan lifted his brows. "Maybe with a friendly game of cards, and a little whiskey, Baker's tongue will loosen." He slapped the private on the back. "Come on. I'm feeling mighty lucky tonight."

In the barn, wagons and other conveyances lined the north side, and stalls, filled with horses, covered the south. Orange lantern flames flickered, and the earthy odors of tobacco, horseflesh, and saddle leather created a masculine domain.

Lieutenant Baker, Sergeant O'Rourke, and Private Bailey sat circled around an upended water barrel with a flat board for a playing surface and one open place.

"Good evening, gentlemen." Ethan straddled the empty chair facing the double doors and studied each man. "Glad you gents could join the game."

The brown-haired Bailey squirmed in his chair. "I feel kind of funny playing poker with officers, sir."

"I always like to get to know my men." Ethan tilted his lips upward. "I've found if I can't trust a man at the poker table, then I can't trust him on the battlefield." He swung his gaze. "If anyone is uncomfortable, he is free to leave."

Everyone remained seated.

"Let's play poker, gentleman." Ethan took control of the deck.

Soldiers gathered in the background and talked in hushed tones. An occasional *nicker* fluttered from one of the horses.

Each player anted up, *clinking* silver coins into the center of the table.

Ethan shuffled the cards several times and nodded at Baker across the table. He tapped the edges of the cards on the surface of the board, before passing the deck left to Bailey.

The private divided the deck into two parts, placed the bottom half on the top, and returned the deck to the dealer.

The sergeant, positioned on the captain's right, shot a stream of tobacco juice into a tin can.

Ethan dealt each player five cards. "Private Bailey, what's it going to be?"

"Two bits, sir." The private tossed the silver coin into the pile.

While bets were being called, Ethan studied his cards. At the end of the first round, he laid the first card on the deck aside. "How many cards, Bailey?"

"Two, sir."

Ethan dealt two cards. "And you, Lieutenant?"

Baker pushed his eyeglasses higher on his nose. "I'll take one." He studied his cards. "Where are you from, Captain?"

"Missouri and you?" Ethan bunched his mouth.

"Pennsylvania." Baker rearranged his cards.

Ethan darted his gaze to Todd standing over to one

side.

The private nodded.

Staying with his story. "Dealer takes three." Ethan counted the cards onto the table.

"Tell me, Captain." Baker fingered the stack of coins in front of him. "Who did you serve under during the war?"

"I bounced around." Ethan positioned his cards in a fan. "And you?"

"McClellan."

"Did a little marching in Washington, didn't you?" Ethan chuckled as he switched a card.

Baker pursed his lips. "A little."

"The Clay family comes from Washington." Ethan scratched his chin.

The thick-lipped lieutenant compressed his lips into a straight line. "Unfortunately, I never had the pleasure of meeting them before the picnic the other day." Baker adjusted a card. "I did catch Miss Vivian in a performance once. She played Lady Macbeth." He smiled. "I swear one glance into those green eyes and I would have killed for her, too."

Interesting. Ethan studied his cards. "Our last post surgeon was from Washington, William Nelson, did you know him?"

"No. Can't say I did." Baker narrowed his gaze and tightened his jaw, then wiped his left hand over his mouth. "Is this an interrogation, Captain?"

"No, just a friendly game of cards, mister." *So, why are you lying?*

The night progressed, different hands were played, different winners declared, and the whiskey flowed.

Private Bailey tossed his cards on the table. "Too

rich for my blood."

Baker pinched his lips. "Looks like it's up to you and me, Captain. What have you got?"

"A full house—three ladies and two aces." Ethan fanned his cards on the table. "And you, mister?"

"A straight." Baker gave a slight smile. "Thought I had you that time, Captain."

Ethan pulled the pot over, and the coins shifted and *clinked*. "Private Todd, refills all around."

Corporal Davis marched in and saluted. "Cap'n, sir, couple of drunken soldiers got into a fight. One of them's bleeding like a stuck hog."

"Did you send for Doc?"

Baker shuffled.

"Not yet, sir." Davis stood at attention.

"Private Todd, take over for me." Ethan rose. "I'll get Doc." He scratched the side of his nose and tossed a final glance toward Baker. What were the odds this guy, Nelson, Vivian, and Booth were all in Washington at the same time, and their paths never crisscrossed? *Sabrina was there, too.*

Chapter 17

Minutes later, Ethan pounded on the hospital's back door. "Doc, open up." He heard her moving around.

"Ethan?" Sabrina cracked open the door. "What are you doing here?" She wore an untied lacy wrapper over a matching pink nightgown. Her dark hair hung in a single braid over her left shoulder, and tiny strands of hair feathered around her face.

Grrrr. Wolf emitted a low guttural warning from the floor.

"Hush, Wolfie." She flapped her right hand behind her back.

A vision of womanly perfection stood before him and a sweet burn kindled in his chest while he drifted his gaze downward and twitched his lips up.

"It's after midnight, Captain." She yanked her robe and tied the edges. "And…you've been drinking."

"I have." Ethan leaned his left shoulder against the door frame and recalled their first kiss in the moonlight. He ran his tongue over his bottom lip and craved a taste of those sweet, soft lips again. "I need you to check on a couple of my men." He advanced.

She stepped backwards and shoved her mussed hair from her face with her right hand. "What happened?"

"A little misunderstanding." He maneuvered his way inside.

"You mean they got drunk and got into a fight." She flattened her palm over the top of her robe.

"That's one way to put it." He felt his chest vibrate with a chuckle.

"That's the only way." She turned and lit the wick of a white candle standing in a brass holder. "I'll only be a moment." Carrying the candle, she stepped behind a white bedsheet serving as a dressing screen and set the flame on a table.

"No rush, Doc." Ethan scratched his neck and sank into a rope-bottom chair. He angled back on two legs and rested the chair's crest against the wall, then crossed his arms over his chest and expanded his mouth at the sweet scene.

Sabrina's shadow shifted and jiggled in a provocative dance while the bottom edge of her nightgown floated upward. The dark silhouette of her nude little backside outlined against the white screen.

He swallowed while his imagination flared white-hot, and his manly senses kicked into full-throttle. His heart pounded, and he forced air into his lungs. His wife had not enjoyed their marriage bed. *But Doc would.* "Damn." He dropped forward, and the front chair legs *thumped* the floor.

"Ethan?"

Outside, he gulped large pockets of the nippy night air. The investigation must come first, but his obsession for her was hurling him into an emotional whirlpool. He needed answers and soon.

A few minutes later, Sabrina joined him. "Are you all right?"

"Needed air."

"Drinking will do that."

He chuckled. "So will other things."

They headed across the fort grounds toward the guardhouse located near the west gate. Torches burned strategically and provided loops of light. Somewhere toward the south, a coyote pack *yipped* and the *grackle-click* of a barn owl called from the shadows.

Arriving at the guardhouse, Ethan entered first.

A bushy-bearded soldier jumped to attention and saluted his commanding officer.

Ethan returned the salute. "I understand you have two of my men, private."

"Yes, sir. Brown got whacked over the head with a whiskey bottle, but McDougal ain't hurt, sir."

Ethan grabbed the large skeleton key and a burning lantern from the top of the desk, then led the way down the slim corridor to the containment area. Rank odors of sour sweat and curdled vomit permeated everything. "Good God, it stinks in here." He shoved the double-notched key into the lock, and metal grated on metal. "Private Brown, on your feet."

Brown rose on wobbly legs, imitated the motions of removing a hat which wasn't on his head, and gave a half-hearted salute.

Ethan held the lantern closer to the prisoner's face. "Private, this is Doctor Clay." Bits of glass glittered along the torn edges of skin, and dried blood marked a trail over Brown's cheek.

"Ma'am." Brown wilted into a slanting position on the side of the cot.

"I need clean water." Sabrina wrinkled her nose. "This place needs to be scrubbed, before we have an outbreak of cholera or something else we don't want to deal with."

Ethan booted his way over the layer of filthy straw strewn over the floor, exposing a fermented stench, and stepped into the corridor and shouted orders to the guard.

A few minutes later, the soldier arrived with a bucket of water.

"Get that stinking slop jar out of here. Tomorrow morning, I want this place scoured from top to bottom. Do I make myself clear?"

"Yes, sir." The private snapped a salute, then left.

Opening her medical bag, Sabrina removed a pair of tweezers. "Most of his cuts are superficial." Using the tip of the tweezers, she pointed to a jagged gash. "This one will need a couple of stitches." After picking the glass shards from the bloody opening, she flooded the area with a dipper of water, then stitched the cut. She placed a whiskey-soaked bandage over the area.

"Dad-gum-it, ma'am." Private Brown roused to full consciousness. "That's burning hotter than any fire."

"Be still." She tied the bandage in place.

"Ma'am, you're wasting good whiskey," Private Brown mumbled before passing out.

Ethan kneaded the back of his neck. "As soon as he's sober, he can help with the cleanup. Nothing like a hard day's work to help a hangover."

She snapped her medical bag shut. "What about him?" She pointed with her head at the man snoring on the other cot.

"He's okay. I've got to talk to Brown's wife. Why she puts up with all his drinking is a mystery to me."

****

Outside, Sabrina pulled her dark green cape tighter

and hooked the frog fasteners. She matched Ethan's pace around and between the buildings to the enlisted men's quarters near the north gate.

He knocked on the door of a small cabin.

A thickset woman, with red puffy eyes and brown hair, opened the door. She wore a faded-yellow dress with tiny flowers.

Ethan removed his hat. "Mrs. Brown, this is Doctor Clay." He rotated the brim.

"What's happened to Curtis?" Mrs. Brown blinked and wiped her cheeks with her hands.

"He got drunk and got into a fight, ma'am, but he's okay."

"Thank the Lord. I've been so worried. I haven't been able to sleep." Mrs. Brown pushed her stringy brown hair back from her face. "Forgive my manners, Cap'n. Y'all come on in, and I'll fix some coffee." She turned toward the round stove in the middle of the room.

"None for me, Mrs. Brown." Ethan put his hat on. "Thanks anyway." He glanced at Sabrina. "Doc?"

"Doctor, ma'am. I'd surely welcome a chance to talk to you." Mrs. Brown coiled her fingers into a knot.

Sabrina curved up the corners of her mouth. "I like my coffee black." She approached a sawbuck table and pulled a ladder-back chair from beneath the edge. "I can assure you, your husband will be fine. Only a few cuts, nothing serious."

"Thank you kindly, Doctor. I don't know what I'd do if anything happened to Curtis." Mrs. Brown opened the lid of the coffeepot sitting on the table and checked the contents.

"Have you been at Fort Greer long?" Sabrina

scooted her medical bag under her chair.

"Came out just before the war ended." Mrs. Brown used a metal poker and stirred the embers inside the stove, then set the coffeepot on.

She glanced around. "If you like, you may call me Sabrina."

"No, ma'am, but I'd like you to call me Mary Beth."

A rocking chair sat near a shuttered window and on the floor, was a wicker sewing basket. A sampler, with *Bless our Home* embroidered in green threads, hung on the wall above the chair. On the north side of the room, a small alcove served as a bedroom with a sagging gray curtain providing limited privacy.

Mary Beth set two blue cups on the table. "Do you like gingerbread, ma'am? I made some yesterd'y."

"I love gingerbread. Thank you."

Mary Beth set a floral-painted tin on the table and smiled weakly, wiping her hands over her stomach. She opened her mouth, but no words came out.

"Honestly, your husband is fine." Sabrina folded her hands and patted her thumbs together.

"Thank you, ma'am, but it ain't that." Mary Beth set saucers and forks on the table.

The scent of boiling coffee puffed from the spout while Sabrina rotated her right thumb around her left. *Why is she so nervous?*

Mary Beth filled the cups, then popped open the tin, releasing the pungent, spicy aroma of cinnamon and ginger. "My husband likes my cooking. Gingerbread is one of his favorites." With a final glance around the room, she dropped into the chair across the table.

Sabrina cradled the cup in both hands, allowing the

warmth to seep into her hands. "Mary Beth, I hope we can be friends. If something is bothering you…"

Fingering the handle of her cup, Mary Beth let out a deep breath. "I'm with child."

"Congratulations. Mr. Brown must be very happy." She set her cup down.

"He don't know nothin' about it. And, when he finds out…he ain't going to be none too happy." Mary Beth wrinkled her chin, rotating the bottom of her cup on the table.

"Some men are a bit nervous at first." Using a fork and her fingers, Sabrina scooted a slice of gingerbread onto a saucer.

"He won't be nervous neither, ma'am"—Mary Beth shook her head and mashed her lips—"he's going to be mad as an old wet hen."

"I don't understand." Sabrina licked her fingers, tasting the delicious blend of spices.

Mary Beth pinched her bottom lip. "Weren't him did the planting, ma'am."

She is confessing an affair. Sabrina nibbled on the gingerbread.

"I ain't no Jezebel." She swiped her tears with her hand.

"Mary Beth, I'm a physician. I help people. I don't judge them." She wrinkled her forehead. "But I'm not sure what you want from me."

Over the table, Mary Beth grabbed Sabrina's left hand. "I want you to fix it."

Sabrina sealed her lips and felt her stomach clench.

"I love my husband." Mary Beth eyed her wedding band. "I'd just as soon be dead as to be without Curtis." She rotated the thin gold band, and her tears continued.

"If you are having relations with your husband"— Sabrina took a deep breath, and then let the air float out—"I don't see how you can be so sure the baby isn't his." She raised her palms. "Perhaps…"

"The baby ain't his." Mary Beth swiped her face with the heel of her hand and sniffed. "Curtis was injured, and he can't…you know."

"How far along are you?" Sabrina agitated the bottom of her cup against the tabletop.

"I only…you know…once. Sometime in March or maybe April. I can't remember exactly."

"Does the father know about the baby?" Sabrina calculated the time. Mary Beth was about seven or eight months, and her large size conveniently concealed her pregnancy.

"He was killed." Mary Beth wiped her face on the hem of her dress.

"If you spoke to your husband…" Sabrina ran her tongue over her front teeth.

"Ain't no man gonna understand what I did." Mary Beth straightened her back. "I know what I done was wrong, and what I've got to do now is make it right."

"How do you feel about children?" Sabrina felt the broken edge of a missing chip, from the cup's rim, against her tongue.

"Sometimes I ache from wanting one so bad." Mary Beth laid a slice of gingerbread on a saucer. "When me and Curtis was first married, we planned on a big family. Then our little Penny died, and my whole insides hurt for the longest, and sometimes, they still do." She licked the crumbs from her finger. "My baby was only two, when she come down with a fever." Mary Beth lifted her fork. "I wouldn't let Curtis, you know, for almost a year. It weren't long after, he got hurt."

A lump of gingerbread dissolved over Sabrina's tongue. "Mary Beth, you need to talk to your husband."

"If you won't help me"—Mary Beth pointed with the tines of her fork—"I'll get the laundry woman to do it."

"What woman?" Sabrina narrowed her gaze.

"I ain't telling. The last doctor we had wouldn't do nothin' to help poor Lila."

Sabrina exhaled. "Mary Beth, I want you to come and see me in a few days." Was William trying to save Lila Minton? She retrieved her bag and headed to the door. "In the meantime, speak with your husband." She opened the door, and cold air blasted inside.

Mary Beth followed. "Getting colder." She hugged her body and rubbed her arms. "Won't be long and it'll snow."

"I promise we will figure this out." She squeezed Mary Beth's cold left hand and then stepped into the maze of dark buildings and her thoughts zinged.

She wants a child and if her husband can't father one, why can't she keep this one? The baby's father is dead, and no one would question the child's paternity. The real question was…could Mr. Brown forgive his wife?

Sabrina stopped and checked her surroundings. The area was unfamiliar. She swallowed the sudden dryness in her throat. She probed the deep nooks of murkiness.

A match flickered.

"Excuse me. Can you point me in the direction of the hospital?" She gripped the handle of her medical bag.

Silence answered. An ominous red glow of burning ash, from the end of something being smoked, dotted the darkness.

She slowly backed away, one foot then the other. Adrenaline pumped as she bolted toward the nearest building and skidded on pebbles and turned the corner. Her heart hammered while she panted and squinted back into the gloomy darkness.

A tiny speck of light sputtered.

No... She sprinted, jamming her left fist into the sharp stitch knotting in her right side. Rounding another building, she smelled hay and horses. *The hospital is on the other side.*

The barn's double doors yawned wide.

She rushed toward the opening with the tail of her green cape whipping around her ankles. She flew by the horse trough, and her hem caught on a nail, jerking her to a stop. Her body snapped forward, and she slammed chest first into the ground. *Oomph.* The air knocked from her lungs, and her medical bag skidded away. Pain cracked over her face and radiated into her chest. She gobbled gritty air and scrambled to her feet.

Someone snatched her from behind.

"Let me go." She twisted, then shoved and kicked her attacker.

"Doc. It's me."

"Ethan?" The haze cleared, and she stared into his amazing blue eyes and frowning face. "A man"—she pointed—"over there."

Ethan half-carried and half-dragged her into the barn, then he tucked her into a pocket behind his shoulder. "I don't see anyone." He shifted and folded her into the circle of his arms.

She felt her body sag and grabbed his waist. With her ear over his heart, she heard the soft *thud-thud-thud. Safe.* She blew out a trembling breath and burrowed her face deeper into his chest, smelling the masculine scent of man, horse, leather, and spicy soap.

"Whoa." He tightened his hold, drawing her closer. "You're not fainting…are you, Doc?" He massaged her back.

"Certainly not." With each stroke of his hand, she felt glimmers of heat burst into her heart. Suspended in the moment, like a raindrop on a leaf, she absorbed his warmth. "I don't faint."

He chuckled, then leaned back and looked into her face. "I know you don't." Using his teeth, he removed his right gauntlet and cradled her left cheek in the palm of his hand.

Taking a deep breath, she closed her eyes, and tears eased out from beneath her lashes.

"Are you all right?" He gently fingered the top of her left cheekbone and wrinkled his brows.

She felt the warmth in his hand and tilted her head in a *yes*, watching the blue in his eyes shift while her heart thrummed, and a quivering sensation jangled in her lower stomach.

Using his right hand, he stroked the dirt from her left cheek, then traced her lips. "No matter what, I will always protect you." He lowered his head and pressed his lips against hers, soft and firm.

She melted into him. *If only Vivian didn't exist.*

Chapter 18

Ethan retrieved her bag. "I'll walk you home." He protectively slipped his left arm around her shoulders. Who was chasing her and why? Does this mean she was involved in the conspiracy and someone knows her connection to Nelson?

A few minutes later, they arrived at the back of the hospital and found the door swinging back and forth.

"I know I closed my door." Sabrina started up the steps.

"You did." Ethan blocked her from entering. "Stay here." He sidled into the ransacked room and surveyed the mess. The mattress lay on the floor with crumpled clothing thrown everywhere.

"Ethan?" She tiptoed behind him.

"*Shhh.*" He crouched and threaded his steps over the chaos. Edging the hallway door open, he coiled his muscles while his heart hammered against his ribs. He focused and listened for any scrap of sound, but only heard the steady *tick-tock-tick-tock* of a clock. He eased out a deep breath and rested his hands on his hips, then rotated. "Whoever did this…is gone."

Sabrina snatched a handful of letters from the floor and shoved them back into the drawer of her trunk. "They dumped everything." She squatted and stacked her books. "Even Grandfather's journals. I can't believe this."

"Someone was definitely searching for something, Doc. The question is…did he find it?" He stepped over a wad of clothing and jerked the mattress back onto the network of ropes. "Can you tell if anything is missing?"

"I don't have anything of real value." Grabbing a crumpled blue dress from the floor, she shook the garment, and bath powder puffed into the air creating a flowery-scented cloud.

"Someone thinks you do." He scooped the pile of bedding from the floor. What would have happened if she had been here?

"Grandmother's necklace." She froze. "Oh, Ethan, what if they took her necklace?" Kneeling in front of her trunk, she opened a hidden compartment. At the sight of the black velvet jewelry box, she rested her hand over her heart. "Still here."

"What about medications, opium, stuff like that?" He dropped the bundle in the middle of the bed and rubbed the back of his neck.

"You think someone wanted drugs?" She brushed the powder from her hands.

He darted his gaze around the room. "They sure as hell wanted something, Doc."

"Supplies are stored in a closet across from the main ward." She pushed her hair back from her face.

"Show me." *The stakes in my investigation have ratcheted higher. Damn.* He felt his chest squeeze.

In the hallway, she opened the cupboard door to the supplies and exposed a well-stocked cabinet. On the top shelf were rolled bandages, followed by labeled bottles of medications, and on the bottom shelf, bed linens. Nothing disturbed.

"I don't understand any of this." She removed her

hair comb, scraped the falling strands, then repositioned the comb.

He met her gaze and plastered his lips together. What could he say? Nothing. He stepped into the main ward, rows of cots, neatly made, and lined side by side. "No patients?"

"I released the last one a couple of days ago."

"And, Fowler?" He raised his brows.

She shrugged. "His services weren't required."

"You mean to tell me"—he jerked off his hat—"you were here alone?" He slapped his hat on his thigh. "Good grief, Sabrina."

"I wasn't exactly alone." She widened her gaze. "Oh, no…Wolfie" She rushed to the front door and stepped outside, then whistled. "Where are you, boy?"

The large, silver-furred animal bounded toward her with his tail waving and his tongue out.

She knelt and enveloped her friend in a bear hug. "You're so sweet." She kissed Wolf's nose.

Ethan crammed his hat back on his head. *If I got down on all fours, would she kiss my nose?* Her bun drooped to one side of her head and her left cheek was turning blue from her fall. She was in danger, and he had no idea what to do.

"Are you hungry, fellow? Let's find you something to eat." Sabrina ruffled the wolf's ears.

"You can't stay here alone." Ethan licked his lips and scrubbed his hand over his face.

She flattened her lips and jutted out her chin. "I can, and I will." She flipped her back and marched from the ward.

"Someone broke into your quarters. Followed you. And…scared you half out of your wits." As he trailed, the thud of his boots emphasized the churning in his stomach. "And me, too, I might add." One second he wanted to embrace her and kiss her senseless, and the next, he wanted to shake some sense into her lovely little brain. "I will assign a sentry to the hospital."

"To guard me?" She headed into the kitchen.

"To protect you." He tossed his hat in the middle of the kitchen table. "Damn it, Sabrina."

She removed the lid from a cast-iron skillet sitting on the stove and found a leftover turkey leg, and tossed it to her pet.

Wolf caught the leg in mid-air, then promptly trotted away.

He clenched his jaw. *Stubborn woman.* He rammed his right hand through his hair and exhaled. "I haven't eaten. You wouldn't by any chance have another one of those, would you?"

She smiled. "No, but I can fix breakfast."

Seeing her sweet smile, he felt some of the tension circling in his gut release. "That's an offer I won't refuse." He shoved a mixture of grass and dried cow chips into the stove, then lit the mass. "Doc, is there anything you haven't told me?"

"Like what?" She opened the lid of the coffeepot and lifted the cheesecloth with the old grounds out and dumped the stale dark-brown liquid into a dishpan. She dipped water from a bucket into the pot, then added a fresh bundle of coffee.

"Oh…" *You were Nelson's sweetheart.* "Anything to help me get a handle on what's happening."

"Maybe someone was searching for something belonging to William." She added a pinch of salt to the coffeepot.

He removed his gauntlets and fixed his gaze on her every movement. "Do you know something?"

"Not really." Sabrina retrieved a bowl from the shelf near the stove and hen eggs from a basket. "I hope you like your eggs scrambled. I'm not good with fried." Whacking the first egg on the side of the bowl, she split the shell apart and dropped the contents into the bowl, then repeated the process four more times.

"Quit stalling, Doc." He shoved his hands onto his hips.

Using a fork, she whisked the egg mixture to a frothy glob. "I found William's diary."

"Where is it?" He cocked his head to one side.

She poured the eggs into a skillet. "In my medical bag." She stirred the yellow blob with a large metal spoon. "I had it with me last night."

"Who knew about this diary?"

"I mentioned finding the journal at supper the other night. Colonel and Mrs. Hunter, Graham, Mother, and Vivian, of course." She stirred the eggs, scraping the bottom of the cast-iron skillet. "And...Mr. Fowler and Lieutenant Baker."

"Just dandy." He focused his gaze on her. "Anyone else?"

With both hands, she hoisted the skillet from the stove. "No. I don't believe so." She scooped the eggs onto a platter. "Honestly, Ethan, William only recorded his medical notes."

"Get the book." He exhaled. *She is in danger.*

Sabrina left, and when she returned, she handed him the green-cloth covered diary.

Flipping the pages, he landed on *December 31, 1865*, the night Nelson was killed. "No entry, but the page is dated."

"I often predate my pages to keep track of the date." She set well-used cups and plates on the table.

Scooting a chair closer to the table, he dropped into the seat. *"December 26. Treated Lucy Crawford for a sprained ankle. Fell while skating."*

Sabrina placed a jar of plum preserves and a spoon on the table.

"December twenty-seven. December twenty-nine. Wait a minute. What happened to *twenty-eight?"* He examined the page. "The paper is thicker." He pulled his penknife from his pocket and sliced the edges apart.

"What does it say?" She craned her neck, trying to read upside down.

"I discovered someone's secret, and now, someone knows mine. God help me, I never wanted the president killed."

"The president?" She tilted the coffeepot, and some of the liquid missed the cup. She swiped the spill with a tea towel.

"Sabrina, you are calling Doctor Nelson, William." He snapped the diary shut. "Explain."

She wilted into a chair. "We were engaged."

Finally. "Why didn't you tell me?"

"I wanted to…really I did. But I needed to know the truth." She locked her gaze with his and swallowed. "And keeping our relationship secret seemed the best way."

"Nelson was murdered." Ethan rested his elbows on the table and studied her face. "The question is why? Was it because he was a Confederate spy involved in the conspiracy, and his identity was discovered, or was he killed because of something else?"

She widened her eyes. "There was a cover-up?"

He lifted his stoneware cup. "There was." He blew on the coffee.

"Why?" She frowned.

"That's what I want to know." He filled his mouth with coffee and a jagged piece of a coffee bean struck his tongue, and he chewed, releasing a strong, bitter taste. "Sabrina, what's going on?"

"The letters I wrote William"—she picked her fingernails—"someone has them."

He released a deep breath. *When this is over, will she forgive me?*

****

A couple of hours later, Sabrina returned to her room and gathered the remains of a broken white vase. She studied the slivers, then dropped the fragments into the wastebasket. Shaking her head, she stared at the shambles of her room. Dresses and undergarments were dumped from her trunks, and Grandfather's medical journals were piled on the floor. She wrapped her arms around her body and scraped her fingernails along her upper arms. Some unknown person broke into her room and touched her most private things. Goose bumps slithered along her spine, and she swallowed. *Who?*

The other night, when she had announced she had found William's diary, Lieutenant Baker asked if she had found any secrets, then he laughed. Was he the man in the shadows? And if he was—she glanced around her quarters—did he do this? *Baker is an imposter.*

She grabbed the wad of bedding, then carried it to the hospital's soiled linen basket at the end of the hallway. *I was gone three...no...more like four hours last night.* She gathered clean sheets from the supply cupboard and returned to her room. *Someone had plenty of time to do this and then follow me.* She floated the covering over the mattress and recalled Ethan's words. *No matter what, I will always protect you.* She twitched her lips up. He had the most amazing blue eyes which were always changing with his emotions. When he was angry, dark-icy blue, and when he was happy, sky-blue, but the one she loved best was the primal silvery-blue, right before he kissed her. Feelings of golden sunshine flowed into her heart.

"Doctor." Private Brown banged on the outside door. "My wife, come quick." The barrel-chested man wiped his mouth with his hand.

"Private, what happened?"

"Best you wait and see." He adjusted his forage cap on his head.

Sabrina left a note for Taddie and retrieved her medical bag.

The large man set a power-pace across the parade ground.

She trotted behind while questions peppered. Did Mary Beth go into early labor and miscarry? Did she fall?

Mr. Brown shoved the door to his quarters. "I come home just a little while ago and found her."

In the couple's bedroom, Mary Beth lay on the bed with her wrists slashed and blood dribbling from the cuts. A butcher knife lay on the floor.

"I'll need a pan of water." Sabrina checked the carotid and found a strong, steady beat. "Mary Beth, can you hear me?" She checked her pupils.

Mr. Brown set a basin of water on the nightstand. "How is she?"

"She's unconscious, but I don't understand why. She hasn't lost much blood." Spying an empty amber bottle on the floor, Sabrina lifted the bottle and sniffed. The spicy odor registered. "Laudanum. Do you know how much was in the bottle?" She began washing the blood away from Mary Beth's wrist.

"Not much. The last doctor gave her half a bottle for some cough she had." Tears filled the man's dark-brown eyes. "She deserves a lot better than me." He rotated and trudged away, sniffing and wiping his face with his hands.

Sabrina wrapped Mary Beth's wrists with strips of fabric, then covered her with an afghan from the foot of the bed. "Mary Beth, I'm sorry." She drifted into the main room.

Mr. Brown slumped at the kitchen table, staring into the bottom of an empty cup. "My wife couldn't stand being with me no more. That's why she done it." He released a shaky breath.

"Your wife loves you very much." Sabrina stepped to the stove and used a folded towel on the handle of the coffeepot, then streamed boiling coffee into his cup. She poured another for herself, then returned the pot to the stove. Unsure of what to say or do, she inched into the chair on the opposite side of the table.

"Then why?" He rested his folded arms on the edge of the table. "I don't understand."

Should I tell him? "Once there was a wife and husband who loved one another very much." She traced circles on the tabletop with her right index finger, feeling every groove and gouge in the wood. "They had a little girl. A fever claimed the child, and the husband and the wife became strangers."

227

He squinted and frowned. "You're talking about me and Mary Beth, ain't you, ma'am?"

She held her cup in both hands and rested her elbows on the table edge. "They were a couple trying to survive their loss"—she sipped the hot liquid, feeling the burn slide down the back of her throat—"together, but alone." She set her cup down. "In her grief, the wife turned to another man for comfort...only once." She watched the muscles in Mr. Brown's face shift. "The woman conceived a child."

"Mary Beth is having a baby?" He clunked his cup on the table and glared. "Who's the pa?"

"I don't know. But I do know he's dead." *I broke Mary Beth's confidence.* Sabrina bit her top lip.

"When our little Penny died..." Tears trickled down the big man's cheeks. "All I wanted was to hold Mary Beth and be close, but she didn't want me no more." He smeared his tears with his right hand. "Then, I wasn't man enough for her."

"Your wife told me"—Sabrina handed him a tea towel—"you were the most important thing in her life, and she would do anything to save her marriage."

He pushed away from the table, then stood.

"Mr. Brown. Please talk to your wife."

He shook his head, "Ain't no use talkin', ma'am." He hunched his shoulders and left the cabin.

Dear Lord, what have I done? Sabrina returned to the bedroom and untied one of the bandages. The clotted blood formed a ring around the patient's wrist. Mary Beth would live. *But will she forgive me?*

Someone rapped on the front door.

"Mrs. Brown?" Mother's voice floated. "Sabrina?"

"Mother, what are you doing here?" She stood in

the opening.

"Mr. Fowler told me where to find you." She set a woven market basket, its contents covered by a square of blue-and-white-checked fabric, on the table. "What's wrong with Mrs. Brown?"

Sabrina closed the curtain. "She's not well."

"And what happened to your face?" Mother peeled off her gloves, laid them on the sawbuck table, and then lowered into a chair.

Sabrina touched her tender left cheek. "I fell this morning." She retrieved the coffeepot from the stove and filled a cup for her mother, then refreshed her own. "Someone broke into my room last night and searched it." She wilted into a chair and filled Mother in on what had happened.

"You shall have your things brought to Millie's immediately." Mother firmed her chin.

"No. Captain Reed will post a sentry."

"Very well. I shall move in with you." Mother sipped her coffee and rested her elbows on the edge of the table.

"Not necessary." Sabrina lifted the corner edge of the checked napkin and sniffed. "*Um-mm* something smells good."

"Lovey made muffins. Daughter, I don't like this." A knock interrupted, and Mother crossed and opened the barrier. "Captain."

"Mrs. Clay." Ethan removed his hat.

Sabrina sailed across the room, grabbed his arm, and pulled him outside, then firmly shut the door.

"Good to see you again, too, Doc." He grinned.

"I have made a serious mistake." She explained what happened.

"Will Mrs. Brown be all right?"

"Physically, yes." She released a thin breath. "But mentally…? I'm not so sure."

He rubbed his jaw. "And the baby?"

"No signs of a miscarriage. But, Ethan, we must find Mr. Brown. I should have never said anything."

An hour later, mounted on horseback, Sabrina trailed Ethan, heading southwest toward the sutler's store. The noonday sunrays spotlighted the front of the shotgun building. Vertical cedar posts reinforced the front, and wooden shingles covered the sloping roof. Dried red peppers, tied with cords, hung along the edge and *shushed* like whispers in the wind. A crudely made sign, identifying *Mangum's Store and Saloon*, creaked back and forth.

They dismounted, then stepped inside.

"I'll only be a minute, Doc." Ethan disappeared through the batwing doors at the back of the room.

The combined scents of roasting coffee beans and refreshing peppermint swirled in the air. Sabrina closed her eyes and transported her mind back to her girlhood. On coffee-roasting day, she helped Grandmother layer the green coffee beans in a perforated pan, and then Grandmother would place the pan on a rack in the fireplace. The rich aroma would linger for days.

The peppermint reminded her of the big sticks of white candy Grandfather always bought at McGregor's and handed out to his young patients, and she always got one, too. *Grandfather, how do I fix this?*

A well-rounded woman wiped the dust from a nearby shelf with a rag. "Afternoon, Doctor Clay."

"It's nice to see you again, Mrs. Mangum." Sabrina meandered down the narrow aisles, passing shelves stocked with canned beans, salmon, oysters, and condensed milk. She paused at a large jar of boiled eggs floating in a yellowish fluid.

The rosy-cheeked proprietress followed. "Them's quail eggs." She pointed to the jar. "Ever had one?"

"No." Sabrina shook her head. "I haven't."

"They're a little creamer than chicken eggs." Mrs. Mangum adjusted the jar and swiped the shelf with her rag. "Is there somethin' you might be needin'?"

"Maybe another time. I'm waiting on the captain." She drifted and then stopped at a shelf holding several music boxes. "These are exquisite." She lifted the lid of a heart-shaped silver one. A miniature couple revolved while the simple *pings* of a waltz played. The purple-gowned woman spun around in the arms of a blue-uniformed soldier. Flickers of a campfire memory embraced her and held her by silken threads while she recalled Ethan's strong arms and firm body guiding her through their waltz.

"Them music boxes come all the way from St. Louie."

She closed the lid, and the music ceased. "They're very pretty."

The frizzy-haired woman swiped a cobweb from beneath the shelf. "One of them girls down on laundry row bought one almost like it. Only it weren't silver, and it played a different tune." Mrs. Mangum peeked around, then lowered her voice. "Men pay those women to do things. As a matter of fact, we had one who got herself in a motherly way, but when the doctor tried to fix it, she died."

"I have heard rumors…" Sabrina trailed the fingers of her right hand along the shelf.

"Lila Minton was a flighty little thing. She come here with her husband, and when he was kilt, she didn't have no money to get back East to her folks."

"I heard she was involved with Graham Hunter?" Sabrina lifted the lid of another music box and listened to a lullaby.

"If it wore pants…she was involved. When Mrs. Hunter found out about her precious son taking up with Lila, she was as mad as a hornet. If I didn't know better, I'd swear Mrs. Hunter kilt Lila herself. She was mad enough to do it."

"I can't picture Mrs. Hunter hurting anyone." Sabrina closed the lid, and the baby's song stopped.

The woman gave a snort-like laugh. "You don't know her very well, then. She and Lila were arguing once. And Mrs. Hunter slapped the woman senseless before the doctor pulled them apart. I suppose that's why Mrs. Hunter tries to be nice to me. I ain't never told nobody; only you."

Was Graham the baby's father?

Mrs. Mangum swiped another cobweb. "Your ma asked me to be on the auxiliary committee."

"I hope you told her *yes*. I need all the help I can get."

"Doc," Ethan called from the other side of the room. "Let's go."

Maybe William wasn't involved with Lila Minton.

Chapter 19

Outside, Ethan settled his hat firmer on his head. "Brown bought a bottle and headed north along the river." He boosted Sabrina into the saddle. "He's got a good head start on us, but he's on foot." Mounting his horse, he headed toward the sandy bank, inspecting the shifting ground for tracks.

The sword-shaped leaves of the yucca jabbed into the air, and the summer's green grasses had dried into brown, bushy broom-like stalks. Prickly pear cacti, with tiny bristles, branched along the top of the gritty soil.

Without a warning, a jackrabbit popped up from behind a clump of shin oak, starling Lily into a side-stepping jig.

Sabrina quickly controlled her mount and flashed Ethan a smile.

He pursed his lips and nodded. "Not bad." Riding along the edge of the clay-red water, Ethan puzzled over the fact someone had ransacked her room. What would have happened if she had been in the hospital? *How in the hell can I protect her? I have no idea with whom I'm dealing—the colonel, his son, Baker, or someone else?* He clenched his left hand, feeling the rough leather of the gauntlet rub against his fingertips. "I can't believe you were engaged to a man you didn't know well." He slanted his gaze on her. *Has she told me everything?*

"William was a brilliant surgeon." She rocked in the saddle, her body coordinating with her horse's movements.

"Brilliant." Bitterness rolled over his tongue. *At least, the bastard is dead.*

The horses climbed a sandy rise.

"Our medical team performed fewer amputations during the war than any other, thanks to William." She gripped the front of her saddle with her left hand.

As Ethan leaned sideways and studied the terrain for tracks, he adjusted his weight, and the leather saddle *creaked*. "He might have been a good doctor, but he wasn't a good man." He surveyed the landscape. "Sing his praises all you want, Doc, but in my book, Nelson was a traitor."

The northwest wind increased, whirling sand into spinning clouds.

"The war was complicated." Sabrina squinted and covered her mouth, blocking the blasting grit.

"Most important things usually are." He bounced his gaze over the environment. The dim October sun vanished behind a rolling bank of blue-black clouds and the temperature plummeted. "We need shelter."

"Can't we go back to the fort?" She gripped the reins of the agitated mare in one hand and clung to the crest of the military saddle with the other.

"Too far. We've got a blue norther coming down on us." He yanked Lily's reins forcing her to follow.

The horses lurched, battling the wall of wind. They jerked, whinnied, and footslogged, climbing higher in the bottomless sand.

At the top of the summit, gunmetal-blue clouds released a hard-driving rain and within seconds, the rain morphed into sleet encasing everything in a shell of ice.

Are we north or west of the fort? Ethan stared into the storm, seeing nothing but ice and snow whipping sideways. He turned in his saddle.

Sabrina hunched forward, clutching the saddle's edge with both hands, but not moving.

Ethan pushed deeper into the tempest. *Where is that soddy?* Frozen pellets nipped and stung his face while he glared into the whiteout. Seconds later, dead ahead, through the frozen mist, a shadow loomed, then an outline of a structure materialized. *Finally.* Towing Lilly behind, he rounded the house and moved away from the body-hammering wind and dismounted. He tethered the horses to a rusty wheel, then reached and removed Sabrina's frozen body from the saddle. "I've got you, darling."

She whimpered.

Ethan wrapped his body around hers and cradled her against his chest. The soles of his boots skated over the crust of ice, and he slipped-slopped to the front of the house and kicked the barely-there door with his right foot.

A one-room dwelling, veiled in shadows, smelled earthy, dank, and deserted. Along the edges of the grass roof, sleet slushed down the adobe walls while the wind screamed over, under, and around the cracks and crevices.

He set her down, then produced a candle and matches from his pocket, and lit the wick.

"I'm so c-cold." She hugged her soaked body, and her teeth *chattered* while her dark hair hung in frozen tangles of rope.

"H-hang on." He forced his stiff, cold body into

motion and crossed to the stone fireplace. Frigid water trickled down his jaws while he searched for kindling. Inside a wooden box, he found a pile of aged buffalo chips and broke several of them apart. He rubbed his shaking hands together, then used the candle flame and lit the mass. Snatching a wooden chair, with a busted cane bottom, he snapped off the legs, then positioned the splintered edges near the flame. When the wood caught, he added more chips, nurturing the sparks into larger tongues of heat. Within minutes, the promise of a warm fire emerged. He brushed his gloved hands on the seat of his pants and turned to check on Sabrina.

"I'm f-f-freezing."

With his teeth, Ethan nipped off his right glove, then removed his left. "We have to get you out of these clothes." He blew warm breath on his hands and flexed his half-frozen fingers, then reached for the top button of her blouse.

Sabrina swatted his hands away. "I-I don't have anything to p-put on."

"Take off your top layer and get over by the fire."

"I-I won't. N-not decent."

"Get…your…clothes…off." He tilted his head and made eye contact. "Or I will take them off."

"W-wouldn't d-dare." She blinked.

"Try me." He firmed the muscles in his face. "I'll be damn if I'm going to let you die, Sabrina."

"F-fine." She flipped her back toward him.

"Fine." Ethan threw his hands up. "If I can't help you"—he shoved his hands back into his gloves—"I'll see to the horses." Outside, the slap of winter did little to cool his frustration. "Damn stubborn woman." He swiped frozen crust from his face while he led the horses to a shed along the back of the soddy. Using the bridles, he hobbled the horses' front legs together, then dumped grain from one of his saddlebags onto a rotten piece of wood. He removed the saddles and stroked the horses' necks. "This is the best I can do, girls." He tugged his rifle from its scabbard and returned to the house. Entering, he ducked his head and halted.

In the shifting firelight, Sabrina finger-combed the snarled mass of hair hanging over her left shoulder. Her right shoulder arched, bare and creamy, above the edge of a patchwork quilt. "Ethan, do you think Wolf is all right?"

Tiny sparks rose behind her and disappeared up the chimney. "I do." He leaned his rifle against the wall. "Some of Mrs. Bailey's cats might come up missing, or some of the chickens might disappear." He cleared his throat and smacked his black hat against his thigh, slinging water into the air.

She wrinkled her nose. "*Oooow*...I hadn't thought about them."

He chuckled and drifted his gaze downward, not missing any curve or dip of her tempting body. At the sight of her exposed thigh, he felt his mouth blast dry. He shoved air into his tight lungs. *This is going to be a long night.*

****

Sabrina tossed her hair back and pointed to her left. "I found some quilts in a trunk over there next to the wall." If she had to spend the night in a cold dilapidated building, she was thankful Ethan was with her. "You need to get out of those wet clothes." She tilted her head to one side and curved her lips up.

"Yes, I do." He twitched his mouth into a devilish

237

grin. "Want to help?"

In the limited light, his blue eyes darkened, which sent tiny goose bumps stumbling over her body. "I have a feeling you've been undressing yourself for years." She revolved her back and faced the fire, relishing the hypnotic movement of the yellow and orange tongues separating, then interlacing like lovers. She sharpened her auditory sense and focused on the sounds of his every action.

One boot hit the floor. *Thud.* The other hit the floor. *Thump.* His belt buckle *jangled.*

Visions of him removing his trousers sent a funny little quaking into her stomach. As the special place below his navel flashed, Sabrina bit her top lip and shut her eyes, glowing warm from the inside out.

Ethan emerged wearing a multicolored quilt tucked around his waist and riding low on top of his hips. In the firelight, he squatted and spread his garments beside hers on the hearth. As he coaxed the dwindling fire into a burst of flames, his wet, bare back displayed a moving canvas of well-developed muscles.

She watched a droplet of water slide from a strand of his dark-brown hair, coast along his spinal column, and disappear underneath the edge of the barrier. She stroked the front of her throat with her right hand, then nibbled her fingers. *What if I touched him?* Her heart stuttered. Would his skin feel like supple leather? She lowered her head and hid her face behind a curtain of hair, forcing lumps of air from her lungs.

"As soon as the weather breaks, we'll head back. I wouldn't want to ruin your reputation." He stood and brushed his palms together.

"My reputation...as a lady, Captain?

"What else?" Ethan grinned.

"This is no lady, soldier." She deepened her voice and mimicked him, then peeked between the strands. At the sight of his perfectly formed navel, her heart rate sprinted and she felt her cheeks flash hot.

He chuckled. "Nothing like having my words come back and kick me in the gut." He lifted the candle.

"Where are you going?" She tossed her hair back.

"Over here. My belly thinks my throat's been cut. Maybe I can find some boot leather to chew on."

Sabrina lifted her heels and tiptoed behind him. "If I step on something wiggly…"

"We'll skin it and cook it." Ethan set the candle on a small table and yanked a rotten, wicker basket from a high shelf, releasing a shower of dirt and dust. Tin cans *rattled*. "Maybe…just maybe there's a can of beans." He peered inside and rooted through the empty cans, producing *clunking-thunking* sounds. "Nope. Nothing."

Sabrina tiptoed to a crudely constructed hutch and gripped the handle and jerked, but the compartment didn't budge. She tugged and wiggled, *jingling* the contents until the drawer gave way, then peeked inside. "Hallelujah."

"Did you find something to eat?" He peered over her shoulder.

She held a fork. "I found this."

Ethan put his hands on his hips and scanned the top of the hutch. "Great. Now all we need is some food to use it on."

"Don't you see?" She held the fork in front of his face. "I can comb my hair."

"Good grief, woman. I'm hungry enough to eat that buffalo hide over there, and you're worried about your hair." Ethan heaved a bushel basket from the top of the cabinet, and inside glass *clinked.* "Now…what do we have here?" He pulled a dusty stoneware jug into view. "God might be listening after all." He wiped the top with his palm, then popped the cork.

"What is it?" She scrunched her face.

He sniffed. "Wine. Maybe. Care for a swig?" He offered her the jug, sloshing the liquid inside.

"Maybe?" She lifted her brows and slowly shook her head. "You first."

"Might take the chill away."

"Might kill you." She caught her bottom lip with her teeth and watched him tilt the round-bodied jug.

Ethan filled his mouth, then swallowed.

"Well?" She raised her brows.

He clutched his chest and coughed. "I'm dying, Doc."

"Ethan?" She grabbed his shoulder, and her heart kicked into a gallop.

He burst out laughing.

She swatted his arm. "Captain Reed." She released a pent-up breath. "You have heard the old proverb about the little boy who cried wolf?"

"Sorry, Doc." He flashed a grin. "I couldn't resist." He smeared his mouth with the back of his hand and then offered her the bottle. "It's wine."

"I don't know if I can trust you." She cut her gaze to his cocky smile. "If you're lying to me"—she jabbed her fork into the air—"remember…I'm armed." She placed her mouth on the rim of the thick bottle, experiencing the warmth left by his lips, then flipped her mind to their first kiss by the creek. The tart flavor of strawberries hit her tongue, and she puckered her lips. *Will he kiss me tonight?*

"Well?" He arched his thick, right eyebrow.

"A taste of pure summer, me dear." She imitated Sergeant O'Rourke's accent, then quirked her mouth up and handed him the jug.

He threw back his head and laughed. "Doc, you never cease to surprise me."

She rotated away, and reacting to the heat of his gaze, she put an extra wiggle in her backside. In front of the fire, she knelt and bowed her head, then used the tines of the fork like a comb.

"How's that working?" Ethan added more wood to the fire.

"Not well." She struggled with a snarl.

He scooted a rickety stool over, arranged his quilt, and dropped behind her. "Here…give it to me."

She handed him the fork and shifted between his knees.

The insides of his barely-covered thighs were level with her bare shoulders with only a fabric barrier blocking his most intimate area from her exposed back.

Sabrina felt her breath slam in the back of her throat, then blew a mouthful out. "I hope you know what you're doing." She tossed the mass of tangled hair over her left shoulder.

"Never combed a woman's hair before, but I have brushed a few broomtails."

"Since I love horses, I guess I can trust you." She fiddled with the corner of her quilt. "Are the horses all right?"

"Better than us." He drew the fork through her hair. "They've been fed."

"I never thanked you for picking me such a sweet

horse. I'm glad you named her Lily." She scraped her fingernail over the fabric. "Which just so happens to be my favorite flower."

"Is it now?"

Was he smiling? Something in his tone puzzled her, and she tried to turn around.

Ethan sucked in his breath. "Sit still."

She settled back into position. Why did his voice sound so strange?

He exhaled.

"My first pony was named Muffin. When she died, we buried her in her favorite meadow, and Grandfather bought a granite headstone with her name engraved. Grandmother tried to help me understand, but…"

"Did your family live with your grandparents?" He used his fingers and gently untangled the snarls.

"No, just me."

"Why just you?" Using the tines of the fork, he worked a knot from the end.

"I was born crippled, so my mother left me with my grandparents."

"Crippled?" He shifted his body. "From what I can see, everything appears like it should, Doc. Of course, if you would like to open the quilt up a little more…I might get a better idea."

"Behave yourself." She shouldered his inner left thigh. "Grandfather made a special brace for my leg, and since I had trouble walking, he taught me how to ride. I loved galloping over the fields and having the wind in my face. No one could make fun of me, and if they did, Muffin and I left them spitting dust." She hugged her knees.

"You were bullied?" He stopped combing.

She heard a catch in his voice and felt her body warm at the thought he cared. "Sometimes." She rested her chin on her knees. "My favorite times were being with Grandfather on medical calls. He called me his little assistant. Grandmother didn't approve, 'Charles, she's a little girl. She doesn't need to be seeing all those things.' Grandfather smiled, and away we went." She picked the frayed edge of the quilt. "Then Grandmother died, and Grandfather's heart was broken, but the war gave him a new purpose. He built a pavilion hospital in Washington City."

"What kind of hospital?" He fluffed her hair with his hands.

"Pavilion." She released her knees and made a fist with her right hand. "This was the main part." Beneath her fist, she flattened her left hand. "Grandfather's design had the wards branch out like spokes on a wheel, creating isolation areas which allowed for ventilation. We were able to keep infectious patients away from one another and stop the spread of diseases."

Ethan pushed into a standing position.

As his left knee skimmed her bare right shoulder, she sucked air. Tiny stars of heat ignited and sparked at every pulse point in her body. She released her breath in short bursts.

He jabbed wood into the dwindling flames. "Your grandfather sounds like a smart man."

"He was. I miss him a lot." She focused on the area at the base of Ethan's spine, fascinated by every muscle ripple while an intense trembling churned inside. "Did you know this house was here?" She ran her fingers through her hair and fluffed the semi-dry mass.

"I did. I was hunting one day and ran across it." He

poked the wood with the iron poker.

Fiery embers blinked like fireflies on a summer's night. "What do you imagine happened to the people?" She hugged her knees and rocked back and forth.

He fed the fire a clump of buffalo chips. "Probably packed up and went back to wherever they came from." He brushed his hands together, then scooted over beside her.

"They came here with hopes and dreams and then gave up. So sad." She rested her chin on the tops of her knees. "I found if you quit, you cannot be successful."

"True. But some people aren't as strong as you are, Doc."

Sabrina cocked her head and met his gaze. "You mean stubborn."

He chuckled and held his hands out, palm side up.

"I hope Mr. Brown will be all right." She retrieved the jug from the floor and sipped, keeping the sweet, warm taste of summer in her mouth for a moment.

"I'd bet a month's pay old Curtis is back at the fort sleeping…after he had a good meal."

She set the jug on the floor. "I don't mean about today." Like rays from the sun, his body heat arced from his left shoulder and warmed her right one. "I mean about his wife."

"I don't know, Doc." Ethan twiddled with a piece of straw. "Having an unfaithful wife would be a hard thing."

She tossed a sprig of dried grass into the flames. "Dealing with someone's infidelity is difficult."

He frowned. "You were married?"

"No, engaged." With her chin resting on her knees, she bounced her feet against the floor. "Before William.

His name was Mathew Stark."

"Didn't he marry Vivian?"

Sabrina bit her lip while memories gushed. "My sister tricked my fiancé into marrying her. Vivian didn't love him." She scratched a loose thread on the quilt. "Not like I did."

He looped the strand of straw into a knot. "The way I see it, Doc, it would be pretty damn hard to trick a man if he didn't want to be tricked."

"All I know is"—she tapped her knee with her right fist—"Vivian got pregnant and said Mathew was the father." Sabrina grabbed the heavy crock, splashing the wine inside. "He married her not because he loved her, but because he was an honorable man."

"Honorable?" Ethan shook his head. "Not in my book, Doc." He formed his mouth into a grim line.

She gulped a mouthful of wine. The liquid rushed the wrong way down the back of her throat, strangling her, and sending her into a coughing fit.

"Easy, Doc." He patted her back.

"Grandfather told me I would meet someone who would love me for who I am, but look how that's turning out." She slowly sipped, feeling the fluid slide down the correct way.

"Give things just a little more time." Ethan stroked his lips with his right index finger.

"What's your story?" She passed the jug, *sloshing* the wine.

He held the chunky bottle. "Not much of a story." He sipped.

Sabrina licked her lips and playfully bumped his shoulder with hers. "When you were little, I bet you were a handful and always into mischief."

"Sometimes…" He chuckled. "We lived on a small farm in Missouri. I was about twelve when Pa died. We never had much, but Ma did the best she could."

"Do you have brothers or sisters?" She folded the edge of the quilt accordion-style.

"Brothers. John and Vincent." He traced the handle of the jug with his index finger. "I was the oldest. One day when we were fishing, John fell into the creek. I jumped in, but I couldn't save him. Three days later, his body washed up downstream." He stared into the fire. "After the war started, I lost track of Vincent. Heard he joined the Confederacy in Texas. He's probably dead, too."

She recalled what Sergeant O'Rourke had shared. "And your mother?" She released her pressure on the folds and the quilt sprang back.

"Died. Cholera epidemic."

He is in pain. Maybe if he will talk to me… She fidgeted with the edge of the quilt. "While you were ill…you spoke of Alice."

"My wife." The muscles in his face hardened, and he pinched his lips with his right hand. "Alice and my son died with my mother."

She dipped her head. "I'm sorry. I shouldn't pry." *How can I help him?*

"No." He faced her and placed his right palm on her left cheek.

She tipped her head up, seeing the blue in his eyes shift with raw, primal pain. *What can I do?*

He dropped his hand. "I want you to know"—he faced the fire—"I was twenty-two when we married. Alice was sixteen. Our families were neighbors." He inhaled and then exhaled. "When the war broke out, I joined the army. Alice begged me not to go. She feared I wouldn't come home. But neither of us thought she wouldn't be there when I did." He tilted the jug. "Our son was my whole world. That little guy followed me everywhere. Always wanting to ride on my shoulders. 'Giddyup, Pa, giddyup.'" Ethan closed his eyes.

Sabrina laid her right palm on the back of his left hand. *If only I could take his pain away.*

He flipped his hand and laced his fingers between hers.

She felt his callouses, hard ridges across his palm, pressing against her hand while strands of intimacy bonded her to him. *Only him.*

"I stayed drunk most of the time." He rubbed his temple with his right hand.

With her free hand, she massaged a strand of dried grass between her finger and her thumb. "Did alcohol help?"

"God no. Made me feel worthless." He released a thin breath. "Not knowing what to do, I rejoined the army—and tried to forget."

"Grandfather was a doctor, and he couldn't save Grandmother. I am a doctor, and I couldn't save him." She felt her body throb with an awareness of the man beside her. "If you had been there, you couldn't have saved them."

"I know." He deeply inhaled. "The old doctor said the disease spread like wildfire."

She sensed an awaking deep inside her chest, like petals unfurling in the dawn's light. *If I kiss him, will he accept or push me away?*

Chapter 20

Hypnotized by the movement of the flames, and the desire to make love to this beautiful woman, Ethan listened to the storm while the night trickled away. He turned and watched her sleep. The thought of another man touching her intimately, twisted his stomach into knots. *My sleeping beauty, I will not share you.* Had she and Nelson whispered love words through the night and watched the dawn paint the eastern sky? *Damn.*

He retrieved more quilts from the trunk, and as he unfolded one, he saw dried rose petals flutter free, and smelled the faint scent of a long-ago summer. Images of his mother's lilies, with their lovely fragile blooms and tough roots, reminded him again of Sabrina. If she had not cared for him at the mail station, he would have died. He covered her with the quilt.

Feelings of guilt, over the deaths of his mother, wife, and son, had frozen his heart in winter. But this bullheaded, smart, and definitely beautiful woman had marched into his life, bringing with her the promise of a lush spring laced with golden hints of a new beginning. He nudged the corners of his mouth up. For the first time, in a long time, he felt alive.

He stoked the fire and tossed more dried chunks into the dying flames. When he read her first letter, he had been searching for evidence. But when he read the second one, he felt an affection surge in his heart for a woman he had never met and wondered if he ever would. In his heart, he didn't believe she had spied or had anything to do with the conspiracy, but…someone followed her yesterday morning—he clenched his jaw—and invaded her privacy. *If the person who killed Nelson, knew him before Fort Greer, then chances are good, the son-of-a-bitch knows Sabrina's connection.* He wanted to confess he had her letters, but her safety was in jeopardy. *If I have to keep some things secret, then I will.*

Outside, the squall pounded the walls of the soddy while icy-rain *thudded* on the dirt roof, intensifying the earthy scent.

Ethan scrounged for more fuel. Near the trunk, he found a stack of wooden bed boards. Using his knee, he busted the planks into smaller sections and fed the fire. The flames burst brighter, chasing the dampness, and creating an umbrella of warmth over the buffalo rug. He eased down behind Sabrina and lengthened his body.

She wiggled her backside closer to his stomach.

Her bottom teacupped into his lap, and his lungs locked. He groaned and slowly puffed small bursts of air.

Ummm. She flipped toward him, and the corner of her quilt dipped.

A perfectly shaped breast appeared. He swallowed, tasting the lingering zing of alcohol and strawberries. *Oh…so…tempting.*

The fire popped and crackled. Sparks shot into the air. Sleet *slushed* and peppered the outside of the door. The wind whistled around the edges of the doorframe breathing cold into the room.

"Ethan?" Sabrina circled her arms around his neck

and pressed closer.

He sucked air into his lungs, feeling his body throb with a firestorm of desire. No other woman had ever touched his soul. *Only her.* He lowered his head and inhaled the rain-scent clinging to her hair. He kissed her and tasted the summer strawberries on her lips, sweet and tart. He inched his hands down her back and kneaded the softness of her hips, drawing her closer. *This needs to stop.* Like flower petals strewn on a pathway, he butterflied kisses along her collarbone. *But I can't.* "Love me, Sabrina."

She cradled his head in her hands. "I already do."

With only the wish to please her, he opened her quilt and skimmed his hands over her silky-textured skin, exploring and memorizing every dip and valley of her sweet form. *Sabrina loves me.*

She floated her hands over his shoulder blades.

He felt a line of fire igniting along his spine and drawing him deeper into the spiraling heat of a lover's web. "My sweet, sweet obsession." *When you learn my secrets, please don't hate me.*

****

Fingers of morning light poked between the dirt bricks. Sabrina fastened her gaze on the strong, rugged face of the man sleeping beside her. She propped her head in the palm of her left hand and leaned on her elbow. She never imagined her body could feel such lovely and enjoyable sensations. He was her first, and he would be her last. *I had a perfect night with a perfect lover.* She wrinkled her brow. But were last night's words from his heart or the wine?

A lock of dark-brown hair fell over his forehead, giving him a boyish, almost innocent appearance. Using her right index finger, she smoothed the curled tendril back and trailed her finger along his whisker-darkened jaw, and then over his lips. She felt an internal sunshine sparkle from within. In the restricted light, she noticed his warrior-body and traced the crescent-shaped scar, at the right edge of his thick brow, then planted a kiss on his temple.

"Ummm." He wound his right arm around her and gathered her closer, then kissed the corner of her mouth and nibbled his way down her neck. "I like waking up like this."

"What happened"—she stroked the scar at his temple—"here?"

"Got kicked by a guy wearing mule-eared boots." He nuzzled her ear.

She kissed his shoulder. "I'm sorry."

He chuckled. "What are you sorry for, Doc?" He kissed the tip of her nose. "You didn't kick me."

"I'm sorry you were hurt, silly." She floated the fingers of her right hand through his chest hairs.

He formed his mouth into a lopsided grin. "Made me tough."

"What about this one?" She traced the puckered ridge along his left side, slightly above his waist.

"My war medal." He lay back and folded his left arm beneath his head, then stared at the dirt ceiling.

"What happened?" She felt her pulse quicken.

"We were pinned down by a company of gray-backs." He drifted his right hand along her upper arm. "We ran out of ammunition, and like a fool, I jumped up and charged with my bayonet."

"Oh, Ethan." She covered his scar with her hand.

"I don't remember what happened next, but when I

woke up, I felt my side bleeding and burning."

She pulled back. "You could've died."

"But I didn't." He grinned.

"Were you transferred to a hospital?" She kissed his chest, and his dark hairs tickled her nose.

"No." He chuckled and drew her closer. "I grabbed some tree moss, mushed in some moldy bread, added a little rotgut whiskey, then shoved the whole mess into my side."

"We often made poultices with moldy bread and water." She slid her hand over his chest ruffling his chest hairs with her fingers. "And...tree moss is good for staunching bleeding wounds."

He nibbled her right earlobe. "Let's not talk about medicine."

Sabrina savored the warm line his lips created down the side of her neck. Then, an image of Vivian's face flashed. *Never again.* Sabrina flipped upright. "We have to get dressed." She untangled her body from his embrace.

"Now?" Ethan slowly slipped his hand over the back curve of her hip. "Are you sure?" He cocked his eyebrow.

Recognizing the wicked glint sparkling in his eyes, she scooted away. "We have to get back to the fort. Someone will be looking for us."

He rested his left elbow on the floor and cradled his head in his palm. "We have to talk."

"No, we don't." She wrapped a quilt around her body and stepped toward the hearth.

"Sabrina..."

"We allowed our animal instincts to rule our heads. Nothing more." She scrunched her clothing. *Still damp.*

"Animal instincts?" He jumped from their pallet. "Our lovemaking was a hell of a lot more than that, Sabrina." He grabbed her arm and turned her around. "Look at me."

She mashed her lips together, fighting for control over her body—the rapid heartbeat, squeezing lungs, and melting bones. She fastened her gaze on his mercurial-blue eyes, then dipped downward to his firm mouth, which was twitching into a smile.

"Tell me you don't like what you see, darling." The texture of his tone smoothed to a velvet murmur.

"Ethan, please…" The wall inside tumbled, and she could no more deny him than she could stop breathing. She loosened her grasp on the quilt. The multicolored barrier, in a pattern of connecting rings, pooled into a puddle on the floor, and she surrendered to the sweet bliss he offered.

****

Outside, horses' hoofs pounded.

Ethan halted the kiss. "Damn." He leaned over and grabbed his damp trousers from the floor.

"Hello in the cabin," Graham Hunter shouted.

"Get dressed." He jerked his pants up and shoved his arms into his shirt. "Hurry." Barefooted, he stepped outside. Cold shot through the soles of his feet and up his legs. He shut the rickety door, with gaps between the planks, and faced his first lieutenant and a patrol of mounted soldiers. "What is it, mister?" He manipulated the buttons on his shirt with cold, stiff fingers while his face burned.

"Sir, Doctor Clay is missing. She left yesterday and did not return."

Ethan stuffed his shirttail into his trousers. "She's

fine."

"But, sir."

"Ethan, what is it?" Sabrina's voice floated through spaces between the boards.

He clenched his jaw and gritted his teeth.

"Permission to dismount, Captain Reed, and speak with Doctor Clay." The lieutenant's mouth thinned into a grim line. "Sir."

Ethan squeezed the corners of his eyes and glared into Graham Hunter's face, then opened the door, and peered into the shadows.

Sabrina stood dressed in front of the fireplace with her hands folded at her waist.

Was she having regrets about last night? He sure as hell didn't have any. "Make it quick, mister."

Graham dismounted and slipped-slid over the icy patches covering the ground. He flashed his gaze to his commander, then ducked his head beneath the top of the door frame, and entered. "I've been worried sick about you, Miss Sabrina." He removed his forage cap. "Before the storm, your mother went to the hospital, and when she didn't find you, she contacted me. She said you had gone with the captain."

Ethan squinted into the darkness with each muscle taut and ready to spring.

Sabrina calmly folded a quilt. "We were searching for Private Brown and got caught in the storm." Cutting across the room, she laid the quilt inside the trunk.

"He returned to the fort last night." Graham rubbed his mouth, darting his gaze to the buffalo rug and crumpled quilts, then reached for Sabrina.

Seeing Graham's action, Ethan started but halted in mid-step.

Sabrina raised her hands and whirled away from the lieutenant.

"We have an understanding." Graham knocked his hat against his leg.

"The captain found us a safe place to wait out the storm"—she returned to the rumpled quilts and jerked another one up—"or would you rather I had stayed on the prairie?"

"We found shelter, Lieutenant." Ethan clenched his fists. "Nothing more. Do I make myself clear, mister?"

"Perfectly, sir." Hunter formed his mouth into a smirk and looked at Sabrina while he crammed his cap on.

An understanding? Ethan glanced at Sabrina. *What the hell does that mean?* "Lieutenant Hunter, return to the fort, and as soon as Doc's ready, we'll be along."

The lieutenant paused in front of his commanding officer. "There's something you should know. Sir."

Ethan arched his brows. "And that would be?"

"Thomas Fowler was murdered last night. Sir."

"Taddie?" Holding a folded quilt, Sabrina stepped into a shaft of sunshine. "Was killed?"

Ethan darted his gaze to her, then back to Graham. "Who found the body?"

"I did. In his quarters. Sir"—the lieutenant shifted his gaze to Sabrina—"when I was looking for Doctor Clay."

"Who else knows?" Ethan wrinkled his lips.

"Sergeant O'Rourke. Sir."

"Return to the fort and close the room. I don't want anything touched. Understood?"

"Yes, sir." The lieutenant saluted, then butted his boot heels into the ice, stomping to his horse. From the saddle, he narrowed his gaze on Sabrina, then led the patrol away.

The muffed sounds of horses' hoofs died away into the frosty air.

Ethan crossed his arms over his chest. "What in the hell is your connection to Fowler?"

"I don't think I like your tone." She flipped away.

"Hang my tone and quit stalling." He jammed his hands on his hips. "Talk."

"Very simple really." She walked to the trunk and added the last quilt. "Taddie was injured and became a patient at City Hospital. While he was recuperating, he helped around the hospital." The lid thumped shut.

"Did he know Nelson?" He grabbed his footwear.

She gathered her stockings from the hearth. "That's a ridiculous question. Of course, he did."

"Ridiculous?" Ethan rammed his left foot into his boot. "And now, he's been murdered just like Nelson. Doesn't that strike you as"—he stomped his foot into place—"oh…I don't know…a possible connection?"

Chapter 21

An hour later, they arrived at the fort stables, and Sabrina followed Ethan across the parade grounds to Taddie's quarters. She recalled one particularly difficult day a patient under her care had died unexpectedly.

Taddie sat with her, not talking, only sitting, and providing comfort with his presence.

She curved her lips up. Other doctors often called him a pest, but he and William developed a friendship. Could they have both been Confederate spies?

At Fowler's quarters, Sergeant O'Rourke slanted his chair back on two legs and rested the crest against the door, and with his arms folded over his chest, he snored.

Ethan stepped closer. "Sergeant."

The front legs of the sergeant's chair *thumped* against the ground, and the man jumped and saluted.

"At ease, Sergeant. How was Fowler killed?"

"A wee bit of lead in the back, sir." The sergeant swung the door open.

"Sergeant, I want you to question everyone in the area. Someone must have seen or heard something last night." Ethan wiped his boots on the rug inside the door, removed his gloves, and looped them through his belt.

The victim lay face down on the floor, his back bloody along his left shoulder blade.

257

Poor Taddie.

A cot lined the opposite wall with the bedcovers tightly pulled and with expertly tucked corners. To the right, a shelf held several books, and below the shelf, a metal trunk with a few plates and cups stacked on top. A cast-iron stove occupied the center of the room, and parallel to the north wall, a slender table stood, with an ink bottle and a few sheets of writing paper.

Taking a deep breath, Sabrina removed her gloves and stuffed them into her pocket, then gathered her damp skirt and knelt. *I'm so sorry, Taddie.* "The bullet entered here"—she pointed to the tear in the military blouse—"and penetrated straight into the back of the heart. Death would have been immediate." She lifted Taddie's left arm. "Rigor mortis has set in, and the skin around his head and neck are greenish-red."

"How long has he been dead, Doc?"

"My guess is…about twelve hours but not much more." She leaned back on her heels.

Ethan pulled his penknife from his pocket. "Time of death would have been around eight o'clock last night." He hunkered on the opposite side of the body, then raised the fabric away from the wound with the tip of his knife. "The wound isn't the same as Nelson's."

"What's different?" She floated her hands over her thighs.

"Nelson's was a star pattern with specks burnt into the skin." He searched Fowler's pockets.

"In order to have a star pattern, the gun would have been pressed against the skin." She rose and brushed her skirt down. "William was asleep, wasn't he?"

"I believe so." Ethan found paper money folded neatly in a rectangle. "This wasn't a robbery."

"Taddie was shot from a distance." She stepped around the body. "By his wound and the way he fell, I'd say, whoever shot him was at least six feet away." She marked the distance to the door. "Maybe from here." She positioned her body at the door and pointed her right index finger like a gun.

Ethan rolled the body, releasing a putrid odor, then yanked his bandana over his mouth.

She opened the door, and chilly air whipped inside. "Why would someone want to kill him?"

"I don't know"—Ethan scratched the nape of his neck—"either he knew something, or someone thought he did."

Colonel Hunter filled the doorway. "Captain Reed, I demand an explanation."

"Sir." As Ethan snapped to attention, he jerked his bandana down and raised his right hand and saluted. "Investigating the murder of Thomas Fowler, sir."

"Murder?" The colonel glared at the body. "Not at my fort." He returned the salute.

"Begging the colonel's pardon, sir. The fact is, sir, the medical steward was shot in the back."

"This is my fort, Captain." The colonel threw back his shoulders and scowled. "And the facts are what I say they are."

Sabrina watched Ethan tighten his mouth and lock his gaze on his commander.

"Sir, there have been two murders at Fort Greer. Doctor Nelson was first, and Fowler is the second, and these murders are connected in some way. If we don't find who is responsible, there might be more. Sir."

The colonel squinted at his subordinate officer, and his face shot to the color of a sand storm, red and gritty.

"Just...one more...word, Captain. And I'll have you court-martialed for insubordination."

Feeling she needed to help Ethan, Sabrina inserted her body between the two men. "Colonel, please listen to Captain Reed."

"My dear woman...if you were a man...I would have you shot for interfering in military matters which do not concern you."

Sabrina crossed her arms over her chest. "Are you saying Thomas Fowler committed suicide?"

"I am." He ground his teeth, and the tiny muscle at his temple throbbed, in, then out. "And no one. Do you hear me? Will question my authority. Not. Even. You."

She glared into the commanding officer's face, tiny beads of sweat gathered along his upper lip. "What are you afraid of, Colonel Hunter?"

"You dare question me?" The colonel's brown eyes glistened, and his lips quivered. "I am a soldier, and soldiers are never afraid. Captain, get this man buried. Immediately." Colonel Hunter spun away and stomped from the cabin.

Sabrina mashed her lips together and narrowed her gaze. "He is protecting someone." She gritted her teeth and watched the colonel's back grow smaller.

"You think?" Ethan kneaded the muscles in at the top of his left shoulder. "My money is on his son."

"I can't believe Graham..." She chewed her lip and darted her gaze to Taddie's body.

"Maybe you don't want to believe." Ethan crossed his arms over his chest and breathed through his mouth. "Maybe you are in love with Lieutenant Hunter."

She felt a blistering heat coat her face. "That is ridiculous."

"Ridiculous? I saw how the lieutenant looked at you this morning, and I heard him say, *you have an understanding.* What the hell was he talking about?" He hardened his jaw.

"Nothing." She wished she could go back and undo what she had said to Graham, but...she couldn't.

Ethan shoved a chair out of the way. "It sure as hell didn't look like nothing to me." He stalked deeper into the room. "I'm telling you Graham Hunter is up to his lily-white neck in all of this. And when I find the evidence, I'll nail his worthless hide to the wall."

She *thumped* her boots over the floor, producing an auditory trail while she combed the room. "I think Graham was in love with Lila Minton." She opened a drawer. Starched shirts were stacked and neatly folded, with nothing disturbed. "I think the baby was his." She rummaged through the clothing. "William noted in his diary he had discovered someone's secret. And this someone must have been connected to Booth."

He glared. "My money's on the lieutenant." He rolled his lips into a straight line.

"All right, but why Taddie?" She put her hands on her hips and rotated.

Ethan sauntered to the cot. "My guess is all three were Confederate spies and on close terms with Booth." He dropped to his knees and hunted beneath the bunk. "Well...well...what do we have here?" He pulled a tin tray, with a half-empty bottle of wine and two dirty glasses, into the open. "Perhaps he was entertaining a lady."

"He was sweet on Vivian." She pursed her lips.

"Your sister...admits to having a relationship with Booth."

"Of course, she knew Booth, they worked together." *Did my sister know something about the assassination?* "Vivian could not have possibly been involved in anything."

He rose and brushed his hands over his knees. "Enlighten me."

"The only thing Vivian is ever really involved with…is Vivian."

"Is that so?" He stalked to the shelf and removed a book. "I don't think you know your sister very well." He flipped the pages, then jiggled the book upside down.

"Trust me." Sabrina returned to the body. "I know my sister." She knelt and turned the victim's right palm up. "His fingers have dried ink on them." She glanced around.

Ethan towered over her. "So?"

"Don't you see? Taddie was compulsive about cleanliness. He would have washed his hands, and the ink would have faded." She stepped to the makeshift desk. "Ethan, look. The ink well is open. He must have been writing." She shuffled the note paper. "I don't see anything."

Ethan scanned the room, then locked his gaze on the stove and stepped around the body. "Maybe…just maybe…" He removed the cold stove lid and peered into the ashes. "Whoa…what do we have here?" He meticulously isolated bits of charred paper and arranged them on the stove's lid. "Looks like someone tried to burn a note." He shifted the pieces. "*You. Meet.* Here's a dollar sign. Money was involved. Perhaps our Mr. Fowler was blackmailing someone."

"Who?" Sabrina stared at the burned fragments.

"The murderer."

"If he was in the process of writing"—she touched the burnt edges— "he hadn't sent the note."

"Try this." With the blade of his pocketknife, he dug deeper into the ashes. "Both victims were shot in the back, and the same person who killed Nelson killed Fowler. New Year's Eve night, Fowler was delivering a baby, but he found Nelson's body. Now for a minute, let's suppose"—Ethan *clunked* the cast-iron lid into place—"he saw or found something identifying the murderer. He decides he can make a little money. So…he writes this person a note, and the man pays off. Fowler becomes greedy. While he is writing his second letter, this person comes to pay a call, Fowler turns his back, and the man shoots him. Graham Hunter found the body. A nice coincidence, don't you think?"

Sergeant O'Rourke clumped into the doorway. "Begging the captain's pardon, sir. I've knocked on everybody's door, and nobody heard a blessed thing last night with the storm and all…"

"Sergeant, see to the burial." Ethan gave the room a final glance. "Come on, Doc, I'll walk you to the hospital."

The wind whipped Sabrina's skirt around her boot tops. Questions rattled in her head. Was Vivian smart enough to have been a Confederate spy?

"We have to talk about last night." He wrapped his hand around hers.

Sabrina felt the warmth from his palm radiate up her arm. *End it now.* She flipped her wrist away and continued walking. "There is nothing to discuss."

"Sabrina, listen to me." He grabbed the upper part of her left arm, jerking her to a stop. "I think we should marry."

"Just because we got a little carried away last night doesn't mean we have to marry." A burning sensation knotted in the middle of her chest. *Vivian wants you.* "Captain, I'm not a little girl. I know these things don't always result in marriage."

"Last night meant nothing to you?" Ethan hardened his face.

The color in his eyes solidified into a darker blue while his neck and face turned an ugly shade of red. Sabrina jerked from his hold. "That's right."

He threw up his hands, then spun away.

Our magical fairy tale night meant everything, but in the real world, Vivian exists. Hot tears burned and flooded her eyes, and all the lovely emotions from the previous night evaporated.

****

Sabrina used an iron poker and stoked the fire in the kitchen stove, then set the coffeepot on. Glancing out the window she watched a soldier huddle deeper into his coat, battling the November wind. The murders remained unsolved, and Ethan had not visited. Their last conversation would be forever carved into her heart. She recalled every moment—the hurt in his eyes, the anger in his voice, and when he stalked away—all the air left her body. *He hates me.*

The front bell *jingled*, and a few minutes later, Mary Beth waddled into the kitchen. "I made you a soda cracker pie. It ain't as good as a real apple pie, but maybe it'll be all right." She set the pastry onto the table.

"I'm sure it will taste delicious." Sabrina grabbed a pot holder and removed the metal coffeepot from the stove. She streamed hot liquid into mugs, releasing the robust flavor of fresh-boiled coffee into the cozy kitchen. "How's the baby doing?"

Mary Beth lovingly stroked her rounded belly. "Tossin' and turnin'." She awkwardly slid into a chair and untied the scarf around her head. "I can't seem to get any rest."

"Cream or sugar?"

"Both." Mary Beth giggled. "I can't believe I'm eating so much. Last night, I couldn't sleep a wink. I kept wanting some watermelon and in the middle of winter." Smiling, she shook her head. "Heavens. Poor Curtis finally went over to Mrs. Bailey's and woke her up. And bless her sweet heart, she sent over a jar of watermelon preserves. It helped but weren't the same." Mary Beth held the mug to her lips and blew over the liquid before drinking. "I reckon my life is just about perfect now." Mary Beth traced the handle of her mug with her left index finger.

Sabrina studied her guest out of the corner of her eye. "But something is wrong." She found a sharp knife and sliced the pie into wedges.

"Pa always said when somethin' bothering you just spit it out. So…" Mary Beth licked her thin lips. "You remember the day poor Mr. Fowler was found killed?" She rotated her mug. "Sergeant O'Rourke come around, askin' questions about anybody seeing or hearing anythin'."

Sabrina nodded and gathered a couple of saucers from the shelf while a warning pounded in her head. "And no one had." She maneuvered a piece of pie onto a saucer and served Mary Beth.

"I didn't exactly tell the truth, ma'am." Mary Beth

sipped her coffee. "That was the day Curtis took off, and he come back right before the storm. We had a long talk, about everythin'. Then he had to leave 'cause he was on guard duty, and I was so happy, I couldn't sleep. Mr. Fowler's quarters were just across from ours." She pinched a bite of crust. "At about seven o'clock, Miss Vivian went into Mr. Fowler's cabin."

"My sister?" *Perhaps the old boy was entertaining.* Sabrina dropped into a chair. *Vivian, what have you done?*

"I didn't want to cause you no trouble. Oh…" Mary Beth doubled over and grabbed her stomach while fluid gushed from her body.

Sabrina supported Mary Beth down the hallway. "I have a room all ready." She guided the patient into a small alcove furnished with a double bed, a small table, a lamp, and a cast-off chair. While she helped the mother-to-be into a gown, questions banged. Ethan said the murderers were the same. When William was killed, Vivian wasn't at Fort Greer, and if she killed Taddie, what was her motive?

Mary Beth clutched Sabrina's hand. "Please, I need my husband."

"As soon as someone comes, we'll send for him. Right now, we need to get your baby born."

"Ma'am, I want you to promise me something." Mary Beth gasped for air. "If it comes down to me, or my baby…save my baby."

Sabrina stuffed pillows behind Mary Beth's back, raising the patient into a half-reclining position. "You and your baby will both be just fine." She retrieved her medical bag from her room and organized the table with the necessary birthing items.

The front door bell *jingled.*

"Doctor Lassie, I've brung ye more cow chips," Sergeant O'Rourke called.

Sabrina sprinted into the main ward. "Mrs. Brown is having her baby, and I need her husband."

The sergeant set the large metal bucket near the fireplace and brushed his gloved hands together. "I'll fetch him."

"And, Sergeant, please get my sister, too." Sabrina returned to the expectant mother.

"I had forgotten how much having a baby hurts." Mary Beth moaned, then another contraction racked her body.

"Your husband is on his way." Sabrina lifted the bedsheet and checked the birth canal. "Push, Mary Beth, your baby's coming." She prepared to catch the newborn.

The mother-to-be leaned forward. "*Mmmmm-owe-ooh.*"

The baby gushed out.

"You have a healthy son." Sabrina positioned the crying newborn on Mary Beth's stomach and prepared two lengths of silk thread from a spool on the table. She moved the baby to the table and checked the umbilical cord. When the pulsing ceased, she tied off the blood flow from the placenta, then tied a second thread three inches from the first and cut between. She swaddled the newborn in a clean cloth, and returned him to his mother's arms.

Mary Beth cradled her son, kissing his head and cooing around his loud cries.

Minutes later, Private Brown arrived.

After reassuring him his wife and son were well,

Sabrina left the family and returned to the kitchen. She poured a fresh mug of coffee.

In a cloud of floral perfume, Vivian flounced in, pulling her fur-trimmed wrap tighter. "I declare it gets colder every minute." She methodically removed her red gloves, laid them on the table, and rubbed her hands together. "I believe I'll have a piece of that pie and a cup of coffee, if you don't mind." She tossed her wrap into an empty chair.

"We need to talk." Sabrina set her cup on a wooden tray and added another mug, two green saucers with wedges of pie, a pair of spoons and forks, napkins, and the coffeepot. Questions swarmed in her head.

"You sent Sergeant O'Rourke for me…just so we can talk?" Vivian flipped her green eyes and wiggled her head. "Really, Sabrina."

"Come with me. I want privacy." Carrying the tray, Sabrina led the way to her quarters.

"What is going on?" Vivian followed on her heels. "You are scaring the living daylights out of me."

"You need to be scared." Sabrina entered her room and kicked the door shut behind her sister. She crossed the room and set the tray on a small table between two chairs. "Now. I want to know what you were doing at Taddie's the night he was murdered." She folded her arms across her chest. "And, don't lie."

"I wasn't at Taddie's." Vivian eased into a chair and touched her mouth.

"First lie." Sabrina dropped her arms and balled her fists. "You were seen. Try again." She pressed her lips into a straight line.

"All right, I was there." Vivian blinked and licked her lips. "But I didn't kill him." She filled her mug with coffee, dropped sugar into the liquid, and followed with a dollop of cream.

Sabrina sank into the other chair and sipped her lukewarm coffee while tiny needle pricks poked into the back of her neck. "What time were you there?"

Vivian stirred her coffee. "I think around seven. Maybe…seven thirty." She laid her spoon on the tray.

Vivian is an actress. Sabrina reached for a saucer, then a fork. *Is she playing a role?* She sampled the pie and turned the bite over in her mouth, tasting the sharp tang of cream of tartar. "Are you certain of the time?"

Vivian rapidly blinked. "Yes…no…I don't know. I can't remember." She tasted her coffee.

"Why did you go to Taddie's in the first place?" Sabrina mashed her lips together and stared at her sister.

"Such a long story." Vivian rolled her gaze and set her cup down.

Sabrina tightened the muscles at the corner of her eyes and scrutinized her sister's every movement. *Why are you stalling?* "Tell me"—she leaned forward—"I like a good story." Her sister's face paled.

"The little toad claimed he had always been in love with me." Vivian shrugged and flipped her hands in the air. "When we were in Washington, he would hang around the theater and stand backstage, always there watching us practice. He never missed a performance."

"Why did you go to his quarters?" Sabrina held her cup.

Vivian exhaled and flicked her gaze upward. "He sent me a note. Said he was going to come into some money, and…he would be a wealthy man. And"—she cocked her head to one side and shrugged—"he wanted to marry me."

"Marry you?" Sabrina tasted the cold coffee. "Do you know how he planned to get this…money?" Maybe Taddie was blackmailing someone.

"No." Vivian shook her head. "Honest…I don't."

"So…you went to his quarters to tell him you wouldn't marry him?" Sabrina set her cup on the table.

"Not…exactly…" Vivian pinched a bit of crust.

"Stop leading me in circles." Sabrina hit the edge of the table with her right fist, rattling the dishes. "What exactly?"

"I said…yes, I'd be his wife." Vivian popped the bite into her mouth.

Sabrina bolted upright and put her hot face closer to her sister's. "You…did…what?"

Vivian widened her gaze and held her palms out. "I had to, Bree. He said, if I didn't marry him, he would tell everyone about my involvement in the assassination of President Lincoln."

Sabrina felt a quaking start in her feet and shutter upward. "What have you done?" Ethan's words blasted. *Your sister had a relationship with Booth.*

"Nothing. I swear." Vivian swallowed and bounced her hands in the air. "You have to believe me."

"I don't have to do anything." Gulping air, Sabrina paced toward the bed. "Now, explain." She settled on the edge.

"I often accompanied Johnny to Mrs. Surratt's boarding house." Vivian twisted her fingers together in her lap. "He would meet with some of his friends, and they would get drunk and start talking nonsense about kidnapping President Lincoln. One day, Johnny made up his mind to do something. He decided they would overtake the president's carriage and hold him until some rebs were released from prison. But the president wasn't inside. So, it was all for nothing."

Sabrina expelled a deep breath. "You knew this, and you didn't tell anyone?" She paced.

"What could I have done? If Johnny couldn't trust me...he would've killed me." Vivian rubbed her throat. "Besides, no real harm was done."

"No harm was done? He killed the President of the United States." She stopped in front of her sister and flattened her lips. "What exactly did you know about the assassination plan?

"Nothing"—Vivian raised her right hand—"I swear."

"How did Taddie find out about this?"

Vivian scratched her cheek. "A couple of times, he was over at the boarding house, and I suppose...while he was there...maybe he overheard some things." Vivian grabbed Sabrina's hand. "I swear when I left the toad was alive. Please, believe me. I didn't kill him."

Sabrina heard a tremor in her sister's voice. *Is she telling me the truth?* "Did you see anyone when you left?"

"No." Vivian dropped her sister's hand. "But I did notice he was writing to someone."

"Who?" Sabrina dropped into a chair.

"I couldn't see. But as he was pouring me a glass of wine, I did partly read the letter. The words were...*I saw what you did.* I don't know what that means, I swear." Vivian jiggled her head.

Sabrina stroked her lips with the fingers of her right hand. "I can't believe you would marry a man you didn't love."

"Wouldn't have been the first time." Vivian rotated her mug on the tray and watched the coffee wave.

"Vivian…?"

"I didn't love Mathew, either"—Vivian closed her eyes—"and he didn't love me."

Sabrina jumped up and fisted both her hands, then leaned into her sister's face. "He loved you enough to have a child with you."

"It wasn't like that." Tears gathered in Vivian's green eyes. "Sit down, you're making me nervous."

Dazed and shaken, Sabrina stiffly walked toward the bed, then slumped onto the edge of the mattress and crossed her arms and hugged her body. Old pain stabbed and twisted.

Vivian followed. "You were on a medical call that night." She pressed the palms of her hands together. "I heard Matt come up the stairs. I suppose one of the maids let him in." With measured steps, she drifted back and forth, and her satin dress rustled with each shift. "Anyway…he was drunk. So, I slipped into your room." Vivian dropped to the floor in front of Sabrina, her red dress puffed outward like the petals of a red rose on a warm, summer day.

"Stop." Sabrina rocked. "I don't want to hear this."

"Matt stumbled into the room and called me by your name, and I answered." Vivian swallowed and placed her left hand on Sabrina's knee. "He said he wanted to make you a woman. I didn't know what he was talking about." Tears glistened down Vivian's face.

"No…no…no…" Sabrina covered her ears with her hands and swung her head back and forth.

Vivian rose on her knees and pulled Sabrina's hands away and held them. "I thought he only wanted to kiss me. So, I let him. Even though he was drunk, he knew I wasn't you. He backhanded me and knocked me to the floor." She slumped and sobbed.

Sabrina oozed downward, and all the air left her lungs. Breathing hurt.

"I begged him to stop, but he kept saying I was getting what I deserved, and I believed him. I shouldn't have gone to your room."

Heaviness shoved into Sabrina's chest. "Why didn't you tell?"

"He said he would kill me." Vivian smeared her tears with her hands. "He's the reason I lost the baby. He got drunk one night, dragged me out of bed, and kicked me in my stomach. Said I had ruined his life. He said if he had married you, he would have money."

Is that all I was to him? Money? Sabrina squeezed her burning eyes and breathed with stutter-breaths. She pursed her lips. *Maybe Vivian's lying. Wouldn't be the first time.* "Why did you continue hurting me after he died?"

Vivian swallowed. "I was jealous."

"Jealous?" Sabrina moved her face closer to her sister's. "Of me?"

Vivian clutched Sabrina's hand. "You don't know what it was like living at that dirty old fort. I wanted to wear fancy dresses and go to parties and eat something besides biscuits and gravy made from weevil-infested flour." She released her sister's hand. "Besides, you were Mama's favorite."

"Now, I know you are lying. Mother. Didn't. Want me." Sabrina felt her cheeks burn and drew back.

"All I can tell you is…every time Grandpapa's letters arrived, Mama cried and took to her bed for days. Papa said she was grieving. But I couldn't figure out why, because no one had died."

Confused by what Vivian was saying, Sabrina took a deep breath.

"I'm so sorry I hurt you, Bree. Truly I am." Vivian clasped her hands together and rested her chin on top. "I know I don't deserve your forgiveness, but please try."

Sabrina heard the anguish in her sister's voice and saw the raw pain in Vivian's green eyes. *Do I believe her?* She let her shoulders slump while emptiness throbbed in her chest. *What would have happened if I had been home? Would Mathew have ruined me and forced our marriage?*

"If you tell anyone I was at Taddie's, then they'll think I killed him, and I swear, I didn't."

"I believe Taddie was blackmailing someone, and that person killed him."

Chapter 22

"Reveille" blasted and catapulted the soldiers from their warm bunks for roll call.

Ethan strode across the parade ground, his boots clunked against the frozen terrain, and his warm breath created smoke around his mouth while the December sun struggled through a wintery haze. Staying away from Sabrina was one of the hardest things he had ever done, but the sooner the murders were solved, the sooner he could explain everything. He tucked his head deeper inside his coat. "Lieutenant, assemble the men."

Graham Hunter stepped forward. "Atten...*hun*."

For a moment, Ethan watched the American flag snap at the top of a pole and recalled all the lives lost while keeping his country united, and his throat burned. "Sergeant, call roll."

Sergeant O'Rourke stepped forward, raised his right arm, and saluted. "Yes, sir." He turned and faced the men. "Mason."

"Yo."

"Bailey."

"Here, sir."

Roll call continued, and Ethan clasped his hands behind his back and sauntered down the line, studying the soldiers' faces. Bailey, Todd, and Butterworth were young. They had peach fuzz instead of whiskers, and he hoped they would survive the Indian Wars heating up across the territory. On the other hand, Parker, Davis, and Shoemaker had seen the war inside out, and like him, their memories contained scenes they wanted to forget but couldn't. He stopped in front of a soldier whose coat was buttoned wrong.

"What's your name, private?"

"Crawford, sir."

"You're out of uniform, soldier." Ethan glared into the man's blinking eyes.

"Sorry, sir."

"Sergeant, this man will stock the fuel bins." Ethan formed his mouth into a grim line. "Understood?"

"Yes, sir."

"The hospital auxiliary is making preparations for a Christmas party"—Ethan pressed the heels of his boots into the frozen ground—"and everyone is invited. All of you will be on your best behavior. Understood?"

"Yes, sir," the soldiers answered in unison.

"Sergeant, we need fresh game for the celebration. Ask for volunteers."

"Privates Shoemaker and Butterworth, ye'll do as the cap'n says."

"We'll need Christmas trees for the families and a large one for the hospital. The rest of you men are on cleanup duty. Understood?"

"Yes, sir," the group answered.

"Lieutenant Hunter." Ethan clenched his jaw, and a knot grabbed in the pit of his stomach. *Understanding? I'll give you an understanding.*

Graham stepped forward and saluted. "Yes, sir."

Ethan tasted the sharp bite of bitterness on his tongue. "You're officer of the day, mister." He snapped a return salute. "Dismiss the men."

"Dis…missed." Graham Hunter's voice boomed over the parade ground.

Sabrina is mine. Ethan headed to the mess hall while the freezing wind whipped the brim of his black campaign hat. Inside, the warm scents of coffee and freshly baked biscuits floated in the air. He hung his hat and navy-blue frock coat on a nail beside the door, then sat at the officer's table and reached for the pot of coffee.

Private Brown arrived with a plate of hot, salt-preserved scrambled eggs and fried venison slices. He scooted the breakfast meal in front of his superior.

Ethan unfolded his napkin. "How are Mrs. Brown and the baby?"

"Mary Beth's fit as a fiddle and busy as a little bee in a field of clover. And the boy"—Private Brown's cheeks turned pink and his eyes misted—"I mean, my son…is growing like a weed."

"I'm happy for you, Private." Ethan sampled the eggs while scenes of a buffalo rug and a desirable woman, with a mane of dark hair and kissable pink lips, replayed. He wondered if…maybe…

"Since I found out about the babe, I ain't touched a drop of whiskey. I don't know what would've happened to me and Mary Beth if Doctor Clay hadn't helped us. She's a fine woman, sir."

"She is." Ethan sipped his coffee.

Brown set a basket of sourdough biscuits and a crock of butter on the table, then returned to the kitchen.

When his investigation was over, he would ask Sabrina again to marry him, and *no* was not an option. He sprinkled pepper on his eggs. Knowing she truly loved someone before him hurt, but he was the first to love her in the physical sense, and that fact gave him hope for their future. *Animal instincts? Sure, Doc, if you say so.* He chuckled, recalling her seductive moans of pleasure.

"Begging the cap'n's pardon, sir." Private Brown stood at his elbow.

"Yes, Private."

"Cap'n, I'm mighty sorry." Brown handed his commander a crumpled envelope. "Hank give me this, but with the baby and all, I plumb forgot."

Ethan tightened the muscles between his brows and broke the seal. *Meet me at the Washita Trading Post, December 24. Have the information you requested.*

"Damn." The trading post was a full day's ride. He bolted for the door and grabbed his hat and woolen overcoat, then headed to his quarters. He changed into a pair of faded-black pants and a red-plaid flannel shirt, then shrugged into a well-worn mackintosh. Rushing to the stables, he yanked a floppy brown hat low over his brow. No time to request permission to leave, and if he missed tomorrow's roll call, he would be labeled a deserter. He mounted and rode to the west gate.

Sabrina entered through the portal with the hood of her green cape covering her head, and carrying a basket of frozen clothing.

"Morning, Doc." He stared into the lilac eyes he loved.

Sabrina propped the laundry basket on her left hip. "Why are you out of your uniform?"

"I'll explain when I get back." He leaned down and traced the left side of her jaw with his gloved fingertips. "There's something I need to tell you." With a final glance, he stiffened his back and kicked his horse into a lope. He rounded the northwest corner of the fort, then headed toward the Red. He had her letters, and the sooner he confessed the better. Sabrina had brought color into his world, where there had only been corners of darkness, and warmth where there had only been cold, and he would have no future without her.

He galloped across the ice-crusted prairie, mile after mile, in a northeasterly direction. Camouflaged prairie dog holes created a treacherous situation, one wrong step and his horse could break a leg, leaving him on foot. Slate-blue clouds stewed along the horizon, and he knew there would be more snow by nightfall. He arrived at the trading post, and evening shadows formed specks of darkness. Long strings of dried red peppers, hanging along the edges of the slapped-together building, *shushed* strangely in the wind. Two mares, a sorrel and a black, were tied to the hitching post. He dismounted and tethered his horse next to the black mare, then massaged the bristling at the back of his neck while he scanned the area, then crossed the threshold into the dingy darkness. Overhead, a kerosene lamp *squeaked* and wobbled in the gust of wind while the rank odor of unwashed bodies reeked.

Three trail-worn men sat playing cards at a center table.

Ethan traversed around the chairs to the northeast corner of the room, feeling the itchy sense of being watched.

"What'll be, mister?" The barrel-chested bartender rolled a wad of chewing tobacco around in his mouth. "Got some leftover stew." He swiped his hands over a dirty cloth fastened around his waist.

"Fine." Ethan wondered just how left over. "And, a beer." He stroked his cheek with his right thumb, observing the men out of the corner of his eye. They seemed tame enough, but one could never be too sure.

The bartender returned and set a mug and a bowl on the grimy table.

"I'm meeting a man by the name of Stewart." He used the general's code name and tossed coins onto the table.

"Ain't been nobody in here but them three over there." The bartender pointed with his head, raking the *clinking* silver into his right hand.

Sipping his beer, Ethan observed the scraggly trio and pondered his history with the general. They had met at an encampment near Washington. The general had never married and called himself an old bachelor. Over a few months, their relationship deepened, and he thought of the general more as a father than a commanding officer. He sampled the thick concoction and identified bits of onion, potatoes, and some kind of meat, rabbit, deer, or something better left unidentified.

"This seat taken, cowboy?" A broad-shouldered man, wearing a floppy hat pulled low on his forehead and a dark, heavy coat, stood behind the slat-backed chair.

"General Callison." Ethan curved his mouth up and sprang to his feet. "Good to see you, sir." He shook the general's hand.

"Damn good to see you, son." Nathanial Callison unbuttoned his overcoat, revealing civilian attire. "I'm so hungry I swear I could eat a horse, hooves and all." He dipped his head toward the bowl of stew. "That any good?" He pulled the chair out.

"No, sir." Ethan resumed his seat and slanted his mouth up. "But…it's hot."

"Barkeep, I'll have the same as my friend." The general pushed his hat back and slanted forward. "Does anyone know you're here?"

"The post surgeon saw me leave."

The bartender scooted a bowl of stew on the table.

A wide grin spread across the general's lined face. "Sabrina Louise Clay. Beautiful and very stubborn."

Ethan tilted his head to one side and pursed his lips. "Sounds like you know her, sir."

The general shifted the bite around in his mouth. "My brother's daughter. And, my niece."

"Begging your pardon, sir." Ethan drew his brows together and stroked his lips. "Her name is Clay."

"My brother and I had the same mother, but different fathers." General Callison washed the food from his mouth with his beer. "I was about a year old when my father was killed in a wagon accident. Mother married Harvey Clay. Harvey was a good father, and Warren and I were close."

Sabrina is the general's niece. Ethan crinkled the edges of his lips. *Damn.* "Did you know she was keeping her relationship with Nelson a secret?"

"I did." The general took another bite and raised his bushy brows. "And, the answer to why I didn't try to stop her is simple. Once Sabrina makes up her mind, she doesn't unmake it. She's smart, and something about Nelson's suicide didn't smell right."

So you pulled the strings. "Weren't you concerned about her safety, General?" Ethan lifted his mug.

"I was." The general grinned. "But I knew you were at the fort."

281

Ethan wiped his mouth on the back of his right hand and felt his lips stretch.

"I'll be damned, son." The general tilted back and crossed his arms over his chest, then smiled. "Judging by the sappy expression on your face, I'd say you're a man in love."

"After the investigation is over, I intend to marry her, sir." He finished his beer. "If she'll have me."

"Have you talked to her about this?" The general shoved his bowl aside and put his elbows on the edge of the table.

"I've tried, but with the investigation...I can't be completely honest." He laid his folded right arm along the edge of the table.

"Sabrina never loved Nelson." The general angled back. "If she had, she would have married him before he left Washington." He frowned. "Something wasn't right about that man." He shook his head. "Can't put my finger on it, but something...never noticed him with a woman before he proposed to Sabrina." He jiggled his mug against the table. "And, Stark was a worthless son-of-a-bitch." He sipped his beer. "Vivian never said... but I know he forced her. She was just a kid. He wasn't anything but a pile of worthless scum."

"Sabrina said..."

"Sabrina was too damn young to know anything." The general shook his head and rolled his chin. "Would not have been a good match." He raised his salt-and-pepper eyebrows. "But you and her..." He flashed a broad smile. "I'd like to dance at your wedding." He leaned forward. "Maybe I could be the best man."

"Most definitely, sir. If only I can convince her."

"I have no doubts you can." The general emptied

his mug. "After all, you convinced an old sawbones to keep me alive."

Laughter drifted from the threesome.

The bartender approached. "If ye gentlemen are stay'n the night, cost ye a dollar a head. Ain't got no rooms, but got plenty of chips to keep this'n warm."

As the general tossed coins on the table, the silver *clinked.* "Another round, and see to our horses."

Ethan pulled his leather cigar case from his pocket and offered one to the general.

The general bit the tip off, then spat it out. "You're right. Baker's dead." He lit his cigar in the flame of the candle burning in the center of the table.

"Exactly who am I dealing with?" Ethan slithered the candle to his side, then stuck his cigar into the flame and puffed until the end glowed red.

Smoke flowed from the general's nose and mouth. "Sources tell me, he's a Pinkerton. Man by the name of Duncan Cramer. Not sure why he was sent or who sent him." He puffed. "At least not yet." The general flicked his ashes into his bowl. "Came through Fort Hex. Now, I want to know everything you didn't tell the colonel."

The bartender set two mugs of beer on the table.

Ethan pressed his back against the chair and waited until the man was out of earshot. "I searched Nelson's things and found some newspaper clippings on the assassination and a couple of notes with the name Gray Hounds on it." He filled his mouth with smoke and tasted the earthy flavor.

"We only recently discovered a Confederate group called the Gray Hounds." The general rubbed his right index finger over his lips, then scraped his jaw with his thumbnail. "We found evidence Nelson was a member.

The Hounds robbed Union trains and disrupted supply lines. The group started in Maryland." The general inhaled and then released a cloud of smoke.

"Nelson's home"—Ethan rotated the cigar in his mouth—"and Booth's."

The general formed his lips into a line and nodded. "We found letters with dates of supplies which were destined for the Union troops but never made delivery. Probably stolen by the Hounds."

"Sabrina found Nelson's diary, and just before he was killed, he wrote, *I discovered someone's secret, and now, someone knows mine.* And then something about not wanting the president killed."

"Interesting." The general scratched his chin.

"The case has another side. Nelson and Graham Hunter were both involved with the same laundress." Ethan drifted his index knuckle along his brow line. "She became pregnant, and Nelson botched an abortion. The woman died. Then, Hunter threatened Nelson in front of witnesses."

"I've never considered Graham Hunter a cold-blooded murderer." The general tilted his head. "Jimmy Hunter, yes." He scratched his chin. "Knew Jimmy as a boy. He was raised by Millie's family, and you never wanted to turn your back on him."

Ethan blew on the end of his cigar, watching the tobacco burn red. "We've had another murder. The medical steward, guy by the name of Thomas Fowler was shot in the back, same as Nelson. Both kill shots came from a small caliber gun. I'm guessing it was the same shooter." He flicked ashes into a bowl.

Frowning, the general revolved the name. "Thomas Fowler? Sounds familiar."

"Sabrina said he worked around City Hospital." Ethan sipped his beer. "Called him Taddie."

The general tapped the table. "I remember him. He had kind of a pointed nose and beady eyes and was always cleaning something."

Ethan angled forward. "Here's where the case gets interesting. I found pieces of paper in the stove in his quarters that weren't completely burned. From what I read, I'm guessing Fowler was blackmailing someone."

The general shifted in his chair, resulting in a series of *creaks*. "Blackmailing?"

"But I don't know who…or why."

"Is it possible he witnessed Nelson's murder?" The general drew tobacco smoke into his mouth.

"Possible. He found Nelson's body."

"Here's another theory." The general exhaled a layer of smoke. "If both Nelson and Fowler were involved with the Gray Hounds, and they could identify the group's leader, maybe Fowler was blackmailing this person." He flicked his ashes into his bowl. "We've had our eyes on Jimmy Hunter for a long time."

"And, if his son was involved with the group…they could be covering for one another." Ethan filled his mouth with the leather-flavored smoke and held it while he breathed through his nose.

"During the war, Millie stayed with a relative in Maryland." The general smiled. "She and Doctor Mudd are cousins or something."

"Mudd?" Ethan arched his brows. "That's a hell of a connection." He flicked his ashes into a bowl. "You believe the colonel organized the Hounds?"

"I do, but…we don't have any proof." The general finished his beer. "One of the reasons I'm coming to

285

Fort Greer is to take a closer look at him."

"And the other?" Ethan inched his brows up.

"I want to see my family." The general smiled.

Ethan heaved his tired body up, scraping the legs of his chair on the floor. "If I'm going to get back before roll call, I have to head out now."

The general pushed into a standing position and stifled a yawn. "Since it is past midnight, I guess I'll see you later today."

Ethan shook the general's hand. "Take care, sir." He flipped his collar up, then stepped outside and staggered against the body-slamming gusts of wind to the lean-to angling along the backside of the trading post.

Wind shrilled around the boards while his mother's words ricocheted from the past. "Beware, son. On a night like this, the devil is calling the sinners from their graves."

Chapter 23

As Ethan rode into the fort stables, he noticed a frosty sun struggling in the dawn's muted gray light. *I missed roll call.* He hunched forward in the saddle with his shoulders coated in a layer of snow, and his hat fringed with icicles. After caring for his horse, he headed for his quarters. Whatever he planned to tell the colonel had better be good. He rounded the corner of his cabin but stopped and ducked back.

Sabrina, wearing her dark-green cape and dressed in his favorite shade of blue, faced Colonel Hunter, blocking the door into Ethan's quarters.

The red-faced colonel pushed forward. "Out of my way, woman, before I have you arrested."

Sabrina threw her hands up, blocking the colonel's advances. "Captain Reed has been quarantined. Until I know exactly what the problem is, no one enters his quarters."

Thank you, Doc. Ethan sprinted to the rear of his quarters and shoved the shutters, then propelled into his room. Tossing his hat aside, he dove for his bunk.

The door flung open.

He jerked the blanket to his chin. "Colonel, don't get too close." He coughed and covered his mouth with the edge of the blanket, gasping for breath around the pounding in his chest.

Sabrina widened her gaze, focusing on the man in

the bed. "As you can see, he is ill. Now, please leave."

The colonel jerked his lips backward into a slim line and glared. "Next time, Captain Reed." With a final glance at Sabrina, he spun and marched from the room.

The door slammed.

Sabrina stuck her hands on her hips. "Where have you been?"

"I've missed you, Doc." Ethan crinkled the corners of his mouth and crossed the room in two strides. He scooped her under her arms and spun her around.

Her feet arced outward, and she laughed. "Put me down." She shoved against his shoulders.

He stopped and loosened his hold.

She shimmied downward.

A trail of heated bliss warmed his cold, exhausted body in a seductive dance, and he tightened his hold and kissed her lips, slipping his tongue between her teeth and tasting coffee.

She reared back and broke the kiss. "Don't change the subject."

"The subject is…I'm quarantined. Doctor's orders. I can't leave my cabin. How about you spend the day in bed with me?" He cupped her sweet backside and nuzzled her left earlobe, feeling nothing but pure joy. He enclosed her left hand with his right and guided her toward his bunk.

"Oh no, you don't." She shook her head and firmly locked her feet. "*Uh-uh.*" Drawing her hand free, she backed away. "Not a good idea."

He wiggled the corners of his lips up, then lunged. "You can't escape."

She laughed and scuttled around the table, then shifted the obstacle between them. "Yes, I can."

"You know you want to spend the day in bed with me, Doc." He laid his hands on the table, preparing to shove the barrier.

"Beside the point." She flicked her gaze to the door and scrambled toward the portal. Suddenly, the toe of her left boot caught on the table leg. She stumbled and fell.

The evidence box crashed, tumbling the contents onto the floor.

Ethan dropped to his knees and snatched her bundle of letters, but one fluttered free. He felt his heart slam against his chest. "Sabrina, don't."

She held the envelope, examining the handwriting. "I wrote this." She covered her mouth with her left hand, and crumpled her face. "Ethan?" Tears welled in her eyes. "How could you?"

"I wanted to protect you." His heart pounded, and he felt every muscle in his body harden.

"Protect me?" She crushed the letter in her fist. "By deceiving me?"

"I never meant to hurt you." He fisted her bundle of letters while his joy curdled into a raging monster of pounding pain. "Please…believe me."

"I thought you were different. But I was wrong." Pushing from the floor, she tossed the letter. "You lied to me."

"I had a job." He grabbed her hand but remained on his knees.

She jerked her hand free. "Stay away."

"Please…" He sprang up and held his arms out. "I can explain."

"No"—she slowly turned away—"you can't."

A howling wind whipped around the corners of the

cabin. The broken shutters whacked. The door closed.

The finality of the wooden bar dropping echoed through the chambers of his heart. *She's gone.* He felt his chest muscles harden into stone, and he struggled for air. Her scent lingered in the room like the aftertaste of a fine wine. Pain gutted, ripping his insides apart. He shot his fist into the board door, feeling nothing, then crumpled to the floor.

$$****$$

The sky boiled dark and gloomy. Battling the wall of wind, Sabrina grasped the edges of her cape and headed toward the hospital. *I love you, and you lied to me.* She felt shattered and broken into tiny bits of nothing. All her lovely dreams evaporated, leaving only the residue of betrayal. *Again.* She entered the hospital through a side door and stepped into the kitchen.

Mother, Mrs. Hunter, and Lovey were busy with food preparations for the evening's celebration.

"There you are." Mother cracked eggs into a bowl.

Everything appeared normal, but nothing would be normal again. Sabrina draped her cape on a nail inside the door. "I had an early medical call." She rubbed her hands together.

"Mighty cold outside." Lovey stood in front of the stove, pouring popcorn into a pot. The hard kernels pelted the metal and sizzled in the hot grease. "Looks like you could use a cup of hot coffee and a slice of apple bread." Lovey clunked a lid onto the pot.

Sabrina removed a clean cup from the shelf near the stove and landed her gaze on the broken edge. Using her right index finger, she traced the cup's lip and paused on the rough surface of the missing piece. *Chipped and fractured, just like me.* She closed her eyes. *After Christmas, I shall return to Washington.*

"Everything all right, Daughter?" Mother held the coffeepot.

"Fine." Sabrina dropped into a chair at the end of the table.

Mother streamed the coffee into the cup, then served Sabrina a slice of apple bread.

The happy chatter of the women, the smell of popcorn, and the taste of cinnamon dancing across her tongue gave Sabrina some comfort, but the voices in her head were snarled and tangled in a knotted mess.

"You could be in danger."

"Captain Reed's a good man."

"No matter what I will protect you."

"Reminds me of the times at Homewood," Lovey's voice penetrated. "Don't it you, Miz Millie?" She didn't wait for an answer and dumped another pot of popcorn in a bowl for stringing garlands. "I recollect Mr. Tom used to send them boys out to cut down the biggest old pine tree theys could find. Then we popped corn, just like we're doing now. Yessiree, our old house would pack with people, and the smell of them piney woods on a damp morning would fill our hearts with pure happiness."

Mrs. Hunter gathered a handful of popcorn. "All before the war." She put a piece of corn in her mouth and chewed. "Polly, do you recall that one Christmas you stayed with us?"

"I'll never forget." Using a spoon, Mother scraped icing from the bottom of a crock bowl and then plopped it on top of the double-layer vanilla cake. "Warren gave me an engagement ring for Christmas." Using a butter knife, she spread an icing of boiled egg whites and sugar over the cake.

"Hansford cut down the biggest tree I believe we ever had. And we decorated with long strings of holly berries from Mama's garden."

"And do you remember what Warren and James did?" Mother laughed.

"As if it were yesterday." Mrs. Hunter leaned back in her chair. "They took Pa's landau and decorated it with red and green ribbons and added an old cowbell. At midnight, we *clanked* all the way to Duck Creek. The old moon was a shining down all milky and white. Made the dirty old creek waters shimmer like liquid silver." She lined a piece of popcorn up with the needle. "After our ride, James asked me to marry him." She poked her needle through a piece of popcorn, and it crumbled in her hand.

"Everything was moving fast." Mother set the bowl into the dry sink. "Warren had received his orders to report to Fort Smith, and I wanted to go with him." She flipped a clean bowl upside down over the cake. "All in the past." She wiped her hands on the paisley apron covering her red-and-brown-striped dress.

"Holidays are the times I miss Hansford the most." Mrs. Hunter pushed a new kernel of popcorn onto her needle and pulled the white sewing thread. "After he joined the army, I never saw him again." Taking a deep breath, she frowned and massaged her temple. "I'm getting one of my headaches, Lovey."

Sabrina set her cup down and scooted her chair back. "You are welcome to use my quarters." She skirted the table.

Mrs. Hunter stood and pressed the needle into the pincushion. "I should go on home, dear. My headaches can last for hours."

"I'll take real good care of her. The best thing for Miz Millie is a cup of my special mint tea. And I knows just how she likes it." Lovey wrapped a heavy cape around Mrs. Hunter's shoulders, then slipped into her brown coat.

Sabrina followed them into the main ward, feeling a sense of heaviness in her chest. She bit her bottom lip. Coming here had been a mistake. Tomorrow, she would make plans and return to Washington City. Tears filled her eyes, and she quickly blinked them away.

The ladies' auxiliary was decorating for the party, and the main ward hummed with excited chatter and laughter. Mrs. Mangum and Mrs. Shoemaker wrapped the buffet tables with red and green fabrics, and in front of the warm fireplace, Mary Beth nursed little Curtis. The radiant glow on the mother's face shifted Sabrina's thinking. *What would have happened if I hadn't helped them?*

In a blast of cold air, Mrs. Bailey, her cherub face glowing red, rushed in with a tray of cookies, bringing the delicious scents of cinnamon, cloves, and nutmeg into the holiday mix. "Why bless me, everything looks so pretty."

Sabrina hurried to close the door but stopped when she heard tingling bells.

A moment later, an open-bed wagon, pulled by two horses and filled with freshly cut cedar trees, rolled into view. Bells, attached to the horses' collars, jingled with the Christmas spirit every time the animals trotted.

Private Bailey held the reins and Private Johnson, a much larger man, sat beside him. Both men smiled and waved.

"Merry Christmas, Doctor Clay."

"Merry Christmas, soldiers." She darted her mind back to that October day and recalled treating Private Bailey's arrow wound and his successful recovery. "Do you have a tree for the hospital?" Maybe coming here had not been a mistake, but staying would.

Private Bailey swung down. "We got you a seven-footer, ma'am. Cap'n ordered the biggest one we could find." The two men clumped their way through the snow to the tailgate and unloaded the bushy evergreen. Carrying the tree into the main ward, they left a trail of melting snow and the scent of cedar. "Ma'am, where can we put this?"

"Over there." Sabrina pointed to the front window and a large bucket of sand.

After the cedar tree was properly displayed, Private Johnson removed his harmonica from his pocket and played "Deck the Halls." The toe-tapping beat wrapped the room in a festive spirit.

Vivian sat in the corner, swaying to the beat of the music while she tied satin bows for the tree. "Fa la la la la…la la…la la…" She waved. "Come help me, Bree."

"All right." Sabrina scooted a wooden chair closer to her sister.

"This is going to be the most beautiful and glorious Christmas party ever." Vivian dropped a finished bow into the bushel basket near her foot. "I remember one Christmas the snow was so bad, we didn't have a Christmas tree. Mama was sick, and Papa was on duty. Bobby tried to cook us something, but he burnt the bread." She cut a section of red ribbon. "I do believe that was the saddest Christmas I ever had."

Sabrina measured a length of green ribbon while

she jogged her thoughts back to her childhood holidays in Virginia. Grandmother loved Christmas. She started in early November gathering things needed to fill gift baskets for their neighbors. Grandfather and Sabrina were the official taste testers of all candies and cookies, and she was in charge of writing festive wishes in all the cards. After Grandmother died, the spirit was gone. She twisted the ribbon into a loop.

"I used to lay awake at night, praying Mama would leave me with Grandpapa the way she had you. You had everything."

"Not really." Sabrina dropped the green bow into the basket. "When I was a child...no one wanted to play with me, like being crippled was disease you could catch."

"Children can be so mean." Vivian added another bow to the basket. "I wasn't always as pretty as I am now. My eyes were too big for my face, and my mouth wasn't right. So, I started acting. I just pretended their cruel jokes didn't matter, and after a while, they didn't. And guess what? Those same boys wanted to court me. Like I'd have anything to do with them."

Sabrina raised her eyebrows and lifted the edge of her mouth while strands of serenity stitched through her heart. She snipped another section of the ribbon. "We have new Christmases to celebrate."

"Starting tonight." Vivian reached for the scissors. "Guess who my escort is?"

"I haven't a clue. Could be anyone." Sabrina coiled the ribbon. "They're all smitten with you."

"Lieutenant Baker."

"Vivian...his name isn't Baker. I don't know what it is, but it isn't Baker."

Vivian glanced around and leaned closer. "You're right. His name is Duncan Cramer, and he came to dinner at Carter Hall once."

Sabrina scrunched her facial muscles and clenched her fist around the roll of ribbon. "I knew it. What is he up to and why is he lying about his name?"

"*Shhh.*" Vivian scanned the room. "He's working undercover for the Pinkertons, and no one is supposed to know. You can't say anything."

"A detective?" Did Cramer know her connection to William, and was he the one who searched her room? Was Ethan right, and she was in danger? Sabrina bent forward. "Why is he here?"

"I don't know exactly." Vivian tied a bow. "Said he was investigating something."

"Do you think he's here because of William's and Taddie's murders?" Sabrina swallowed the dryness in her throat.

"He can't tell me 'cause it's all hush-hush." Vivian shrugged. "But if he finds out about me and Taddie, I'll just die." Her cheeks tinted a bright pink. "I'm in love with Duncan."

Sabrina fluttered her gaze upward. "Heaven help us. Here we go again."

"No, really. I am. When I'm not with him…I can't stop thinking about him." Vivian dropped a green bow into the basket. "Don't you feel the same about the captain?"

Sabrina jerked the basket up. "He lied to me." She marched to the tree, punching her boot heels against the floor.

"You lied, too, Bree." Vivian followed.

She spun around. "I did not."

"You kept your relationship with William secret." Vivian tilted her head. "Isn't that the same as lying?"

Was it? Sabrina tied a red bow to a cedar branch and watched the limb wiggle. *Am I guilty, too? Ethan never said he didn't have my letters.*

Vivian fastened a green bow on the opposite side of the tree. "Did he tell you why he lied?"

"He said he was protecting me." If Taddie was killed by the same person who killed William—and if someone had found her letters—they could have connected her to both men.

"Maybe he was." Vivian hung a red bow on the tree. "Here's a truth. Matt didn't love you or me. And I don't know about William, but Captain Reed..." her sister's voice grew dreamy. "He loves you."

"How do you know?" Sabrina felt her cheeks grow warmer.

"Anyone with eyes can see how he watches you." Vivian tied a small green bow above a large red one. "Every time you're in the room, he gets a hang-dogged expression on his face." With her hands on her hips, Vivian created a comical version of the captain's face with her mouth hanging open.

"Really, Vivian." Sabrina laughed. "I think I would have noticed."

"I'm serious. Captain Reed would face the devil for you." Vivian rounded the tree and hugged her. "That kind of love only comes around once in a lifetime, Bree. You've got to grab it and hang on." She stepped back, smiled, and wiggled her eyebrows. "My Duncan doesn't have a chance."

Laughing at her sister's antics, Sabrina stepped to the window. Snow layered the rooftops and blanketed the ground while giant flakes floated like tufts of cotton from a gray, bleak sky. Using her right index finger, she traced the watery line of a melting flake sliding along the pane. Intimate scenes from the soddy flipped in her head and ignited her body with an intense fire only her blue-eyed captain could extinguish.

Mother headed across the ward, carrying strings of popcorn. "These should finish the tree." She handed her youngest daughter the holiday garlands. "Sabrina, I left a Christmas gift in your quarters this morning."

"A present for me?"

****

In her room, Sabrina balanced on the side of the bed and unknotted the red satin ribbon. The skirt of a purple ball gown spilled to the floor and released the fresh scent of new fabric.

Mother fluffed the ruffled neckline with her right hand. "The material came from Saint Louis and Lovey and I worked on it together."

"It's beautiful, thank you." Sabrina slid the fabric over her cheek, feeling the slick texture of the satin. "I can't recall the last time I had something this special."

Mother finger-pressed the tiny wrinkles along the bodice. "I remember a special Christmas long ago...and a dashing young man I met before your father." She smiled, and her cheeks pinkened. "I think he loved me quite a lot. I sometimes wonder if I should have married him."

"You were in love with someone before Father?"

Mother nodded. "I believe I was." She released a hard breath. "But when you're young, you don't know what real love is. I had a good life with Warren, but he carried a torch for Sarah Jackson. I told you about her and Millie's brother." Mother stroked the fabric. "Your father needed me, and for some reason, I needed to be needed." She pursed her lips. "But, if I hadn't married Warren, I wouldn't have my children…all of whom I love dearly."

Buried emotions bubbled. Sabrina felt the muscles in her chest squeeze. "Bobby and Vivian, but not me."

"Good grief, Daughter." Mother rose and moved in front of Sabrina. "How can I make you understand?" She held her palms out. "If I could go back, there are many things in my life I would change"—Mother took a deep breath and released—"but…leaving you with Father is not one of them."

"You abandoned me." Sabrina felt her eyes burn and tears appeared while she shoved the gown from her lap onto the bed.

"Not true." Mother grabbed Sabrina's shoulders.

Sabrina wrapped her arms around her chest and felt her tears dribble down her face to her chin, leaving a heated trail over her cheeks. "I was crippled, and you didn't want me."

"For once…in your life"—Mother angled her face closer and gently shook Sabrina's shoulders—"listen to me. Please."

"I never would have abandoned my child." Sabrina dashed the tears away with the palms of her hands.

"I did not…abandon you." Mother slid her hands down Sabrina's arms and clutched her hands. "I gave you a chance. Your father was being transferred to Fort Towson, and my first duty was to my husband. Can't you understand? Leaving you tore my heart out, but Father was an inventor, as well as a physician, and he was always trying new things. I knew he was the only one who could help you. I made the decision to do what was best for you, Sabrina"—Mother blinked—"even though you weren't in my arms, please understand… you were always in my heart."

Tears gushed and Sabrina sagged into her mother's arms. "You really do love me?"

"Of course, I do." Mother laid her cheek on the top of Sabrina's head. "I love you very much. And I am proud of you and what you have accomplished."

Sabrina wiped her tears and sniffed. "Purple is my favorite color."

"I know. Try it on." Mother wiped Sabrina's cheek with the palm of her hand.

Sabrina flipped her back, feeling Mother's fingers unfastening the buttons of the blue dress. When the top fell forward, she withdrew her arms from the sleeves. The dress dropped and created a pool around her feet. She ducked beneath the edge of the ball gown and guided her arms through the cap sleeves. The purple hem cascaded to the floor, and she twirled, swinging the bottom of the gown like a giant bell.

"You will need a couple of underskirts." Mother adjusted the gathers. "If Captain Reed doesn't propose the minute he sees you, then the man is blind."

"I doubt if he'll come." Sabina swallowed through the taut muscles in her throat while emptiness fluttered in her heart. "We argued."

"Only a fool would give up over an argument, and Captain Reed isn't a fool, Sabrina."

"Mama, Big Sister." Vivian's voice floated from the hallway. "Uncle Nathan's here."

"Nate?" Mother smoothed wayward strands of her brown-gray hair up into the braided bun on her head. *Mother and Uncle Nathan?*

Chapter 24

Preparing for the party, Sabrina soaked in a tub of lilac-scented water. She leaned back against the rim.

Wolf snored softly on the floor.

Questions about the murders reigned. William's last entry in the diary verified the fact he was a Confederate spy, and someone at this fort knew. Who was Taddie blackmailing, Graham or the colonel or someone else? Who are the Pinkertons investigating?

Sabrina stepped from the tub, hearing the water *swish-swoosh* along the sides. She shrugged into her floral wrapper and brushed her hair, then pulled the sides up and secured the strands in place with jewel-studded combs, leaving the back hanging free. *Just the way he likes it.* She shimmied into the purple ball gown, then hung her grandmother's amethyst necklace around her neck. The stone settled slightly above her cleavage. "What do you think, Wolfie?" She curtseyed in front of the canine.

The animal raised his head and stretched, then lumbered to the door.

"A man of few words, eh?" She lifted the corners of her mouth and opened the door, then watched her pet disappear into the chilly darkness while her thoughts centered on Ethan. *If you love me, you will come.*

Sabrina entered the main ward and stopped at the end of the first food table. Unable to resist the chunks of peppermint candy displayed in a crystal dish, she popped a piece into her mouth. The sweet, sharp bite tingled over her tongue while she scanned the room.

Long tables displayed a multitude of savory dishes. A cheery fire popped and crackled in the granite-stone fireplace while the regimental band played softly in the background. Dozens of candles and oil lamps dyed the room with yellow light, and large cedar wreaths, tied with bright-red ribbons, saturated the chamber with an outdoorsy scent. People, who had become her friends, gathered around the room, laughing and talking.

Mother and Uncle Nathan stood near the Christmas tree, holding hands. Mother wore a soft-cream-and-gold gown while Uncle Nathan, in his immaculate uniform, displayed the smile of a man deeply in love.

Thank you, Mother, for doing what was best for me.

Hearing laughter over her left shoulder, Sabrina pivoted.

Vivian, dressed in a green satin gown and wearing red ribbons tucked into her blonde curls, and her beau embraced beneath a mistletoe ball.

In hindsight, I had refused to see behind the mask Mathew wore. Through the veil of girlhood, I ignored witnessing him drunk on more than one occasion, and I knew he gambled. In my young mind, I created the idea man, but what he did to Vivian revealed the truth. Mathew Stark was not a good man. She inhaled deeply, then exhaled, giving flight to her seeds of anger and felt a surge of hope for a future with Ethan. *Please, come.*

The front bell jangled.

The colonel escorted Mrs. Hunter into the room and helped his wife remove her navy-blue cape which revealed a royal-blue ball gown with gold trim, and the perfect complement to his uniform.

Graham trailed his parents and brushed snow from his shoulders then removed his leather-brimmed forage cap and linked his gaze with Sabrina's.

She turned away. Was Colonel Hunter protecting his son, or was Graham protecting his father? Without a doubt, they were involved in William's death.

The fiddle player struck a lively tune, and couples quickly paired. The ladies' dresses created an ocean of reds, greens, blues, and yellows and waved in patterns of gingham, floral, and paisley.

Private Todd claimed Sabrina for a quadrille, and when the song ended, she danced a polka with Private Bailey. She bounced, quickstepping to the beat of the music, and laughed, but in the back of her mind one question taunted, would Ethan come to the party?

The song ended, and the band played the first slow notes of a waltz.

Graham approached and gallantly bowed. "Miss Sabrina, may I have the honor of this dance?"

Should I? They hadn't communicated since the cabin, and she certainly didn't wish to speak with him now, but…this was a social gathering. She mashed her lips together and stepped rigidly into position and held her body away from his.

"I've missed you." He jerked her closer.

She flinched and locked her knees. "Graham, you mustn't." She focused on the small muscle at his right temple popping in and out.

"I must say…when I found you at the cabin with Captain Reed…I was a little disappointed." He screwed his lips into a smirk and forced her into a turn.

She felt the fingers of his right hand dig into her left side. "My relationship with Captain Reed is none of your business."

"We had an understanding, my dear." He squeezed his left hand.

Feeling the pain crush into her right hand, she flinched. "I'm not your dear." She rotated her body, resisting his vise-like hold.

"I've decided...I shall have a future with you." He wrenched her around and led her into another direction. "I will rebuild Homewood and you will be mistress." His muddy-brown eyes turned cold and vacant.

"You've decided?" Sabrina revolved her right wrist and attempted to break his hold. "You're hurting me." *I have to get away.* She bent her arm and yanked.

He increased his grip. "We will raise our children to be fine Southerners." He glared into her eyes. "If you conceived, I shall claim the offspring as mine."

"Let me go." Panic jangled along her spine. "I will scream."

Suddenly, Ethan shoved between the couple with his back to her and providing protection. "If Sabrina is with child"—he thrust his nose into the lieutenant's face—"the baby is mine...and I will damn sure claim my child, mister." His nostrils flared while he poked Graham's chest with his right index finger. "Stay...the hell away...from Sabrina."

The lieutenant knocked the captain's hand away. "This isn't over, Captain Reed. Not by a long shot."

Ethan shoved Graham. "In here or outside?"

The two men glared while happy Christmas music played in the background.

Graham spun away.

"Ethan." Sabrina smoothed her right hand on his right shoulder, feeling the rough texture of his damp uniform.

He revolved and faced her while he released a hard breath. "My darling." He cupped her bare elbows with his gloved hands. "Please tell me you are all right?"

As the color of his eyes thawed from arctic-blue to warm silver, bliss purred into her heart. She eased the corners of her mouth up. "I am now. We need to talk."

"We do..." He flashed a broad smile. "About a lot of things, Doc. But right now"—he swept her into a waltzing position—"I need to hold you." He put his lips near her left ear.

She molded her body to fit his and danced on a sparkling cloud of happiness.

"Is there a baby?"

She felt the kiss of his warm breath on her ear and released a deep sigh. "No." She wanted to say *yes*. Having a little boy with Ethan's dimples and blue eyes would be pure joy, but then, so would a baby girl.

He cocked his left eyebrow. "We could go back to the soddy and work on...making something happen."

Bolts of desire crackled over her body. She licked the corner of her lip. "We could."

"Darling." He pressed his forehead against hers. "Don't ever walk away again." His voice broke into a soft whisper. "Promise me."

"I promise." She cupped his left cheek with her right hand.

"You love me, don't you?" He turned his face and kissed her palm.

She tilted her head, and the muscles around her mouth twitched. "No."

He grinned and crushed her into an embrace. "Ah, darling, no more lies."

The clean fragrance of his shaving soap wove into her nostrils. "Ethan, people are staring."

"Let them."

"Come. We need privacy." Holding his left hand, she pulled him into the hallway and into a dark corner. Flipping around, she faced him and pressed her back against the wall, then took a deep breath. "You had my letters and realized who I was from the beginning."

"I did." He placed his left hand on the wall beside her head and leaned closer. "I was sent here on a special assignment to ferret out any Confederates involved with the Lincoln Conspiracy."

"And William was one?" *I saw only what I wanted, just like with Mathew.*

"He was." Ethan shifted his weight. "When he was killed, I scoured his quarters for evidence"—he dipped his head closer to her ear—"I found your letters."

"And read them." She felt his warm breath fan over the side of her face while she trailed her fingers down the front edge of his jacket.

"I did." With his right index finger, he traced the surface of the amethyst. "I fell in love with you by the words you wrote to another man, always wishing you had written them to me."

Honeyed sensations sluiced over her body. *He loves me.* She felt the strength in her knees soften and clutched his waist.

"When I met you at Fort Hex, all I could think was…you were as beautiful as your letters. And at that moment, all I wanted to do was kiss you." He skimmed her left cheekbone with his right index finger.

"Really?" She toyed with a brass button on his coat. "As I recall…you tried to make me leave."

"I swear…all I wanted was to keep you safe."

She downed her head and played a seductive game of eye-tag, glancing into his blue eyes, then darting her gaze away.

A deep rumble vibrated in his throat. "You've got to stop looking at me like that."

"Like what?" She cocked her head to one side and tilted the corners of her mouth up.

He nuzzled her left ear. "Like you want to make love."

She flicked her brows up. "Oh, but I do."

"Ahem," Mrs. Hunter cleared her throat. "Pardon me, Captain."

Ethan dropped his arm from the wall. "Ma'am?"

Sabrina peeked around Ethan's shoulder. "Are you all right?"

Mrs. Hunter massaged her temple with her right hand. "No, dear. I'm getting one of my headaches. I was wondering if I could lie down in your room."

"Of course." As Sabrina stepped from the shadows, she cut her gaze to Ethan. "Wait for me. I'll be right back."

Ethan formed a seductive smile. "Hurry."

"I will." Sabrina cloud-walked, and her heart sang. *Ethan loves me. He really, really loves me.* Clusters of candles burned along the passageway, and she plucked one from the brass holder. "I'm sorry you're not feeling well, Mrs. Hunter. I do hope you will be able to rejoin the party."

"We shall see, dear." Mrs. Hunter held her blue-velvet evening bag close to her chest.

Entering her quarters, Sabrina crossed to the bedside table. Lifting the lamp's chimney, she bumped the globe on the base, causing a tingling sound, then lit the lamp's wick with her candle. "Would you like some headache powders?"

"Not necessary, dear." Mrs. Hunter's gown rustled.

"Are you sure?" Sabrina blew out the candle and turned, then froze. All the air whooshed from her body.

Mrs. Hunter pointed a gun.

"What are you doing?" Sabrina's thoughts flashed in rapid-fire succession and tangled into a cold hard knot. Was the woman hallucinating?

Mrs. Hunter steadied the small gun. "I want Doctor Nelson's diary."

"Why?" Sabrina wrapped her arms around her suddenly shivering body.

From the main ward, lovely party sounds drifted, people laughed and music played.

Ethan, my darling.

"I'm not a fool." Mrs. Hunter let out a deep breath. "You know why."

The black gun barrel glinted in the lamplight.

"I don't. I swear I don't." The rotting-egg scent of burnt gunpowder blasted into her brain. Sabrina clenched her arms and dug her nails into her skin. *Not real.* Registering the pain her nails were causing, she squashed the flashback.

Mrs. Hunter narrowed her gaze. "I know you've read the diary." She smirked. "Why else would Nathan be here?"

"Uncle Nathan?" Sabrina blinked.

Mrs. Hunter flipped her gaze toward the ceiling, shaking her head. "People have been underestimating me for a long time. I know…he is here…to arrest me. What are you, dimwitted?"

What is she talking about? Sabrina wrinkled her brow. "Arrest you?"

Mrs. Hunter waved the gun. "I don't want to shoot you, but I will." She laughed with a brittle edge. "I've had lots of practice, dear."

Pieces dropped into place. "You killed William." Sabrina pinched her locked elbows and gulped a lump of air.

"Perhaps you aren't dimwitted." She cocked her head and warped her lips into a smug smile. "Good old Doctor Nelson figured out who I was." With her free hand, she coiled a loose curl dangling on the side of her head. "So, I killed him. He was asleep and never felt a thing. And then that little gopher of a man thought he could blackmail me, and I killed him."

Sabrina toe-crawled her left foot toward the outside door and followed with the right one. If she could get close enough…maybe…

An eerie madness lit Mrs. Hunter's gray eyes. "I still remember that god-awful day. Clear as the ring of a Sunday morning church bell." As she sauntered to Sabrina's dressing table along the north wall, her eyes grew rounder. "Matter of fact, the Yankees rode into our yard just after we'd come back from church." She held the gun in one hand and lifted Grandfather's ivory chess piece with the other. "I wasn't too worried. James was in charge. I thought he'd come home to see me, but I was wrong…terribly wrong." She set the ivory knight down. "I witnessed my loving husband give the order to burn my home in the name of the Union."

"My God." Sabrina slid her left foot closer to the

back door. *I have to get out of here.*

"The flames licked around the boards my great-granddaddy used to build his dream of a better life for his family. And, as my beautiful Homewood turned into a pile of worthless ashes—so did my heart."

"Seeing your home burn must have been difficult."

Mrs. Hunter laughed, creating a haunting empty sound. "Difficult? You could say that. My baby brother dying in a Yankee prison was a little difficult, too." She loosened the glass stopper on a bottle of perfume and sniffed. "Lilacs. I've always liked lilacs."

Sabrina edged closer to the door.

"I tried to save Hansford. I petitioned everyone, even Old Abe." She replaced the stopper. "He told me he sympathized, but there wasn't anything he could do."

"I'm sure you tried." *If I run, can I reach the door?*

"We had a plan to kidnap the president, but Booth botched the kidnapping."

Sabrina wrinkled her brow. *Vivian said something about a kidnapping.*

"We planned to ransom our boys out of prison." Mrs. Hunter leveled the gun. "I see you…" she sang. "Stop moving…" She hardened her tone. "I will shoot."

Sabrina halted. *I have to get away.* "What has this got to do with William?" She hugged her body tighter while images of her life with Ethan wafted away, like dandelion fluff in the wind.

"Doctor Nelson was part of my little group. We called ourselves the Gray Hounds." Mrs. Hunter tapped her left hand along the edge of the dressing table.

"You were part of a spy ring?" *Maybe if I can keep her talking, then Ethan will come.*

"Not only part of it...I...was the leader." Mrs. Hunter cocked her mouth into an arrogant smile. "We robbed the Union trains and sent the supplies to our boys. I wore a disguise, and no one suspected I was a woman. Not even the men who rode with me."

"But somehow, William figured everything out." She shoved her left foot closer to the outside door.

Mrs. Hunter massaged her left temple. "Not at first, but eventually."

"Let me help you." Sabrina started for her medical bag in a chair closer to the back door. "I can give you some headache powders."

"Don't. Move." Mrs. Hunter leveled the pistol, and the bright light in her gray eyes dimmed.

"You have your son. Perhaps..."

Mrs. Hunter snorted. "The biggest disappointment of my life." She smirked, shaking her head. "I wanted him to join the Confederacy, but no...he had to be a Union soldier. Just like his father. And then...he got the laundress pregnant." She sauntered around the room. "And wanted to marry her. I paid the little trollop to get rid of the mistake and leave. Everything would have been fine, but no...Lila Minton had to go and die"—she stopped—"because Nelson had principles." She cocked the hammer and sighted her target. "Give—me—the diary."

"Uncle Nathan has it." Sabrina licked her lips and swallowed the sour taste in her mouth.

Colonel Hunter appeared in the doorway leading from the hallway. "Millie?"

Mrs. Hunter frowned, looked at her husband, and angled her head. "Why are you here, James?"

The colonel treaded deeper into the room and held

his hands out, palms up. "I heard you had one of your headaches, dear." He stopped in front of his wife. "How is it?"

Mrs. Hunter clutched the butt of the pistol in her right hand but dropped her arm. "Better, I think." She rubbed her left temple.

"Mil, I'm so sorry for what I did, and I know about the Gray Hounds." He smoothed his left hand over her right shoulder. "I know you killed Nelson and Fowler. Honey, it's over. Give me the gun."

Mrs. Hunter crushed her lips together and shook her head. "I can't."

"I'll take care of you. Just like I always have." The colonel grabbed the gun.

Bang!

Mrs. Hunter's eyes widened, and a trickle of blood dribbled from the corner of her mouth. Her body sagged lower in her husband's arms.

"Do something, please." Colonel Hunter dropped to the floor, cradling his wife.

Sabrina rushed forward and placed her fingertips on Mrs. Hunter's carotid artery. "I'm sorry, but she's gone, sir."

****

Later, after everyone departed, Sabrina returned to the main ward. A small fire burned in the fireplace, and the magical scents of Christmas drifted like a morning mist disappearing on the horizon. Several candle flames bobbed. She approached the closest table and blew out the first candle.

Ethan stepped from the shadows and set a familiar music box on the table. He opened the lid, the sweet melody *pinged*, and the handsome soldier and beautiful

313

lady rotated. Smiling, he held out his hand. "May I have this dance?"

She placed her right hand into his left one and floated into his open arms. "This is exactly where I want to be, Captain."

"Sabrina, I love you. And, I want to spend the rest of my life with you. Will you please…be my wife?"

Epilogue

One year later, Washington City

The orchestra played Christmas songs, and the lights blazed in Carter Hall. Friends and family gathered in small knots, visiting and celebrating the holiday season. Tables, laden with food, lined one end of the dining room.

Sabrina wore a sapphire-blue gown and bounced to the beat of "Deck the Halls." She spied her nephew near the end of the food table.

Little Bobby reached into the candy bowl.

Carolina grabbed her son's pudgy hand and shepherded him away from the table.

Laughing, Big Bobby scooped the toddler into his arms and kissed his wife's cheek.

From behind, Sabrina smelled the sensual scent of her husband's shaving soap, fresh and clean. She lifted her mouth, feeling joy, peace, and happiness bound together into a love knot.

Ethan embraced her from behind, folding his arms around her shoulders.

She felt encased in a warm cocoon while he nibbled her right earlobe. Granules of desire skidded along the back of her neck. Laughing, she spun in his hold. "Major Reed, you must behave yourself." She dusted the military patches on his left shoulder with her right hand. "I cannot believe how happy I am." She seductively traced his jawline with her fingertip. "Did I tell you? Vivian and Duncan are buying the house next door, and Mother and Uncle Nathan are leaving on their honeymoon." She leaned back in his arms, pursed her lips, and wrinkled her brow, studying the color changing in his eyes. "Something is wrong. What is it?"

He kissed the tip of her nose, then holding her left hand, he tugged her into the library.

Wolf lifted his head from the braided rug in front of the warm fire, wagged his tail a couple of times, then returned his chin to the floor.

"Tell me." She faced him and smoothed her hands over his chest.

"I've received a new assignment." He extracted the hairpins from her chignon and one by one tossed them to the floor.

She felt her hair falling over her shoulders. "Which is?"

He buried his hands in her hair and massaged the back of her head. "Commanding officer at Fort Greer."

"I see." She sighed, relaxing into the magic of his fingers. "I need to speak with Drew, but I suppose I could have everything packed...and ready by week's end." She settled into his caress. "When do you have to report?"

"Darling." He touched his forehead to hers. "You are not coming." He kissed her nose.

She cupped his left cheek in her right hand, and a warm creaminess pooled in her stomach. She twitched the corners of her mouth up. "You sir, are mistaken."

"My darling wife, I am not only concerned for your safety"—he caressed her rounded stomach with his left hand—"but for the safety of our child, too."

"Our baby can be born at Fort Greer." She closed her hand over his.

"Sabrina…"

"Ethan…"

He drew her into his chest. "Doctor Reed, you are one stubborn lady."

She pulled back and cocked her head, then lifted her chin. "You forget, Major, I'm no lady."

He jiggled his mouth into a devilish grin. "So…" he arched his brows, "we agree on the stubborn?" He lowered his head.

She floated her eyelids down. "Maybe." She heard his chuckle and raised her gaze.

He kissed her chin.

She felt complete happiness breeze into her heart and opened her mouth. "I…"

He sealed her lips beneath his and tightened his hold.

She surrendered to his seduction, and her words melted like snowflakes on a warm hearth. *"…love you, Ethan."*

Praise for Twilla Kay Lamm

"An excellent read…loved the characters and the suspense."

~Paul Carter

~*~

"I finished this in one sitting, couldn't put it down! Super compelling all the way through! The ending really got me!"

~Pam Graddy

~*~

"Lamm's book, HIS SWEET OBSESSION, is an intriguing tapestry woven with history, mystery, and romance. The main protagonist, woven through the whole tapestry, is a strong, intelligent, female doctor. And the *who done it* ending was a revelation."

~Judy C.

~*~

"HIS SWEET OBSESSION has it all…mystery, intrigue, history, and romance. The characters and setting are vividly real as if the reader is right there. I thoroughly enjoyed Sabrina's journey of discovery. She is a brave, warm, and loving character, brought to life with all her humanness and insecurities. The book incorporates the era after the Civil War in Oklahoma Indian Territory with ease and accuracy. I was left wanting more from this author!"

~Pam Crookham

A word about the author...

Twilla Kay Lamm is a graduate of Northeastern State University with an undergraduate degree in elementary education and a graduate degree in early childhood. Her favorite books to read have always been historical romance. When she retired, she decided to write one. HIS SWEET OBSESSION is her first. You may contact her at P.O. Box 426 Antlers, OK or twillaklamm@gmail.com.